M000031509

Sylvan's Guise

This is a work of fiction. All characters and events portrayed in this novel are either products of the author's imagination or are used fictitiously.

Sylvan's Guise

Copyright © 2019 Vicki B. Williamson
All rights reserved.

No part of this book may be reproduced in any form, including photocopying, recording, or other electronic or mechanical methods—except in the case of brief quotations embodied in articles or reviews—without written permission by the publisher.

Cover by Driven Digital Services
Map by Vicki B. Williamson
Editing and typesetting by Kingsman Editing Services

First Edition November 2019
ISBN: 978-0-9990605-2-0

vickibwilliamson.author@gmail.com

. . . the believers . . .

OTHER TITLES BY
VICKI B. WILLIAMSON

Finding Poppies

Key of the Prophecy — an Ellen Thompson Thriller

THE PEDAGOGUE CHRONICLES

Book I: *Maya's Song*

Sylvan's Guise

THE PEDAGOGUE CHRONICLES
BOOK II

VICKI B. WILLIAMSON

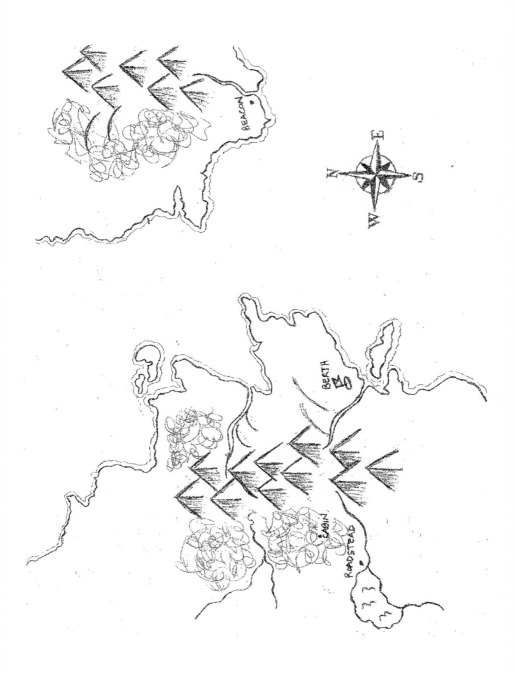

A CRYSTALLINE WIND WHISTLED THROUGH the room of the old manor, snuffing out candles and blowing an ancient tome from the mantel.

Caleb turned without surprise as his sister, Cassandra, marched in with the cold. Every time he saw her, he was reminded of how different she was from the sibling of his youth. In the past, she had loved him. Now she was driven purely by self-interest.

"Brother," she yelled over the howl of the wind. With a flick of her hand, the door slammed shut and the wind cut off. The first moment of quiet was so complete, he thought he'd gone deaf, but then footfalls broke the silence. Uninterested in what she had to say, he shifted to stare into the fire blazing in the hearth.

"Come now. Don't turn from me. I have a proposition for you."

What could she possibly want from him?

When he continued to ignore her, she grasped his arm and swung him around.

"Don't be that way, brother. Come, play with me."

Caleb stared at her, not sure what she was about. "What is it you want of me, sister?"

She laughed and sat before the fire. "It appears as if the pieces are even in our endeavor. Perhaps we could double the stakes."

Intrigued against his better judgment, Caleb sat in the other chair facing his sister. "What do you have in mind, Cassandra?"

"One player is mine, and one is yours, but in the end, there will be three. When I win, you will halt attempts to stop me. All the worlds and their bounties will be mine."

"But what if I were to win?"

She laughed again as he said the words, but in her humor, he sensed fear. Each of them had a fair chance. Each may yet win this contest.

"Ask what you will, dear brother, for you will never win. My player is dark, darker than you know. She has been so from the beginning, and with it she will color all who come near. And with her stain, I will win all."

1

Sylvan's Sixteenth Names Day

BATHED IN THE NOVA BRIGHT light that didn't burn, Sylvan walked to the platform. Her heart raced, and by the time she'd taken the first step, her chest rose with an increased need for air.

Looking over her shoulder, she glanced at the assembly of people behind her. In front of the group of statesmen and citizens, her mother and father sat with the Bathsar family from the adjoining property. With Lord and Lady Bathsar sat their two sons. Mikel, the eldest, was hunched in his seat, his face scrunched and eyes flashing. Her soon-to-be husband, Eldred, watched her with an open expression. His eyes tracked her every movement. When he caught her gaze, a smile tugged at the corners of his mouth, and he gave her a small wink. She returned his smile then took a deep breath, centered her courage, and turned back to the light.

On an ornate table at the center of the dais sat an orb. The vessel glowed from within, and occasionally the light pulsed in a brighter flash.

The pulses became more frequent. The pounding of her heart rose in the vein of her throat until the two pulses created a steady rhythm.

A few steps more, and Sylvan stood directly in front of the table—within arm's reach of the orb. The pulsing vibrated her frame. The blood in her veins became one with the light. Pulled without conscious thought, she laid her fingertips against the sphere. With a hiss, Sylvan yanked her hand back and stuck her fingers in her mouth. Only then did she realize that what she thought was hot, was actually cold. It was freezing.

Daring to—needing to—again she touched the orb. After a second of pain, it warmed. Like a welcoming bath, the warmth flowed through her fingers to fill her body. Sylvan pulled the orb into her embrace and the light intensified.

Watching from below, the crowd gave an audible gasp as the light encompassed the entire dais. Soon, Sylvan was lost within the illumination.

Inside the cocoon of light, Sylvan felt a shift within herself and the orb in her arms. Her entire being opened and grew. For a moment, she knew all things, saw all times, and she gasped as she grew blind to her surroundings.

The ball of light in her arms softened, its shape altering. As her consciousness returned to this day, this time, Sylvan perceived a lessening of the sphere's intensity. It faded, and her vision returned, though for a moment it was speckled with small sunbursts. In her arms, the object shifted, a velvety softness caressing her skin. Taking a deep breath, she looked down into a pair of large, yellow eyes.

When the light faded, she was surprised to see a cat in her arms.

Wide-eyed, she thought back to her expectations of this day. Further back than she could fathom, the firstborn child of her family—the Singh family—had been given the gift of wisdom. It came in the form of a trainer, a mentor. A pedagogue.

As the legend went, a distant ancestor aided a wizard by saving his love, and for this help, the wizard granted a wish. Her ancestor wished for wisdom for his only child. The wizard gave the family much more than that. Each generation, the firstborn child received the gift of a pedagogue on their sixteenth Names Day. This mentor helped the child grow in wisdom to better lead their lands and people.

Her father's teacher, and his fathers before him, had come in the form of an old man. Being born full formed, the pedagogue began their lives already mature and wise. Sylvan had always thought hers would be a woman—with an aged visage and sage mind.

She stared at the feline she held, unsure what to think.

Hearing footsteps coming up the rise behind her, she turned to the crowd. Eyes wide, she looked from her burden to the eyes of her father, the first to reach her.

"Daddy . . ." she began. His gaze dropped to what she held, smile slowly disappearing as he stared at the feline.

Part of the lore of the pedagogue was that it would come in a form and with the knowledge the Singh heir required. What could this cat possibly offer?

Then the cat shifted in her arms. It pushed against her and leaped to softly land on the table next to them. All conversation halted, and people stared as he performed a bow of amazing gentility—considering it was performed by a cat—and said, "My lady. I am Nathaniel."

2

FROM THAT FIRST DAY, ONE lesson Nathaniel knew he needed to succeed at was to teach Sylvan of her magic and how to master it. Of all the Singh heirs, she was one of the more powerful, if not the most.

When she wouldn't use her magic—she wouldn't even try and wouldn't tell him why—he put his considerable intelligence to the problem.

They sat, first for small portions of time, working on manifesting her magic. She maintained that she had no magic day after day. That it had left her long before.

"I don't know why you're so certain I have magic. You know, it is possible for magic to leave a person."

Nathaniel stopped himself from rolling his eyes. "No, actually, it's not possible for magic to leave a person. The magic is always with you, even if you choose not to use it." He approached the padded bench where she sat, leaped on it, and placed a paw on her hand. "Tell me why you choose not to use your magic. I can help you, and I'm a good listener."

She pulled her hand from under his paw, stood, and moved away. With her back to him, she muttered, "I don't know what you are referring to." At his silence, she turned to face him. "Anyway," she mumbled with a shrug, "I had very little magic to begin with. I'm certain I used it up."

This time, his eyes were rolling before he could stop them.

Now she had *him* acting like a teenager.

"I would like you to sit and meditate with me. We will search together, deep within your psyche, and locate your magic."

"I don't want to, Nathaniel. Let's go for a walk by the lake. It's such a beautiful day. I don't want to be inside."

After a few more moments of thought, he concluded that he may get her to do what he wished if he gave her what she wished. "All right. It is a beautiful day."

It went this way for a few weeks; her stubbornness not to attempt her magic always outweighed his efforts to get her to try. When he put down his foot, or paw, she did as he asked. But her efforts were halfhearted and the results halfhearted also. She showed some magic in small things, but none of the promise from when she was a child. None of the true power he sensed within her.

Lying at night, formulating his plans for the next days and weeks, he promised himself he would be sterner with her, but he'd come to love this girl-child. Her fear was palatable, especially when she finally managed to tap into her power. She would perform a small feat and then shut down. He found he just couldn't bring himself to hurt her in any way. Sylvan had become very special to him.

3

Two Years Later

O PENING HER EYES IN THE light of early morning, Sylvan studied the broad back of the man in bed with her. Her marriage had taken place six months ago, and some mornings it still surprised her to find a man in her bed. Most mornings, however, it was he who woke her—in the most delightful fashion—and she had no coherent thoughts at all.

Rolling on her back but keeping her eyes on her husband, Sylvan laid a gentle hand on her belly. She had yet to tell him of their child. Today, there would be a celebration to commemorate his twentieth Names Day, and during that time she would pull him into a private moment and give him his present—the upcoming birth of their baby. A smile crossed her lips at the scene in her mind. He'd be so excited.

A crash sounded outside the room, and Sylvan's eyes snapped to the door, her thoughts pulled from their reverie. Hearing nothing else, she was just relaxing back into the mattress when a shrill scream exploded downstairs.

She and Eldred sat up at the same moment.

"What was that?" he uttered, instantly alert. Like all the men of the land, he'd done his time in the military. That experience had honed the boy into a man proficient with multiple weapons. Before she could answer, he was out of their bed and striding toward the door. Sylvan couldn't help but admire his exposed backside. She gave an inner sigh, her thoughts drifting, before his demeanor centered her attention.

Standing to the side, he cracked the door and peered out. When the barrier opened, a flood of muted sounds flowed in and Sylvan slowly rose to her feet.

"What is that?" she whispered. "What's happening?"

"Shh," he hushed her and, closing the gap even further, placed his ear to the opening.

Her nerves rose every moment. Another scream echoed up the stairs and she jumped. Stepping around the bed and pulling a sheet around her body, she padded silently to him. With a hand on his shoulder, she rose to her tiptoes and whispered in his ear.

"What's happening?"

His eyes focused on her for a moment, his gaze running up and down her small frame.

"Get dressed, Sylvan. Quickly, my love."

The intensity in his eyes had shivers running down her spine to weaken her knees, but she nodded briskly and turned to their closet. Feeling the urgency press down on her with each second, she grabbed a serviceable skirt, tunic, and hose.

Throwing them on, she sat on the bed to lace up her boots. When finished, she returned to Eldred's side. He nodded in approval.

He quietly threw the locking mechanism after closing the door and then listened for a moment more. He took her by the hand and led her away from the entrance. Quickly pulling on a pair of trousers, he again laced his fingers with hers and walked toward a door that adjoined their bedroom to another.

Sylvan went with him, not questioning where he led them, trusting him to keep them safe.

Through the second room, Eldred directed them onto the side balcony. When a troop of riders moved through the inner courtyard, he pulled her back along the wall and into his arms.

"El," she whispered but quieted when his arms tightened. She knew he understood her unspoken question, however. These men, their horses, and the colors they wore were unknown to her, yet they moved through the yard as if they belonged there. When the riders passed them, Eldred stepped forward, moving her behind him to peer over the edge of the balcony.

Sylvan's heart beat heavily in her chest, and she couldn't draw a full breath. Questions ran through her mind. She gripped his hand in preparation to ask him her questions when another scream pierced the air. It was followed closely by a slamming door and raucous laughter. Sliding them back to the wall, Eldred moved to the far edge of the balcony, and after assisting Sylvan over the divider, he slid over and hurried after her. He moved them into the new room, cracked the door, and listened. This location put them farther down the hallway and past the open walkway within view of the main gallery. Sliding out, he moved them along the hall with their backs to the wall. Loud voices reverberated up the stairs and over the divider.

The two of them rounded a corner at the end of the hall. Halfway down the next passageway, Eldred slid his fingers into a previously unnoticed juncture in the brickwork and manipulated a hidden lever. Part of the stone wall slid open, emitting a low grinding sound. He pushed it to widen the gap and directed Sylvan in with a hand on the small of her back.

"Go to the river. Wait for me there."

"No," she insisted, grabbing his waistband. "Come with me. We'll go to your parents and get help. Your brother's men will surely rally to our aid."

Shaking his head at her, he insisted, "You go now. I'll follow as soon as I know more of what's happening. I'll locate your parents and bring them with me."

In a fit of indecision, Sylvan laid a palm on her still-flat stomach. "I don't want to leave you."

"My love." He hugged her quickly and placed a tender kiss upon her forehead. "Stay safe. I'll be right behind you."

Nodding her understanding, she allowed him to move her farther into the hidden corridor. With a final glance, he pulled the portal closed. He stared at the rock, his brows in a scowl as he took a deep breath, then he turned back the way he'd come.

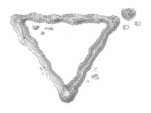

4

WHEN THE DOOR TO THE hidden portal slid closed, Eldred kept the image of Sylvan in the forefront of his mind. She would be safe, he told himself, and they would soon be together again.

When another crash and shout sounded from the main hall, he glanced over his shoulder and listened. He'd kept from Sylvan the fact that he'd recognized the clashing of metal—swordplay. He didn't yet know what was happening, but he was certain people were dying. With Sylvan out of harm's way, he could act without worry for her safety.

Moving back the way he'd come, Eldred slipped into the quarters he shared with his wife. With quick efficiency, he dressed in clothing fit for battle—loose enough for movement but hardy enough to provide protection.

Sliding a long knife into his belt, Eldred grasped the hilt of his sword and moved to the door. He peered out, his eyes and ears attuned to every nuance of sight and sound. Quiet. All he heard was the sound of a breeze blowing outside.

What is happening?

Sliding the door open enough to allow passage, he slipped into the hall. Slow, careful steps drew him toward the opening of the balcony where he peered down into the main room.

A shiver ran up his spine when he viewed a room full of battle-garbed men. Around them, on the floor, lay many of the estate's servants.

The group of men tilted their faces to stare up at him. Eldred turned to flee. More soldiers came up the stairs on either side and through the hall behind him. He was severely outnumbered. Turning to the soldiers, he took a fighting stance and raised his sword.

When the first man got close, he swung out, catching him in the throat and dropping him. Eldred stepped to the side so as not to trip on the body or the blood now coating the floor.

This time when the soldiers approached, they came en masse. He tried, his instincts to fight no matter what, but they soon had him surrounded. Too close for his sword, he dropped it and reached for the long dagger in his belt.

A soldier struck his temple with the hilt of his sword and Eldred fell, blood running down the side of his face. They grabbed him by the arms, wrenching them up and back to lift him to his feet. When they laid his chest on the stone half-wall, his attention was pulled to the room below. In the center of the carnage, alone, with his back to Eldred, stood a man. He glanced side to side and then turned, as if surprised, to look up at Eldred. A large smile split his face and he opened his arms wide in welcome.

"Hello, brother."

5

SYLVAN STOOD FOR A MOMENT in the darkness of the corridor, eyeing where she knew the door to be. Leaving her husband felt wrong, but she was a girl used to obeying the men in her life. First her father in her younger life, and now her husband in the present. She didn't give any thought to disobeying. Still feeling the indecision for a moment, her hand crept back to her belly. She was protecting more than just herself now, wasn't she? She needed to think of their child.

With the image of their babe strong in her mind, Sylvan pivoted and ran her fingers along the rough-cut wall. She took careful steps until she located a small mounted box. Directly above that was a holder filled with the shaft of a torch. Taking it from the wall and matches from the box, she held the torch in the crook of her arm as she struck a match. It burst into flame, and her eyes clenched tightly as she turned her face away. She peered through squinted eyes at the glow then put flame to torch. Old and dry, the material erupted to life as if it had been waiting an eternity for just this opportunity.

Glancing down the hallway in front of her, at the edge of the light, stairs began their descent. With one final glance back the way she'd come, she started forward.

SHE FELT AS THOUGH SHE'D been walking for ages. From the very beginning, the tunnel had been dry, so dry it leached the moisture right out of her. The air was hard to breathe, and even swallowing became difficult, her throat so dry, the edges stuck together. The torch continued its steady burn, occasionally sputtering and dropping bits of flaming material.

When one of these brands hissed upon hitting the floor, she paused and held the torch out, looking around. Rivulets of water oozed from the walls, pooling on the steps.

She continued to move forward, and the stairs soon became slippery with mosses while the air took on a fetid stench. Stepping carefully, Sylvan continued. She'd known of these tunnels her whole life—an escape route built into the heart of the castle—and now they were fulfilling their destiny and permitting the heiress a safe escape.

The farther she descended, the more tired she became. With her next step, she had a fleeting thought of thankfulness that she wasn't having to travel the opposite way. Along with the weariness, the thing that weighed most on her mind was her ever-growing thirst.

Why hadn't Eldred thought to grab a jug of water for me to take?

With no other option but to continue, Sylvan took step after step. Time lost all meaning and the muscles of her legs quivered with each downward motion. Running her free hand along the wall, she leaned into it occasionally to rest. She turned and looked up the staircase. The light disappeared within a few feet, and beyond its circle, there was only darkness. The longer she looked up the stairs, the murkier the darkness seemed. As if the darkness were watching her, a touch of claustrophobia pressed on her mind for a moment.

Shaking her head at her imagination, Sylvan continued downward.

When Sylvan saw a glow farther down the staircase, she paused and breathed.

Finally.

Concentrating on the feeling of air moving in and out of her lungs, she relaxed her shoulders and stretched her back. She hadn't realized how tense she'd become. In the back of her mind, unable to admit it, she'd imaged a never-ending staircase and of being trapped forever.

Forcing her feet to move, she pushed herself despite being near exhaustion. She moved down the final steps until she approached what appeared to be a wall of vegetation.

Sylvan doused the torch on the dirt floor and reached for the vines. They parted, allowing a narrow stream of sunlight to warm her face and fill the area. Somewhere close, she could hear the gurgle of water.

Well, at least I won't succumb to thirst.

She waited a moment longer but heard only the flowing water and the wind high above the trees. Pushing her hands through the vegetation, she peered out, blinking rapidly as the light caused her eyes to water. Nothing — just the sounds of the forest.

With a firm hand, she parted the wall and stepped through to the other side. A brush of sound came from behind her, and she glanced back to see the gap in the vines close. From this side, the curtain appeared to be a wall of rock covered in a growth of wild vines.

A cool breeze danced playfully with tendrils of her hair and the hem of her skirt.

When will Eldred come for me?

The sound of water drew her attention, and since she hadn't heard anything, she decided it was safe to quench her thirst. She started in the direction of the water. Soon, she could smell it, cool and fresh, and she swallowed hard.

When she approached the creek, she found a clear, fast-flowing pool, and she dropped to her knees to scoop cold water to her lips.

After she'd drunk her fill, her hunger had also subsided somewhat, and she sat back on her heels. Looking toward the sun, she heaved a sigh and tried to relax. Eldred would come for her. She just needed to be patient.

Unfortunately, patience wasn't her best virtue.

After a while, and another long drink of water, Sylvan stood, shaking out her skirt and looking around. Birds chased each other through the treetops and hung on currents of wind before plunging down among the branches. The sun, at its apex, warmed her bones, which had chilled during her time in the tunnel.

Her thoughts turned to what was happening at the manor,

and with a start, she realized her parents might truly be in danger.

And Nathaniel. Where was Nathaniel?

If it were up to her, Nathaniel would be allowed to stay within their room, and so he would be with her right now, but Eldred put his foot down on that subject. He refused to even consider the cat spending the night hours in their private quarters.

Warm in the sun, her mind drifted to when the cat had first entered her life, and a small smile curved her lips.

WHEN SHE WAS SIXTEEN AND Nathaniel had just come, Eldred didn't like all the time she spent with the cat and away from him. Directly after his coming, she and Nathaniel began taking walks and spending a great portion of their time together. During this period, they discussed many things. Even the topic of his existence came up.

"Nathaniel," she began.

He sat beside her on a brightly printed blanket. She rested in the shade of a large tree and he bathed in sunlight. When she spoke in such hesitant tones, he glanced at her over his shoulder.

"What is it, my dear?"

"What—I mean, what are you?"

Only distant birdcalls and the breeze moving through the top of the trees answered her question. He looked off into the distance before he turned to face her.

"Your question is a bit impertinent."

When heat flushed her cheeks, she dropped her gaze to stare at her clasped hands in her lap.

"But we are friends, are we not?"

She caught his eye and the small smile that hovered over his lips.

"Come girl, move closer and let me tell you a tale."

She scooted forward on the blanket, eager to hear his story. Nathaniel faced her, his luxurious tail curling around his feet.

"Once, long ago," he began, "the only cats of this world were of the common variety."

The corners of her mouth turned up with this statement. If anything were certain, it was that Nathaniel thought his kind above the "normal" animals.

"Long before men came into being, some of the cats began to change. It was a slow change, wrought with difficulties, confusion, and pain."

The drone of his voice, the cadence of his story, drew her in, and she lay down in front of him, her head on the crook of her arm. A breath of cool air moved over her, and an insect buzzed by, further relaxing her. Unable to help herself, she gave a mighty yawn and her eyelids drooped.

* * * * *

THE FELINE FACED HER PRIDE. They were an unkempt lot, dirty and simpleminded. She didn't know how she could have been birthed from them. And now they were driving her out, biting at her, whipping their claws to move her along.

She was happy to leave. But as much as she no longer wished to be here, part of her felt the fear of being alone. She'd always been part of a group. Hunted as a group. Slept warm as a group. Would she find others like herself, or was she destined to be alone?

She put aside her misgivings, gave one final look back, and with a turn, lopped off into the forest.

TWO WEEKS LATER SHE CLEARED the vast forest and faced the wastes of the dry land. Being alone, she'd only been able to catch small game. Now, though the desert called to her, she looked back longingly to the cool green of the forest. How would she fare in the desert? Would there be food and shelter? What was this force that called her forward?

Turning her life over to fate, she stepped into the hot plains of the desert.

THE CAT CROUCHED AND WATCHED the blue lizard dart among the evening flowers of the rock plant. She hadn't eaten since coming to this place, and the lizard would fill the hole in her belly. But it was quick, and day by day, she became slower. The lack of water was perhaps the most debilitating thing. At times, she imagined an actual voice speaking to her out of the wilderness. Sometimes, she thought she might be losing her mind.

The lizard stopped, its back to her, occupied with the consumption of an insect. She pushed her haunches up slightly, muscles tense. Her hind end swung back and forth, her tail a counterweight to the motion.

When the lizard faced away from her completely, she took the opportunity. With a flash of motion, she leaped forward. She pivoted with her prey, intent on bringing it down, aware this might be her last chance.

She stood, breath heaving, only then to realize the lizard was clenched in her teeth. Triumph filled her, and she moved from the exposed rocks to enjoy her dinner hidden among an outcropping. Small though it was, her meal fueled her muscles, and she moved with a quicker pace through the night—ever on the watch for another quarry to present itself.

Twice more that night she stalked and killed. By the time the sun began its ascent in the morning sky, her belly was full, and she considered a location to sleep.

WHEN SHE WOKE, JUST AS the moon rose, she was rested but once again hungry. A small desert shower began, and she welcomed it, lapping the water from a basin in the rocks. She once again heeded the call in her head, ever vigilant for the movement that would signal a break in her fast.

She felt different tonight. She'd walked for many moments before she understood. With a tilt of her head, she admitted she was no longer afraid.

She stood on a break of rock, looking down at a valley, and the insight and power of being the alpha predator filled her. With her face lifted to the shining moon, she screamed into the wilderness. Her warning for all to beware.

Moments later, a yowl answered her.

SHE HADN'T TRAVELED FAR WHEN a shadow appeared ahead of her. She froze, listening to the night. There was only the flap of distant wings. The longer she waited, the greater her anxiety became, so with a careful pace, she moved forward.

When she rounded a bend, she came face to face with another of her ilk. He stared at her. Dark to her light, he was larger than her, his gaze giving nothing away. Her surprise couldn't be contained. She was the largest in her clan, yet he was the biggest feline she'd ever seen.

When he stepped forward, she crouched with a hiss, her ears laid flat against her head. After a pause, he again took a step. A rumble issued from his chest, and she perked her ears. When he leaned in and sniffed along her neck, she became like a statue, no longer fearful, but wary. His tongue rough, he licked her ear then turned away. She watched his retreat, head up, ears pricked. Just as he was about to round a bend on the trail, she leaped to her feet and padded after him.

When he stopped, she moved right up to him. Head dipped, she butted him and rubbed her length along his. When he continued, she fell into step with him.

* * * * *

WHEN NATHANIEL STOPPED SPEAKING, SYLVAN blinked sleepily and slowly pushed herself into a sitting position.

"Was that your mother and father?"

"No. Distant ancestors. They were the beginning. Through

them, each generation became more until I am as you see me before you. A dirkcat."

Sylvan's mind spun. Dirkcats were ancient. Animals of legend and magic. She had heard tales of them, lore really, but never thought the stories were true. They had abilities, varied and mysterious. Not only was it unique to meet one, but for him to be so important in her life had shocked her. Why her? She was just a girl. Yes, she came from a good family, an important family, but did that really matter?

Her throat moved as she swallowed.

"A dirkcat?"

"Yes. And I am here to assist you. Aid you as you grow. To ensure you are prepared for all that may come."

She nodded, her eyes large and round. "Yes, Nathaniel."

SYLVAN LOOKED UP, ONCE AGAIN catching sight of the birds at play. Their loud banter pulled her from her memories, and she glanced around. Her concern for Nathaniel was real, but it couldn't override everything else. She had nowhere to go, no one to seek out.

She'd wait for Eldred. But where should she do that? Outside the tunnel, she could be seen. Inside the tunnel, it was stuffy and damp. Uncomfortable. But still, better to be safe. Seeking to avoid the dark and dank tunnel for as long as possible, Sylvan sat outside the vine curtain watching the sun move across the sky.

Nathaniel, being a cat, mostly wandered at night or worked on his hobbies—reading or research on his special projects. He could be anywhere, within or without the castle. To calm her mind, she assured herself he would be safe.

Sitting and waiting, feeling proud of her level of patience, Sylvan's imagination worked with the ways Eldred would make this up to her. Through it all, she'd be the gracious and loving wife. A small smile curved her lips to imagine him pleading on his knees. Her fantasies kept her busy, and before she knew it, the sun slipped down in the sky.

She stood and again wandered to the stream's edge. After slaking her thirst, she found a private spot to relieve her bladder. Making her way to the tunnel's entrance, she pushed through then again witnessed the curtain closing as if her passage had never occurred.

THE NEIGH OF A HORSE and rattle of reins woke Sylvan from a deep sleep. She blinked, not at first able to recall where she was. When she shifted, a pain lanced through her shoulder and with a flash she remembered.

Emitting a small moan, she sat and stretched her chilled and stiff frame. The sound of a man's voice pulled her to her feet in a rush, and tripping on a numb limb, she hurried to the entrance.

Thinking the men and horses were surely Eldred coming for her, she was about to pull back the vines and yell a greeting to her husband when a spike of foreboding curled up her spine. Pulling her hand back, fingers curled into a fist, she stopped mere inches from the vegetation, straining to hear.

The hum of men's voices mixed with the sounds of their

mounts and Sylvan knew, somehow, this was not Eldred. The shiver again passed through her. She was in danger.

Lacing her fingers between the vines, holding tightly to them, she created a small opening and peered out.

The entire area bordering the stream, the area she had so recently wandered around, contained men—on horses and off. Men clothed in cloaks of the unknown colors in the courtyard at home.

Her brow wrinkled as she watched the remaining men dismount and lead their horses to the stream. When a voice spoke next to her, she started, almost giving her location away. "The castle is taken, my lord."

"Good. Any evidence of the woman?" The voice was gruff and deeply masculine.

"Not yet, my lord."

"Continue searching. Inform me as soon as she is located."

"Yes, my lord."

Letting the curtain close, Sylvan stepped back, sure not to make a sound.

Am I the woman they seek? Who are these men?

Sitting in the ribbons of light, she waited and listened. After a time, the sound of boots and horses approached the hill face and the vine curtain. She heard the creak of a saddle as a man settled on a horse.

She clasped her hands in her lap in an attempt to still their quaking. She would wait. She was certain Eldred would come for her. They could not know she was here. She was safe.

6

THE SUN SANK AND THE cave chilled. When she stood, her muscles cramped, and she suppressed a groan that tried to push past her lips. Walking around the small area, she worked the kinks out of her sore, cramped muscles until she could do so without limping.

Her small fingers parted the vine curtain by a degree of inches, and she peered out at the encampment of men. She stepped back, allowing the vegetation to close while she contemplated her next move. Even from where she hid, it was obvious the camp had sentries.

How am I to sneak by them?

And the question had to be asked—where was she to go? Backward didn't feel right. Eldred entrusted her to take the hidden tunnel and stay safe. To head back to the manor would make that all for naught. She could go to her in-laws for help. They were most likely unaware of the invasion. Yes, she decided, she would go to Eldred's parents. It would be a hike and would take her the better part of the day and night, but it was there where she would find help. But first—how to slip past these men.

* * * * *

ELDRED COULDN'T BELIEVE IT. TRAINED with the finest warriors in the land, victor of countless battles, and sheer numbers were still able to overpower him and all his knowledge.

When his brother greeted him from the killing field in the main hall, he'd been stunned. Mikel, the underachieving elder son, stood arrogantly, surrounded by his soldiers.

When he'd come to, he was tied and gagged. His arms, legs, and chest were bound to a heavy chair and a cloth stuffed in his mouth with another wrapped to secure it. His chair was pushed up to his in-laws' table. At the head of the table sat his brother as if he were the lord of the manor.

While Eldred watched, his brows drawn close together, Mikel dined on a banquet of meats, cheeses, vegetables, and grains, and slurped loudly on Lord Singh's fine wine.

"Ah." Mikel smiled with his mouth full. "It's about time you woke."

Eldred tried to yell at his brother, but all he emitted was a muffled, unintelligible growl from behind the gag.

Mikel nodded as if in agreement before throwing back his head and laughing. Spittle and bits of food flew across the table, but he didn't seem to care.

"Grr to you, too, little brother." And he laughed again, shaking his head. Sobering quickly, as if he'd never shown his dark humor, Mikel peered hard at him. "What I really want to know is where that little wife of yours has gotten herself off to."

Eldred stilled and eyed his brother as he would a venomous snake. Keeping his fear for Sylvan out of his eyes, he concentrated on keeping his breaths slow and steady and repeated to himself, *He doesn't know where she is. He doesn't know where she is.*

"Hm, interesting," Mikel said quietly. "I know you know where she is." He tapped his finger on his chin. "Now how do I motivate you to tell me where that might be?"

Straining, Eldred again uttered a garbled mix of sounds.

"I can't understand you!" Mikel yelled, and with his cupped hand to his ear, he leaned in. "You'll have to speak up." Picking up his utensils, Mikel again ate as he chuckled at his own humor.

"You know . . . Sylvan was to be mine." He glanced at his brother. "We were in love before you connived to take her, her fortune, and her powers from me. You always had to have everything." With a shake of his head he added, "Gods, how I've always despised you."

Eldred's breath and heart stilled at his brother's words. It was true he and Mikel had never gotten along, but he didn't know the animosity ran this deep. It was sad to admit it, but in Eldred's world, Mikel held little to no importance. As the elder, Mikel would inherit, and Eldred had always known this. Facing life as a second son, he'd gone about making his plans.

Mikel was delusional about Sylvan. She and Eldred may not have been in love as children—at least not as adults define love—but they'd always known they'd be together. The news of her planned marriage to Mikel had put her into a panic. She'd never cared for the elder brother, his sadistic nature all too obvious. She and Eldred talked, even planned on running away, but Sylvan couldn't leave her beloved parents. She decided to speak with her sire. If he loved her as she loved him, she reasoned, he must give her to Eldred, whom she wanted.

She was right—he mused, and his heart warmed at the thought of her—Sylvan was always right. She had an uncanny knack for reading people and situations.

Her father acquiesced, and one marriage was canceled while another planned. Never, in all the changes, did Mikel let on he might be anything more than happy for the young couple. The fathers promised to find him another bride. One just as wealthy and beautiful.

"So, I know how much you loved our mother . . ." Mikel's nasally voice cut into Eldred's thoughts. "And I would certainly use her to get information about my intended if she were still with us." Seeming to be speaking to himself, Mikel stared off into the center of the room.

Eldred stopped breathing as his brother's words penetrated.

. . . loved our mother . . . still with us . . .

Eldred had just seen both his parents yesterday when he'd ridden to the adjoining estate to discuss some business with his father. His mother, who tracked him down to inquire after the possibility of a grandchild, had been happy and healthy—if persistent in her desires.

Eyes flashing to his brother, Eldred again strained against his bindings, moving the heavy chair. The guttural sounds issuing from him, although unintelligible, were full of fury and menace.

His fork aloft in the air, Mikel laughed in delight.

"Oh, this wasn't how I planned to tell you, but it is wonderful." Setting down his utensil, he leaned toward Eldred. "The old cow died at the end. And the confusion in her eyes." In a high falsetto, he mimicked, "Why, Mikel? But we love you, why?" And again, his voice came out normal. "As if that bitch ever loved me."

Tiring of his story, he again turned his attention to the food on his plate.

Eldred's eyes burned at his final words, his heart rending.

With a screech of wood on wood, Mikel pushed back from the table, throwing his napkin onto his plate.

"Come." He gestured to Eldred. "Let's go see your in-laws." Then he paused and spoke to himself in a low voice. "Soon to be my in-laws, right? But no matter — they'll be dead soon." And he walked across the room to the doorway.

Rough hands grabbed at Eldred. Some ropes loosened, and others tightened, and soon he was upright and being dragged through the room after his brother. Though he was familiar with the manor, as he and Sylvan resided here since it would one day be their home, Eldred looked about with barely any recognition. The artwork and beautiful tapestries that once adorned the walls were gone. Great rugs from sister countries were missing from the floors. Bare and scarred walls seemed to weep at the loss of their adornment and the defilement of their beauty. Without the coverings on the walls and floors, their footfalls echoed.

By the time he got his wits about him after the shock of the stripped walls and floors, Mikel was gone. The two men pulled him mutely down the long hall toward the exterior of the manor and to a long-unused door. Since childhood, Eldred had played in these halls and had seen the door with its large, rusty lock. Once he had asked his father what lay beyond and was barely given an answer, which at the time had been enough to quench his curiosity — Lord Bathsar mumbled something about unused rooms locked for safekeeping.

Now, the lock was off, and two more men stood before it. When he and his guards neared, the two waiting silently opened the door. Instinct had Eldred planting his feet and straining backward, but it did him no good. His guards lifted him to carry him forward and then down.

A set of well-lit steps descended, and it was there they took him. He heard voices and strained to understand them. The tones were familiar, and he labored harder to pick up words. He needn't have bothered as the men led him directly to the occupied room.

His brother stood with his back to the door, and across from him, facing the door, were Eldred's in-laws. In the corner of the room was Lord Singh's pedagogue, Samuel, wrapped in binding much like Eldred.

Conversation halted when the soldiers pushed him into the room and with a gasped, "Eldred," Sylvan's mother started toward him. She had to move past Mikel to get to him, and as she attempted to do so, Mikel struck her across the side of her head, knocking her to the ground. A howl erupted from Sylvan's father and he pushed forward, but a wall of soldiers barred his way. While Eldred uttered grunts and strained at his bindings, Mikel sniffed a laugh.

Sylvan's mother sat on the floor holding her head, obviously rocked by the blow.

"So, I was just telling Eldred, I require information on Sylvan's location." At her daughter's name, Lady Singh looked up at Mikel through loose strands of her hair before her gaze streaked to Eldred.

"Please no, Eldred. Don't tell him anything."

Taking one step forward, Mikel bent and again struck Lady Singh. She moaned as she fell prone on the floor. Once again, Lord Singh and Eldred exploded in protest.

"As I was saying before being so rudely interrupted, I'm looking for my future bride and I'm certain my brother can help me. You two will be motivation."

Lord Singh's eyes remained locked on his wife, giving no indication of hearing Mikel. However, when Mikel kneeled behind her, pulling her body up into a seated position, he had the lord's full attention.

Taking a long blade from his waistline, Mikel grasped the lady by her hair to wrench her head back and placed the edge of the blade against her throat.

Eldred stared across the room at the ashen face and panic-stricken eyes of his mother-in-law, but he only focused on how red the blood was at her swollen and split lip.

"Now tell me . . . where is Sylvan?"

Eldred's garbled protests filled the room to mix with Lord Singh's shouts. Attempting to push his words past the gag, Eldred's gaze swept from his brother to his mother-in-law. Her eyes locked on his and then, slowly, she shut hers. In the next instant, the knife moved across her neck, freeing a fierce spurt of blood.

The noise generated by the two prisoners reached a fevered peak for several moments. As Mikel stood to push Lady Singh's limp body forward, a moment of absolute silence was broken only by Lord Singh's soft utterance of, "Matilda."

Pacing around the area, staying well away from the growing pool of red flowing from the body on the floor, Mikel again addressed his brother. Eldred didn't even hear him, his gaze locked across the room on the broken visage of Sylvan's father.

When a large hand hit his face hard enough to crack his head back and split his lip, Eldred focused on Mikel.

Eldred and Mikel had never gotten along—always squabbling in the way of siblings. With the dissolution of his engagement to Sylvan, Mikel became quieter, staying to himself. Then, when her marriage to Eldred was announced, he only mentioned it once. Catching Eldred in the hall, he stared at him for a long, quiet moment, and then thrust out his hand to congratulate his little brother.

Eldred, ever leery of Mikel, tentatively took his hand.

"Thank you, brother," he responded, waiting for Mikel to

do something, but he had simply dropped Eldred's hand and walked away. Now a year later, this.

Mikel gestured to his men. "Bring me the old man." Before the lord stood before him, Mikel stepped up to Eldred and freed his gag.

"Mikel, why are you doing this?"

Throwing his hand in the direction of the lord, Mikel asked, "Do you want to save this man?"

Eldred nodded vigorously and strained against the ropes. "Of course. Please, brother, don't hurt him."

"You know what I want. Where is Sylvan? She, her lands, and the power that runs in her veins is mine. *Mine.* You stole what was mine. I'll have her back and you'll pay for what you've done."

"Mikel," Eldred said, his voice and eyes pleading, "these things you're doing and saying are insane. Let me go and we'll figure this all out together. We're family."

"You're wrong." Mikel paced to Lord Singh and took his arm, dragging him forward. The lord moved like a broken man, the loss of his beloved wife too much for him to bear. "I have another family. I haven't needed you for years."

Eldred's eyebrows furrowed at his brother's words, but before he could question more, Mikel pulled Lord Singh in front of him. Holding him with an arm around his throat and a blade tip pressed to his ribs, Mikel repeated his question.

"Where is Sylvan?"

Lord Singh seemed to stir at the question, and he pulled forward, his eyes blazing.

"Don't tell him a thing. I'll gladly give my life to keep my daughter safe."

Mikel leaned into the lord with a growl. "As you wish, old man." His gaze jumped between the lord's pedagogue and Eldred, and he pushed the knife between the old man's ribs. A gasp of pain came from his lips, and within seconds, the lord's eyes glazed over and his body went limp. Gaze bright with excitement, crooked leer splitting his face, Mikel stared at the bound mentor in the corner. As the old man's breath left his body for the final time, a vacuum of air filled the room and, with a wisp of mist, the mentor vanished. Mikel pushed the lord away and leaped to his feet, the body dropping.

"*Whew!*" Mikel yelled, racing across the floor to pick up the empty ropes in the corner. "I always wanted to see that." Hurrying back to Eldred, he brandished the ropes as if they were snakes. "They always say when the heir dies the pedagogue vanishes, but you just don't realize how incredible it is."

"Why did you do that! They never did anything to harm you." Tears pushed at the back of his eyes. Sylvan's parents had always been a part of his life, almost like second parents. Their deaths struck deep in his heart. And his beloved Sylvan—how was he to tell her of their deaths?

Due to the tears in his eyes, he felt more than saw the figure stop in front of him. In his grief, he didn't register the presence until Mikel spoke. "Now little brother, what shall I do with you?"

7

MIKEL BATHSAR HATED HIS FAMILY.

Before they saw fit to bring another child into his life, his parents barely registered in his world. They were an irritation for him to work around, something that he knew he'd deal with one day. He saw himself as a force of one. And he knew he would be great. The only person he despised more than his parents, though, was his brother.

When the woman appeared to him, even as a child, he knew his time had come.

Mikel wasn't sure if it was the light or perhaps a sound that woke him. In the fashion of the very young, he rubbed his eyes and sat up. At the end of his bed stood a beautiful woman. She was surrounded by a glowing aura. Mikel thought he was dreaming.

"Are you real?" he whispered.

When she stepped around the foot of the bed and moved toward him, instead of shrinking from her in fright, he sat up straighter and leaned forward.

"Mikel, I am Cassandra, and I am here for you." Her voice was like a beautiful symphony to his ears. The words played for him alone.

Mikel always knew he was special, always knew he would do something great with his life, and now, here was the proof.

When he jumped from the bed and walked toward her, the woman held out a hand. Without hesitation, he grasped it, and a charge infused his body.

"You and I, Mikel. We will make this world mine. You will be my dagger, my champion." As she spoke the words, his heart swelled, and his breath quickened.

"What do you ask of me, my lady? I am yours."

The woman smiled, and a feeling of love washed over him to block out everything else.

She placed her free hand on his tousled hair, and for a moment, just staring at him, her smile turned predatory.

"We will make this world ours, young Mikel." She turned with him to walk across the room toward the doors of his terrace. Just before they reached them, a wind from inside the room blew them open. He held his breath, sure the glass would shatter, but they remained intact.

He stepped one foot out the doorway, and the world beyond them changed. No longer was he in his bedroom, just entering the night air. Now he was within a cathedral-like room of a dimly lit cave. Musty smells permeated the area, and the sharp scent of smoke rose from small firepits that encircled the room. When he tilted his head back to gaze at the ceiling, the light disappeared and the ceiling, if there was one, wasn't visible. He thought he saw a silhouette of something pass overhead. A sound drew his attention from the great height, and when he looked across the room, he watched something he couldn't identify scuttle back into the darkness. He was not one to be afraid but found he was glad he still held the lady's hand.

"You tremble, my dear. Do not be afraid. Nothing will hurt you—nothing will ever hurt you again." Leading him, she moved to a large fire in the center of the room. Over the fire hung a kettle filled with a thick, bubbling liquid. An acrid stench emanated from the kettle, and his nose wrinkled.

She released him and scooped some of the liquid with a chipped, aged mug. She handed the mug to him and he accepted it without question.

"Sit. Don't drink . . . not yet. Let the brew cool."

Mikel took a seat on a rock away from the heat of the fire, the mug large within his grasp. Away from the woman, he became fearful, glancing about the room, and started when something ran past or he heard a sound.

Always, his gaze returned to her, watching as she went about gathering herbs and vials of unknown elements.

When she began to chant and the room warmed, he strained forward. Now nothing drew his attention from her, his gaze locked on her movements, his hearing locked on her words. The fire leaped to pulse with a myriad of colors. Her back to him, she raised her arms, the sleeves of her cape falling to reveal skin heavily marked with symbols. When her voice grew loud, he stopped studying her skin and focused on what she was saying.

She spoke in a language he couldn't understand, but the

power was evident. Tearing his eyes from her, he scanned the room to see he wasn't alone in his fascination. Small animals crouched in a circle. Animals unlike anything he had ever seen before. Some, he would describe as a mixture of animal and nightmare, and some so bizarre, he couldn't look at them—his brain refused to allow the study.

With a final utterance, the woman turned from the now-dying fire to face the boy. In her hand she held a small vial that she poured into the mug he still held.

"Drink," she whispered. "Drink and be one with me."

Without hesitation, the boy put the mug to his lips. Over the edge of the cup, he watched her. Her smile grew as he tipped the cup, soon blocking out her visage, but in his mind, he held her image.

8

A S SHE MOVED FROM THE curtain of vines, Sylvan stepped among the sleeping men, making certain to place her feet gently and silently. Thirst had finally driven her from her hiding spot, and she'd had to take a chance at escape.

She hadn't wanted to make this move, to attempt to slip past the soldiers—she was afraid. But in the back of her mind was the time spent with Nathaniel. In their talks, they not only discussed how to be a good statesman; how to be a just steward of her father's land; how to be kind, but firm; how to love her people as her family and care for them in the same way.

They also discussed magic.

Though she disputed it, Sylvan had always had an innate magical ability. Magic, or a power of some sort, was strong within the Singh family. Sylvan had been able to enchant. From the time she was little, she could, if she caught someone unaware and gave it the effort it required, stupefy even the most stalwart person. When she was only a toddler, her mother found her crawling around the field while her nanny drooled in the sunlight. Instructions to the staff and training for her began that day. Her teachers often told her she could be very powerful if she'd only try harder. But trying hard wasn't in Sylvan's nature. The magic that ran through her veins was, to her, a toy. Something to entertain and fill her down hours. Until she was eleven, it was not something to be taken seriously or feared.

While discussing her magic, one of the many things Nathaniel instructed her on was the dirkcat's ability to seemingly disappear. He told her it was his belief that his magic and hers were linked. Since she could enchant, their magic seemed to stem from the same tree. Why else would he be a pedagogue to her? But in all the long months they'd worked, she'd never been able to fully grasp the nuances of the art.

"Concentrate, my lady. It's all in the mind," he'd tell her over and over, but no matter how hard she tried — and she never tried very hard — she couldn't tap into that part of her power.

Though Sylvan's power had always been strong in the past, she'd used it to do frivolous things. By the time Nathaniel began to train her, with her fear of her own abilities, the magic would not come. Always, he would shake his head at her, his ears dropping back in irritation when she'd give up without truly trying and failed to achieve success. Sometimes, late at night, when she was alone, she'd try to make herself vanish, but inevitably, darkness would rise in her mind and she'd turn from the magic in fear.

The next day, she'd tell Nathaniel she'd work on her magic tomorrow, then she'd laugh, scratch his head, and wander away.

THAT DAY—THE DAY THAT Sylvan learned to fear herself—the sun shone brightly, and a breeze moved through the garden. Sylvan was supposed to be studying—reading a tome of history loaned to her by one of her teachers. Easily bored, she was daydreaming when a beautiful birdsong caught her attention. She stood, searching with her gaze among the branches of the trees for the minstrel. When the song came again, she homed in on it and caught sight of the bird.

Beautiful. It was blue, but not just blue. The variegated shades darkened like an evening sky just after sunset. She moved closer, but each time she neared, the bird flitted to another branch. She stomped her foot and, with her hands fisted, glared up at the bird.

Summoning her magic, she slipped closer. The bird hopped to a new branch and watched her. When their eyes met, it was caught. Enchanted, it flew from the branch to land on her finger. Sitting in the grass, she gazed raptly at the small creature. Then, her gaze mesmerizing, she commanded it to sing.

So beautiful was the song, she longed to hear it over and over. The effort soon became too much for the small bird, but with her enchantment, it was unable to stop. When the bird dropped from her finger to fall dead on the ground, she jumped up and ran weeping to her father. He returned with her to retrieve the bird, which they buried. They discussed the incident, and he explained the responsibility that came with their magic. She agreed, but since that day, she would no longer use her magic. Just the thought of the darkness she had felt filled her with fear.

OUTSIDE THE TUNNEL, SYLVAN MOVED around the sleeping men, keeping an eye out for sentries. She knew if she continued with this plan, she may be forced to use her magic. Just the thought of it had her mind shutting down—she didn't want to consider it. She kicked herself for not paying closer attention when Nathaniel had tried to teach her. Fear warred with necessity.

A twig snapped under her foot and Sylvan froze. The soldier nearest her moaned and turned in his sleep, but then all was silent.

She had just reached the outer perimeter when a shout arose. Men woke around her and the shout was repeated.

Her heart pounding and any practical thought gone, Sylvan grabbed her skirts in a fist and ran. Leaping over the legs of men not yet risen and dashing around fires, she pushed into the denseness of the forest. Perhaps she could lose them in the underbrush or by crossing the stream.

With the heat and mass of the horde of men behind her, she pushed energy into her legs and increased her speed. The thought that in the near dark she might trip and fall—truly injure herself—surfaced, but she couldn't slow, the panic of flight now having her fully in its grip.

She was beginning to outdistance them, catching the sleeping men unaware, when from both sides previously unseen soldiers closed in, their dark forms breaking from the trees.

When one grabbed her arm, wrenching her to a halt, she

closed her eyes. Fear skittered over her nerves and a survival instinct took over. A fire began in her belly and then her body burned white-hot. Her eyes popped open when the sensations hit her. As if watching someone else, she saw a black mass exit from her—as if it came from the pores of her skin—and beginning at the hand that held her, it soon wrapped the man in a swirling cloud.

Arching back from him, not knowing what was happening, Sylvan grabbed her own arm and yanked on it, but the man had an unbreakable grip on her.

"Let me go. Oh, please. Let me go!" she wailed.

With a final swirling movement, the mass constricted the man, popping him like a ripe grape. Blood and pieces flew in all directions. With a whimper, she dropped to her knees, scraping the hand from her forearm. Hearing footsteps and the calls of male voices, she looked up, eyes wide, breath straining. Her mind focused when she saw a large group of men surrounding her. When she stood, her boot slipped on the fresh pile that was once a man. She righted herself with a tree limb and again took off at a run.

After a few yards, she screeched to a halt and spun in a circle, looking left and right, unsure which way to go. Craning her head, hair flying in her face, she saw a small opening and bolted to it. Dropping and sliding, she evaded the men. Hands grasped for her, but desperation aided in making her agile and fluid.

Just as she thought she might be captured, a soldier tripped and went down—his sword and shield flew out in front of his prone form. Bunching her legs, Sylvan leaped over him to land firmly on the other side. She dug in to continue her flight.

For a moment, the confusion and noise of the encampment were left behind. Stillness ruled, and the scent of the night was fresh and damp. Moving forward, unable to see much beyond her immediate area, Sylvan's mind spun as she looked for a way out.

Like a calm breeze, Nathaniel's voice filled her thoughts. "Concentration, my lady. It's all a mind game—a game we cats play better than most, but one you too will learn."

Grasping a tree to pull herself behind it, Sylvan closed her eyes. The night sounds and scents filled her being. The image of the black cloud emerging from her pushed forward, but with a will she didn't know she possessed, she shoved it down into the recesses of her mind. The pounding of her heart and rasp of her breath calmed as she reached inward. Nathaniel's eyes—large, yellow, and luminous—filled her mind and with a deep breath, she moved forward.

The snapping of branches and calls of men threatened to break her concentration, but newfound, steely will kept her focused.

Weightlessness filled her. It was as if she were floating above the rocky broken hillside. Worry and stress dissipated, leaving her calm. Empty.

Relaxed, sleepy eyes opened in the darkness. Men moved around her, yelling to each other and searching in the forest for their quarry. The sounds came to her as if she were behind a closed door. Like a wraith, Sylvan stepped forward and moved stealthily away from the fray. Step by step, moment by moment, she moved from those who sought her. The men fell behind, their shouts fading. None followed. None saw.

The quiet of the forest closed around her, flowing through her as she moved. Cool, dark, and secretive. Her senses expanded. Above her the brush of hunting birds' wings reached her ears along with the scurry of feet as their prey fled. She became one with the night. The sound of a breeze when it ruffled the wild grasses, the scent of dew forming as the night cooled, a distant call of a coyote.

Time passed without thought, and Sylvan moved without tiring.

The sun was just poking its head over a distant hill when she came back to herself. She was exhausted but strangely exhilarated. The muscles of her legs and back ached, but her mind was clear and focused. Before her, in the pale morning light, lay the home of Eldred's parents. The gate to the front was open, and giving a soft cry of thanksgiving, she started forward, anxious to enlist their help in returning her world to its normal state.

Almost clearing the forest, she paused. Something wasn't right. Straining to listen, she scanned the area, senses open to pick up the normal sounds of the manor life—the neigh of a horse, low of a cow, clang of metal on metal from the blacksmith, laughter of children, and scolding of women. Nothing. Everything was quiet. The longer the silence lasted, the more the prickles rose on her skin.

When a rider approached the gate, two men stepped from

the interior to confront him, and a shiver ran up her spine. The two men were soldiers, but they didn't have on the Bathsar colors. In fact, their uniforms matched those of the men she and Eldred saw in her parents' courtyard.

The hums of the men's words floated to her, but she wasn't close enough to understand. Stepping carefully, sliding along a side wall, she moved forward until they became clear.

". . . in order. The manor is under our control. I'm here to speak to your commander and to inform you to take control of any girls who pass. They are to be kept safe until the captain comes from the manor to identify and take possession of the one we are looking for."

When the soldiers at the gate just glanced at each other, the rider raised his voice. "Is that understood?" he said, which caused the soldiers' eyes to jump to him and their heads to nod vigorously.

"And they're not to be injured. If *the* girl is harmed, someone will pay."

More nodding followed this, and the rider kicked his horse to continue into the courtyard.

Sylvan realized the area wasn't safe, but she couldn't move. She didn't know where else to go and wondered what came of Eldred's parents. She needed to ensure they were safe. They could escape together. Her beloved would come for them, no matter where they went.

Closing her eyes and looking inward, she again tapped that spark of magic she'd found in her desperation last night. A warmth flowed through and around her. It felt like slipping into a bath or walking into the sunshine. She envisioned the warmth expanding to fill not only herself but also the immediate area around her.

When she again opened her eyes, the day was thrown into stark relief—all lines sharper, colors brighter, and sounds clearer.

Her gaze sharpened on the gate and the soldiers within. She moved toward it while concentrating on the bubble around her. Stepping through the gate, she paused, waiting to hear a warning. So ready for flight was she, that when nothing happened—no warning, no amassing of men—she almost lost her concentration and dropped the camouflage of her bubble.

As she stood in the entry, one of the young soldiers who the man on horseback spoke with walked within a few inches of her. Pivoting so they didn't bump shoulders, Sylvan watched him continue out the gate and around the end of the wall. After the soldier passed from her sight, she turned and looked at the courtyard and the manor house beyond. The yard was empty. There was no sign of the other guard.

The Bathsar estate was markedly smaller than the Singhs'. It often surprised people that Lord Singh would wed his only child into a family less wealthy than his own. But the Singh and Bathsar families had been close for generations, the reigning lords having grown to manhood together.

Sylvan knew the Bathsar estate as well as her own, having visited here many times. With a deliberate stride, she marched across the courtyard to an open door and entered.

A smell permeated the hallway—a smell of old blood,

bodily excretions, and rotting flesh. With a hand to her mouth, Sylvan held back a gag and pulled the neckline of her shirt up to cover her nose and mouth. Stepping lightly, she moved forward and neared the large room at the end of the hall.

Low candles burned on a grand dining table. Around the table, slumped in their chairs, were not only Lord Bathsar and his lady, but trusted servants—the butler, head housekeeper, stable master, and many more.

A full spread of once-sumptuous foods lay before them, now all well into the act of decomposition. The room was silent except for a low-grade humming she couldn't at first identify. When she moved closer, drawn by a morbid sense of curiosity and shock, a swarm of black flies rose from the nearest bodies.

Gagging, she stepped back, almost tripping on something on the floor. She caught herself before going down and noticed a severed stump of a man's hand below her.

No longer able to control her need to vomit, she ran to a corner of the room of horrors and emptied her stomach.

When she overcame her heaves and took a deep breath, she stood straight and wiped at her mouth with the back of her hand.

Footsteps echoed behind her. Without thought or effort, the warmth within rose and expanded. Two men entered the far end of the hallway, stopping short and covering their mouths and nose with gloved hands.

"By the gods, it's ripe in here."

"Sure, and you'd think they'd clean it up, but been told the new master wants 'em left just as they are."

The first man moved closer to her to peer into the dining area.

"Creepy, if you asked me."

His companion joined him and peeked at the scene from around his friend.

"Aye. And to do that to your own family."

His word caused both the first man and Sylvan to whip around, their motions mirroring each other.

"What you mean, family?"

Putting his shoulders back and chest out, the second man proclaimed, "Didn't you know? It were the eldest son of the Bathsar family who done this."

"No," his friend muttered.

No, Sylvan thought. But a thought knocked on the back of her mind. Was she really surprised?

"Ayah. Finally snapped, that one did. Always been a bit of an odd one, I'd say." The man looked left and right to ensure he wasn't overheard. "And you know what else?"

Sylvan turned to look back into the room, thinking of Mikel and the horror her life would have been with him as her husband.

"Heard he left here and did the same at the Singh estate."

"No."

"No!"

The word erupted from Sylvan and the man at the same time. The men gave no indication of having heard her, and they continued to scan the room.

She hurried toward the men to stand directly in front of

them, not sure how to get more information. She needn't have worried, though. The man was only too happy to continue for the benefit of his friend.

"Yup. Overheard the Cap'n and a rider talking when I took him his breakfast. Said somethin' about some girl and the killings at the manor. Said the whole place was dead." With eyes big and round, the one man listened to the tale of the other. "You're a new one here, but the folks in this area been talkin' for years about how crazy the oldest son is. Now he has it all — just lookin' for some girl."

Sylvan backed away from the men who continued to discuss the killings and the mess in the adjoining room.

My parents dead—and Eldred . . .

A sob caught in her throat and her hands found their way to her belly. Their child. He never even knew about their child.

After a moment, Sylvan's shoulders straightened and her chin rose. Eldred's child was now her sole responsibility. Her face grim, she contemplated her future. Her parents were dead along with her beloved and his parents. The closest relative was the monster who committed the slayings. She didn't have a drive other than to take her child far away from here. Far away from Mikel.

Nodding slowly, a plan formed. She would require provisions for a journey of such a length, and this was as good a place as any to get them.

She closed her eyes, took a deep breath, and reached deep within. She felt the warmth of her power where it surrounded her. Where it filled her. It was a skill Nathaniel had spent so many hours teaching her. Camouflage. Enchantment. Guise.

She let go of her fear and it dissipated from within her core. Her magic, after a little over a day of use, was part of her. A part she had voluntarily sacrificed. A part she would not give up again.

She would put her plan in motion. She would stay hidden and find a new life for herself and her child.

Leaving the two gossiping men behind her, she stepped out of the still-open outer door and moved to the nearby kitchen. Eyeing the closed kitchen door, she was just contemplating what to do when the dilemma solved itself. The door was pushed from within to eject a young servant. When she stopped to respond to a yell from the other side, Sylvan slipped in.

Looking around to ensure she was alone, Sylvan grabbed two loaves of bread, a wedge of cheese, and a full water bag from the kitchen. No one worked in the general area, and as she waited again by the door, she felt secure in her camouflage.

It wasn't too long before the door again opened and Sylvan slipped out as the girl stepped in, her arms now full of carrots.

Just outside the kitchen door, Sylvan stopped and looked around the Bathsar estate. She made a vow to herself.

Our child will come home one day to reclaim this land and to give justice to both sets of his grandparents. Mikel will pay for his actions.

9

THE BOY WOKE IN THE alley. Around him the sounds of the city were already loud. This day would be like the last and the next like them. He had no reason to think his life would become any different than it had always been. He didn't know how he'd come to be here. Didn't have a name or a family. Each day was simply a struggle to survive.

When he woke, he listened before moving. When all around his immediate area was quiet, he pushed the rags from himself and stood.

The day was new, the sun barely risen, and the alley was in shadow. Staying to the side of the alley, along the wall of a building, the child moved out to find something to eat. Trash spilled from containers, some of it beyond what even he could consume. But within the mess, he located enough to fill his belly.

For the remainder of the day, he stayed out of the sight of the merchants. One quick enough to see him when he attempted to steal a trinket—something he might sell for a warm bed—

didn't hesitate to act.

"Hey, you, boy!" he yelled and advanced on him, raising a staff.

The boy fled. He was fast, a trait that had saved him many a time. The merchants weren't the only threat in his world. Other orphans, adults in search of an easy victim, and the possibility of starvation or freezing, all made his life hard.

THE NEXT MORNING, HE WOKE much the same as every other. This time, however, he lay perfectly still—something was not right.

Keeping his eyes closed, feigning sleep, he strained to identify what was out of place.

A smell. His nostrils quivered as he picked up a scent he'd never encountered before. Drawing a deep breath, his body warmed and his mind relaxed.

"I know you're awake, boy."

He jumped at the proximity of the voice, unable to control his start. Whoever spoke was sitting right beside him.

When he cracked open his eyes, he saw a man. Sitting, clothed in a robe, the man looked directly at him. His legs seemed to be folded under him. His arms wrapped through the sleeves so that the only part of him visible was his face under the cowl of his cloak. The boy studied him, and the man sat still and quiet, allowing him his time.

The man's face, a pleasant face, wore a short brown beard slightly darker than his eyebrows. After a moment of joint contemplation, the man's lips curled in a smile.

"Do you have a name?" The timbre of his voice resonated

within the boy, relaxing him further.

The boy shook his head but didn't speak.

"Is there one you might like? A name you wish to be called?"

The boy had never been asked this question. For a moment, he kept his gaze on the man. Then, he sat up and shook his head, waiting to see what else the man would say.

Nodding, the man leaned in. "I've always liked the name Patrick. Do you like that name? I could call you Patrick."

The boy thought for a moment and then gave an answering nod.

"Splendid."

With a fluid motion, the man stood. "Come, Patrick," he said, and turning, he walked away.

The boy threw off the coverings of his night, leaped to his feet, and scrambled after the man. He'd almost reached him by the time he arrived at the end of the alley. As the sun broke over the buildings, the rays hit the man. The boy stopped and gaped. No shadow darkened in the man's silhouette. The sun's beams shone through him to illuminate the wall of the alley.

When the boy stopped, the man also halted and turned to look at him, his eyebrow raised. Seeing the astonishment on the boy's face, he looked down at his own frame, a chuckle forming.

"I'll explain everything to you. Let's take a walk and have a talk."

When the man started forward again, Patrick followed him.

10

MIKEL BATHSAR STUDIED THE ROOM in the topmost portion of the tower. Always in the past, his practices had been in secret, performed in the lowest, darkest reaches of his parents' estate.

No longer. The Singh manor was now his home. Its vast grandiose his to enjoy. He'd been free to have his special collection moved to a room of his choosing. He remembered this room used to be one of Sylvan's favorites.

He recalled coming here to play as children, his father on some task with Lord Singh. Sylvan, then just a young girl, had been playing with her dolls. He'd thrown a favorite doll from the window and watched it smash upon the cobblestones in the courtyard. She had crouched, weeping in a corner, afraid to do more than shoot glares at him. He'd contemplated what it would be like to throw her from the window. Would she scream on the way down? Would she shatter like the doll?

When he'd stepped toward her, intent on discovering the answer to his questions, her cries had turned into whimpers.

Just as he reached for her, the door was pushed open and his meddling younger brother allowed her to escape. It was all for the better, though. Soon enough it became evident she would be powerful. To kill her would have been an error. He could use that power—and her beauty.

And it was easy enough to experiment on others.

Now, scanning the room, he felt closer to her with the memory of their times together. He'd find her soon and then he'd introduce her personally to his mistress. He'd show her all the power that could be theirs.

Moving through the room, Mikel reverently touched his things. Among them were candles, knives, and a few precious stone amulets, as well as mortars for grinding spices and powders. Stacked in the corner, cages filled with a variety of small animals and birds awaited his attention.

After the first time, when Cassandra appeared in his room, he'd thought perhaps he'd experienced a dream. Many weeks passed before she again called him. He'd awoke in the night, sweaty, his chest heaving. When her voice sounded in his head, he bit his tongue hard enough to draw blood. With the pain, he'd tasted the metallic tang in his mouth and known he was awake.

He'd climbed out of bed and scrambled to get dressed. Retrieving a horse from the stables, he followed the trail she described into the mountains. He was still physically a young boy, and the trek was a hard one. Fear filled him often, but the allure of her voice wasn't something he could deny.

Deep within a dark cave, in the wet and muck, he'd reached

into a crevasse in the stone to pull out a bundle. Back outside, under the light of a full moon, he'd kneeled to unwrap the package. His eyes had beheld an ancient pendant. Metallic and old, the amulet shone, free of tarnish. He held it up to better see it, tracing the lines. Whispers in his mind caressed him, telling him how proud she was of him. Mikel beamed from the mental stroking. The acceptance—the promises—kept him enthralled and coming back, time and again to do the bidding of his lady. By retrieving the pendant, he'd proven his worth and loyalty. His mistress told him it was important, that it would allow Mikel to come to her, and it had. Since that day, he'd learned many things. Many wonderful things.

The one thing he'd failed at was to secure the girl. His mistress wanted her—well, parts of her—and told Mikel he could have the rest. He was to show her the darkness within. When, as a boy, they were to be married, he thought the pact won. Then Eldred spoiled everything.

Well, he'd pay.

Finishing his circuit of the room, Mikel moved to the center and touched the stone pedestal he'd had hauled up here. On the pedestal rested a porcelain bowl stained red from long use. An ancient knife lay beside the bowl. He caressed it before picking it up. Bringing it to his lips, he whispered sweet words of promise and praise. This blade was one of the first items he'd been gifted with. With it, he'd been able to bring the essence of his mistress closer than ever before. In time, they would again stand together. In time, they would rule the world.

From across the room a whimper sounded. Looking up, he

stared blindly for a moment before glancing over his shoulder. With a spin of his body, he moved to the corner where the sound came from.

Tied, hands to feet and gagged, crouched a man, his eyes huge in the dim recesses. They reflected the light of the many candles. As Mikel stared down at him, his head tilted to the side to better regard the prisoner, and another whimper escaped. The small sound trailed away as Mikel's face broke into a smile. Stepping toward the bound man, he chuckled as the sharp scent of urine permeated the air.

IT WAS A WHILE LATER when Mikel walked through the door, wiping his hands on a cloth. Finished, he tossed the stained fabric into a corner and turned to his servant.

"Who did you say wished to speak with me?"

The servant's eyes stayed glued to the cloth on the floor. A shudder passed through his frame and he answered in a low voice.

"A man from the east, my lord. He says he bears a present for you."

"Hmm." Mikel scratched the edge of his nose. "All right. Bring him into the main meeting hall. I'll be there shortly."

"Yes, my lord."

When Mikel strode into the manor's main hall, the only person present was an unassuming man. Small in stature, he stood against the far wall facing the doorway. His direct gaze had Mikel stopping for a moment before continuing past him and up to a small dais.

"My lord Bathsar," the small man began from behind him. Putting up a hand to halt his words, Mikel took a seat in a large chair and, with a small gesture, had a servant hurrying from the recess of the room to fill a goblet with wine. After taking a sip, Mikel eyed the visitor.

"So, I'm told you bring me a gift."

"Yes, my lord, that is true." The small man walked to the bottom step of the dais.

"Well?"

"My lord. My name is Orson, and I've traveled a long way to meet you. The gift I offer is my services."

Mikel eyed the man. Whatever would he need from him?

"You say you've heard of me, have you?"

With a nod, the small man stepped onto the bottom stair.

"If I might be permitted, sir, to tell you a story." Without waiting for permission, the small man went on. "Some nights ago, I had a dream. In this dream, a voice came to me. The voice was full of power and anger, and with this voice came an image of you."

As the tale spun out, Mikel leaned forward, arms braced on his thighs, and listened intently. His dreams often revolved around a voice full of power. A voice that had directed his life for the past fifteen years. The voice of his lady.

The man's eyes gleamed and he stared into Mikel's eyes. "Of course, at the time I didn't know who you were, but the voice gave me instructions and a direction. It gave me images— wonderful images—that showed me you are the one I would serve. One I could help to become even more."

Mikel met the small man's gaze, and a flitting shadow crossed his eyes. A darkness kindred to the darkness inside of him. His mistress sent this man to him. He would be the foundation he could build his empire upon. Closely watching the small man, Mikel gestured for the servant. When the man rushed forward once again, Mikel halted him.

"Prove your loyalty," he whispered. Keeping his gaze fixed upon the visitor, he told the servant, "Pour our guest some wine." The servant stepped forward with a goblet of wine just as the small man moved. Quick as a striking snake, from under his cloak, a knife appeared in his hand and the servant's neck was cut almost to the bone.

Blood spurted to hit the small man along his face and chest as, without a whisper, the servant fell to the ground, the goblet shattering on the step.

Mikel stood, his fingers clenched, his breath coming hard, nostrils flaring. His heart beat loudly in his ears. His gaze shifted from the body at his feet to the face of his guest, now dripping with the servant's blood. Never had he met another like himself. Never had he seen a man move so fast.

Excited, he walked down the stairs and approached the small man. Taking his face in both of his hands, he smeared the blood over the man's skin. With gore-covered palms, he angled Orson's face up and gazed down at him.

"Welcome, brother."

11

SYLVAN WALKED FOR TWO DAYS. It was night when she spotted a campfire in the distance. Keeping her gaze alert, she approached slowly.

In the light of the flames, she spotted an elderly man and a middle-aged couple. She watched them for a time, and seeing that they acted just as they appeared, and needing provisions, she pulled back her power and allowed herself to be seen. She brushed off her skirt, straightened her shoulders, and walked closer to the campsite.

"Hello to the camp. May I enter?" she called in the universal query when approaching a stranger's camp. At her words, all three heads jerked up, and the younger man reached for a sword resting on a log beside him.

"Who's there?" he called into the night, head pivoting as he peered into the darkness.

Sylvan stepped to the edge of the fire's illumination. She kept her hands open and to her sides, so they could see she held no weapons. They were leery of her, but she was leery of them.

She watched, ready to bolt at a moment's notice.

"Jeremiah, it's just a girl," the woman said and laid her hand on the man's arm. He kept his weapon at the ready as he approached her, the woman on his heels.

"What do you want?"

With a cautious step, Sylvan moved closer. "Just a safe, warm place to pass the night. And some food if you can spare it."

The man looked left and right into the darkness. "Why are you traveling alone? Don't seem right for a young girl to be traveling alone."

He was clearly suspicious of her motives, so Sylvan looked over his shoulder at the woman.

"My parents just passed," she said, her voice cracked with real emotion. "I'm traveling to the coast to the home of my relatives."

The woman moved around the man, placing her hand on his arm. "Jeremiah, it'll be all right. She's just a girl." Turning to Sylvan, she gestured her forward.

"Come to the warmth of the fire, dear. We don't have much, but it's good and filling."

Sylvan walked toward her, keeping an eye on the man and giving him a wide berth. She sat with the woman and gladly accepted a bowl of what appeared to be a meat stew.

Watching her closely, and still scanning the tree line, the man came back to the fire to take his place between the woman and the old man. He laid down his sword but kept it close to his side, within easy reach.

Glancing from one to the other while she greedily ate her stew, Sylvan saw the old man was blind—the white film that covered his eyes reflected in the firelight as he stared off into nothing. As if feeling her gaze, the unseeing one's eyes shifted to her.

"Fare thee well this evening, daughter?"

Since he used an address from the old speak when greeting her, she answered in kind.

"Yes, father. Thank you for your care."

Nodding at her, he added, "You are safe tonight, child. No harm will come to you and the babe."

At his words, Sylvan started and almost dropped her bowl. Her eyes flew to those of the others, who now stared at her. Looking back to the old man, she replied, "Thank you, father," and, burrowing her head in her dish, went back to eating her meal.

When she finished, the woman, who said her name was Glenda, brought her a blanket to wrap in. Lying by the fire, her stomach full, she was soon fast asleep.

THE NEXT MORNING, SYLVAN WOKE to the clank of a spoon on a kettle and the smell of boiling oats. When she stirred and sat up, the woman asked, "Have you a husband?"

She knew the stigma that came with being with child and unmarried but didn't want to tell the woman her husband was dead. Another death within the same family may lead to speculation when the story of the massacre came around—and she didn't need a trail of gossip following her.

Dropping her head and refusing to meet the woman's eyes, Sylvan whispered, "No, ma'am."

The woman didn't say anything—just stared for a moment. Then, filling a bowl with the meal, she handed it to Sylvan.

"Eat. You'll need to keep up your strength."

WHEN THE FAMILY BROKE CAMP, Sylvan helped, and when they headed down the road, she went with them. It seemed safer traveling with them, and if Mikel had people looking for a lone girl, she was less obvious with a group.

They were heading in the right direction—which was anywhere other than the way she'd come—so there was no good reason not to travel with them. They didn't question her moving within their group, and in silent thanks, she did all she could to help.

Over the next few days, Sylvan watched and listened. She'd always lived among servants, so although she knew the fundamentals of cooking and cleaning, she'd never done much of it. And she'd never even thought to cook over a campfire. Staying close to Glenda, she found it simple to pick up on how things were done. She listened to Glenda's instructions. The woman knew what she was doing, and Sylvan knew the woman's cooking was good from experience.

Along with the cooking and cleaning, in the evening, by the light of the fire, she read to the old man from a small, precious book the family owned. She liked this task most of all and would never think of it as a chore. She missed her books, and though reading while spending time with the old man made her heart ache for her father, she found warmth in the memories.

The husband, Jeremiah, never seemed to get over his initial distrust of her, but his wife liked the company and help with the chores, so he didn't complain. The old man was Jeremiah's father, and having Sylvan around improved his days considerably. She took an almost immediate liking to him and often busied herself with finding ways to ease his discomfort.

In her former life, part of the responsibilities of the lady of the manor was to see to the ills of the people. While visiting the citizens under the supervision of her mother, it became obvious that Sylvan had a natural ability as a healer. She utilized those abilities and training now to aid the man with his aches and pains. Part of the pleasure of her day was searching for plants and herbs as they traveled. It was a quiet time for herself.

"Father," she said one night while rubbing his arthritic hand with an oil solution she'd made, "where do you hail from?"

The old man sighed with contentment as the salve worked into his sore fingers. "Why do you ask, my child?"

"I would like to know more about you."

"Now, now, my lady. I don't pry, and neither should you."

Sylvan's heart jumped at his words, her ministrations on his hands stopping.

My lady. How did he know that? And his comment disclosing her pregnancy. *Who is this man?*

"Why did you call me that?" she asked casually, starting her massage again.

"We're alone. Jeremiah and Glenda are down at the river.

You don't need to be coy with me."

"Who are you?"

"Just an old, blind man—but sometimes I'm allowed to see things, very interesting things." Turning his hand in hers, he gripped tightly. When he spoke, his voice took on a faraway quality. "The child you carry will be a catalyst to right the wrongs in the land. You must stay safely hidden—you and your child. One. Two. Three, and they will become One. At the breaking of age, action and bravery will be required."

When he fell silent, Sylvan pulled her hand from his.

"Breaking of age? What does that mean?"

The old man stared at her out of eyes long blind. With a shrug, he said, "That is for you to discover."

Sylvan's head turned as she heard the couple coming back. Through the part of the wagon tenting, she caught sight of them coming up the hill. They laughed and had their arms around each other. The image of them, happy within each other's embrace, made her heart ache with the loss of Eldred. Smiling at them as they neared, she stood and approached Glenda to inquire about helping with the next meal, but her thoughts were on the old man's words.

12

CASSANDRA'S LAUGHTER REVERBERATED IN THE room. A large smile remained even once the sound ceased.

When she stepped back from her viewing bowl, the waters calmed, and the image dissipated. It pleased her to see her two disciples, Mikel and Orson, finally come together. Men with such an obsession for their own desires were easy to manipulate. They would make a formidable team in her quest for triumph over her brother, to make this world hers. And if they didn't succeed, it would be easy enough to replace them.

A harsh call preceded the entry of a huge crow through one of the upper portals of the castle. Its feathers were black as the darkest night. Its wingspan was so large, they displaced air on its circuit to the woman. It landed on a table beside her and ambled to her, slipping slightly where sharp talons met the surface of the slab.

With a slight coo, Cassandra ran a sharp-tipped finger over the head and beak of the bird. It stood still as if basking in her adoration.

"Pretty bird," she murmured. "What do you have for me?"

The bird cawed loudly, and then again.

She placed a knuckle to her mouth as if to contain her words, but then a loud guffaw ejected from her. With a spin of delight, she circled the room.

"Perfect. Absolutely perfect." And she laughed again. "That old man will fill her head with nonsense. Soon she'll be desperate for assistance. Let Caleb try to influence the game. Let him think he can win." It would make her triumph all the better.

13

SYLVAN TRAVELED WITH JEREMIAH AND his family for many weeks, and the time was good. They were common people but hardworking and honest. Though she visited often with the old man, he never again spoke of his sight.

One day, a little over three months in, Jeremiah turned their wagon to the east at a split in the road and, walking behind with Glenda, Sylvan paused.

She stared at the path that led west. The image before her appeared to pulse and elongate. For a moment, it was as if she could almost see her destination at the end.

"What is it, Sylvan?"

She glanced at Glenda and at the slowly departing wagon and again turned to the west road.

Superimposed over the route, she now saw an image. Three equal lines connected at their ends. They came to a point, and that point was aimed down. A feeling of expectancy flowed into her, and she knew in her heart that her destiny was at a crossroads.

"I have to go, Glenda," she said and she ran to the wagon to pull a small bundle from the back. Seeing the old man resting inside, she climbed up and kissed him on the cheek.

"I'll remember your words, father."

Taking her hand, he held it for a moment. "Be safe, daughter." And then he released her. Jumping from the wagon with her bundle, Sylvan ran to Glenda and gave her a hug.

"Thank you. I won't forget your kindness."

"But, Sylvan . . ."

"It's all right. Everything will be all right." Shouldering her pack, she stepped toward the opposite path.

FOR FIVE DAYS SHE WALKED, eating and drinking from the supplies in her bundle, and at night, she lay wrapped in a cloak to remain hidden in the forest. At the end of the fifth day, the trail opened into a small fishing community. As she walked through the streets, she drew stares. She knew it was unusual to see a woman traveling alone but kept her head high.

Near the middle of the village, Sylvan was drawn to a busy building. The sounds of many voices flowed from it along with the clang of dishes and the scent of cooking. Turning to it, she walked up the stairs and pushed through the front door.

The interior was dark, and for a moment she couldn't discern what the inside held. Her eyes adjusted to reveal a busy pub. Men ate, drank, and talked while servers moved among them.

Sylvan walked into the room, sliding along the edge to bring her closer to what she thought to be the kitchen. There an older woman stood, surveying the noise and confusion.

"Excuse me, ma'am."

The woman glanced around and down at Sylvan. She eyed her from her unbrushed hair to her booted feet.

"What you want?" the woman asked with a sharp tone and, dismissing her, turned back to monitor the dining hall. Sylvan swallowed hard at the woman's attitude and pushed herself to go on.

"I'm looking for a job."

The woman looked her over again and said, "Got all the serving girls I need."

"I can cook." The months with Glenda had taught her proficiency in creating meals. They weren't fancy, but they were good and hearty.

Turning completely toward her, the woman stared her fully in the face for a minute. With a gesture, she moved off and threw over her shoulder, "Follow me," while she walked to a door at the back. When they passed through the opening, they entered a room full of chaos. Meals were being prepared and people rushed everywhere.

Raised voices issued from around the room, pans clanked and, in the corner, a young girl, perhaps Sylvan's age, wept. Standing aside with her hands on her ample hips, the woman said, "Show me."

A moment of doubt had Sylvan looking left and right, not sure how to proceed. She'd never been in a kitchen so large. It wasn't clear who was in charge or what was a priority. The counters and floors were dirty with spilled food, while bowls and pans of cooked and uncooked foods sat victim to the elements.

Taking a deep breath, Sylvan marched into the fray. One or two of the workers eyed her with distrust, but no one stopped their work as she joined their ranks. Not assuming the safety of the meats that sat out, she glanced around until she saw what appeared to be an entrance to a cold storeroom and pantry. Selecting her area, she got to work.

The counters were covered with what appeared to be more than just a day's filth. With a wet rag, she did a quick but thorough scrub of her spot. Satisfied with her working space, she went to the storage-pantry area and gathered ingredients for a meat and vegetable pie, which was a favorite of Jeremiah's. On her way back, she lifted an appropriate pan from some clean ones on the edge of a wash bin.

With the woman's eyes on her, Sylvan got busy. Her initial nervousness soon passed as she lost herself in the pleasure of cooking. Without realizing it, she began to hum an old tune, and after looking at her strangely, the women around her calmed and added their voices to her song. A peace filled Sylvan, fueled by memories of home and her time with Glenda. Thinking of the child growing within her, a warmth of love expanded to fill her chest.

Slipping the meat pie into a warm oven, she again went to the pantry. This time she brought a bowl with her and collected ingredients for a coarse, dark bread. After combining the fixings, she flipped the dough out and kneaded it—her hands had grown strong over the past months.

The sounds of the women humming and singing penetrated her thoughts. She joined in with a smile, not realizing it had been her to begin the camaraderie in the first place.

When she placed the formed dough in a pan and covered it with a damp cloth to rise, she felt a presence behind her. Turning, she saw the woman who had led her into the kitchen.

"You're hired."

Caught by surprise, Sylvan sputtered, "Don't you want to taste it first?"

The woman shook her head. "I know good cooking. You need a place to stay?"

Sylvan nodded her head, mute with surprise.

"Come on. I'll get you a room. You'll start tomorrow — sunrise. Room and board, plus a little extra for your purse." Turning to walk out, she yelled at one of the women, "Get that pie out before it burns."

THE THIN MATTRESS GROANED IN protest as Sylvan landed flat on her face. Her workday had ended moments ago, and the most she'd been able to do was to make it back to the room she'd been given. She shared the room with another woman named Martha, and although they hadn't had time to really visit, she seemed pleasant.

Her first day had been exhausting. Though she'd managed to organize her little part of it, the kitchen was in chaos.

Rising before the sun peeked over the horizon, she'd washed and hurried to the inn. The building in which the female employees slept was to the back, but conveniently located. As soon as she'd walked in, the woman from yesterday, who Sylvan soon discovered was named Meg and owned the two buildings, told her she'd be making more, many more, of her meat pie and bread—the inn being a popular destination for travelers and locals alike.

Finding her spot, she once again cleaned it up, scrubbing the counter and moving pans and utensils to a basin to be washed. Meg walked by, handing her an apron from a stack by the door and informing her that first customers arrived late morning, so to get busy.

And get busy she did. Her addition to the usual fare was a big hit, the quality and change making them highly desired. She soon lost count of the number of pies she created, loaves of bread lying before her like waiting soldiers.

Toward midday, she stepped outside with a heel from a loaf of bread to stand in the shade and consume the small meal. Turning her face to the breeze, she'd lifted her hair when a footstep behind her made her jolt.

"Bit jumpy, ain't ya," Meg muttered and stared with perceptive eyes.

"Just a bit tired. I'm not used to working in a busy kitchen—but I'll get used to it," she hastened to add.

"Well, you're doin' real fine. Keep it up."

"Thank you, Meg." The compliment surprised her, being the first she'd heard clear the woman's lips.

"Ah, well . . . don't be out here too long." And she turned to return to the inn.

LYING ON HER BED, WATCHING the sun sink in the sky, Sylvan's tired mind pulled her into thoughts of the past. The loss of her parents, husband, and home. The legacy of her family ending in one horrific day.

A small sob escaped her lips, and tears ran down the side of her face and over the bridge of her nose to wet the pillow.

When the door opened and her roommate stepped in, she turned her head toward the wall and stifled her small sounds. She didn't know what she was doing or where she'd end up, but her instincts told her to keep all personal information to herself. It had been months since she'd seen or heard anything of Mikel, but knowing him, she was certain he wouldn't give up.

Sylvan heard the other woman move around their room for a few moments, the splashing of water in a bowl, and the shifting of clothing. These familiar sounds sang her a lullaby and she drifted to sleep.

14

ELDRED'S EYES CRACKED OPEN WITH the squeal of the door. For the first days—or weeks—he'd attempted to keep track of the time. Soon, though, the days blurred. The beatings became so frequent that his body barely registered the pain from one before another began.

At first, they questioned him on the whereabouts of his Sylvan, but after enough time, even that changed. If he knew, he wouldn't tell them, but the truth was, he had no idea where she'd gone. She was to meet him at the river. He remembered the last moments before closing the hidden door on her. So young, so beautiful. His pulse quickened with the thoughts of what could have become of her all alone in the woods.

Pulled back into the now by rough hands, Eldred barely kept his feet when yanked from the floor. His clothes were ragged—what remained of them—and hung from his emaciated frame. His head hung and his hair, grown long and unkempt, fell about his face to obscure his vision. A large hand pushed from behind and, stumbling, he trod forward, not caring where he was to go.

His feet slid as he moved down a flight of stairs, and some semblance of sanity returned to him. Catching himself on the wall, he halted his forward momentum and then continued. Perhaps he should have let himself fall. At least the torture would end.

At the bottom of the stairs, another man took his upper arm firmly and directed him into a small, dark room. A brazier threw off light and meager warmth, but what caught Eldred's attention were the rings hanging from bolts in the far wall. He stopped only to be shoved forward again.

The first man joined him and the second, and together the men shoved him into the wall face-first and quickly buckled the shackles to him.

With the side of his face laid along the rough, cold stone, he strained to peer over his shoulder. When he heard the whisper of a slithering sound, he wrenched his head to the other side, scraping skin from its surface, to try to see what was coming.

A streak of white-hot pain laced down his back and he knew the pain of before was nothing. Screaming with each consecutive strike of the whip, his sanity flew up and away from his body.

15

O
RSON STOOD IN THE CORNER of the tower room and watched the ritual. Mikel Bathsar chanted, mixing substances into a small bowl.

Orson had observed as Mikel gathered some of the ingredients. The body growing cold in the corner was a testament to the freshness of the items.

Orson enjoyed assisting Lord Bathsar in his rituals. Knowing his own predilection for the torture and use of others, he would have found pleasure in the things that Mikel did even without a higher calling. Had he not heard the voice in his head personally, which brought him to this place, he would have thought this man mad. As it was, there were times he thought they might share the same delusion.

Mikel spoke of his mistress. Her beauty. Her darkness. Orson had never been granted access to her as Mikel had. Always, he worked hard, that reward in the front of his mind. His desire to stand with her something he dreamed of. When Mikel spoke of her, Orson superimposed himself in the story in place of Mikel Bathsar. Someday, he would be one with his mistress.

The flicker of firelight reflecting against the glass of a side cabinet caught his attention and held it. The flames were so beautiful—and hypnotic. There were times when he would stare for hours. When he came back to himself, his body would be stiff from the prolonged inactivity, but his mind would be full of wonderful thoughts. New, imaginative, wonderful thoughts.

In the center of the room, his master finished the final steps of a special ritual. He was fixated, always fixated on finding the girl. They'd been looking for months, but no sign or word of her had come.

That first day, the small man was put in charge of all the soldiers, answering only to this man, and he'd been given a primary job: find Sylvan Singh. Or Bathsar, Orson thought. Once, when he thought to mention that she was the wife of his brother, Mikel had struck him.

His master wanted her—perhaps even needed her. He'd mentioned, again and again, that their mistress wanted her above all things.

Over the course of the past few months, being privy to all information and meetings, Orson had begun to understand the power the girl held within her. He would find her. He couldn't fail at this mission. This place, this home, was the first time he had a goal. Been part of something bigger than himself. Before, it was just existing—and not getting caught.

16

NATHANIEL SAT ON AN OUTCROPPING high above the main hall and listened to the soldiers talk. He'd waited for months to hear news of his girl. For the first time in his long life—his current existence with Sylvan only being a part of his lifetime—he didn't know what to do.

If she were dead, which he refused to consider, wouldn't his life as her pedagogue end, too? Nathaniel thought there was some uncertainty in this since he was more than just a mentor. More than a being that came to be from the warlock's magic. He had been alive a long time, been many places, seen many things. So, his still being here, alive, couldn't guarantee that life still moved through Sylvan.

He considered that she had mastered the art of masking her whereabouts. Masking it even from him. Finally, tapping into her magic. He felt frustration and pride in equal measures. The girl would always do things in her own way—so stubborn.

When the new lord of the lands and his favorite lackey sauntered through the door, Nathaniel's ears pricked, and he shifted forward.

These two, he thought not for the first time. *I'd like to kill them myself.*

The room of men became aware of the entrance of their lord simultaneously, and all conversation halted, the only sound the scraping of chairs as they hustled to their feet.

Mikel and Orson made their way around the assembly, stopping to issue a softly spoken order or straighten a uniform. When they took their places at the head of the table, servants rushed forward with plates laden with the finest foods.

Nathaniel's stomach growled softly as the fresh smells wafted to him. He'd been forced to eat what he could find since the massacre of these lands. Never had he lived such a destitute existence. He could leave, go to where the danger was to a lower degree, but by staying he hoped to hear some news of Sylvan. Now, looking down at Mikel, he saw a change in him—a relaxation that hadn't appeared before. His observations proved adept when Mikel spoke.

"Finish your meals, my good men. I have news, and you will be traveling west."

17

FOR SYLVAN, THE NEXT FEW months passed in a whirlwind of busy days and dreamless nights marked only by the growing child in her body. When her pregnancy became obvious, she took to wearing larger aprons to hide her belly. Soon, even that didn't work. One morning, Meg stopped her and demanded information.

"My husband is dead. His death is what put me on the road." Sylvan raised her chin and blinked rapidly to keep tears from falling.

With a deep breath, Meg said, "A young girl alone and in the family way's gonna raise more than a few eyebrows in this town. Just sayin' your man's dead ain't gonna stop tongues from waggin', and the hounds from sniffin'."

"I don't know what else to tell you, Meg. I need a job. I work hard. You've seen that for yourself. My husband's dead and I'm pregnant. These are my facts and I can't change them."

Meg gave her one last gaze, and as she turned, she threw over her shoulder, "Get ready for work. It's gonna be a long day."

SHE'D LEARNED TO STAY IN the kitchen almost exclusively. The town knew of her condition and her status, but if she stayed out of their sight, it seemed to lessen their ire. No matter the approaching birth of her child, she worked as hard or harder than the other females in the kitchen. A strong work ethic, learned at her father's knee, was instilled in her to the bone.

Today, two of the kitchen women were down with an illness, so the kitchen was that much busier. Everyone stepped up.

After finishing two plates for a table of regulars, Sylvan hefted them on her forearms and headed to the dining area. She pushed the swinging door open with her back and heard the swoosh of it closing behind her. Stepping into the common area, a flash of red and black caught her eye and, reacting to the drop in her gut, she pivoted and stepped behind a wall. Back to the cool stone, she took several deep breaths before turning to look past the corner and into the hall.

Two men sat off to the side, just out of the main area. Their distinctive cloaks filled her mind and heart with memories of her last day at the manor. Suddenly, she could feel Eldred's hand in hers and her lungs became full of his scent. Her throat closed, and her eyes filled as she scanned the room only to look into the all-too-perceptive eyes of Meg.

* * * * *

WHEN THE DOOR OPENED, AND a figure stepped out, Meg's attention caught. Seeing it was Sylvan, arms laden with food for a customer, she turned her attention back to the smooth running of the inn. When the girl almost spilled the food she carried and hid behind a wall, Meg gave Sylvan her full consideration. Eyebrows furrowed, she watched intently as the girl stood for a moment and then peeked around the corner. Following her gaze to the two strangers, Meg watched them and then fixed her sight on Sylvan.

Now, what was this about?

When the girl's gaze caught hers, they stared for a moment at each other, and then Meg walked to the corner. Taking the dishes from Sylvan, she proceeded to serve her customers without question. After inquiring of any additional needs they may have, she walked back near the kitchen, where she grabbed the girl's arm in a tight grip and dragged her into the questionable privacy of the kitchen.

"What was that all about?"

Sylvan swung her head around, not paying attention to Meg. She didn't even seem to remember where she was.

Meg gave her a shake.

"I asked you a question, girl. What was that all about?"

"I have to leave. I have to leave *now*."

Meg was silent. Then, without another word, she pulled her from the kitchen, out the back door, and to the women's quarters. Pushing open the door to the room Sylvan shared, Meg pulled her in and spun her around. Giving her a shake, her eyes flashed.

"What trouble have you brought to my door, girl?"

"I'm sorry. They'll never know I was here. I'll leave right now." Sylvan stared up into Meg's eyes, pleading with her to understand and not turn her over to the men. "Let me gather a few items. I'll go out the back way." She stepped from the older woman to collect her bag and began thrusting her small pile of possessions into it. Done, she pulled off her apron and moved toward the door.

"Wait," the inn owner said.

Sylvan turned from the door, one hand on the side of her belly and the other holding her bag on her shoulder. For a few moments, neither woman said anything.

"You can't leave. That baby will be here any day. And where will you go?"

Her shoulders dropped as some of the tension eased from Sylvan's frame, and her eyes dropped to the floor. "I've stayed too long as it is. I need to keep moving. We'll be fine." Taking one of the woman's hands in hers, she said, "Thank you for everything you've done for me, Meg. You've been a good friend."

As she turned to go out the door, Meg opened her mouth to protest, but no words came out. The door closed quietly, and it was some time before she made her way back into the inn.

* * * * *

WHEN SYLVAN LEFT THE SMALL community, it was through the forest. Her footing was good due to the years of layers of old needles under the pine trees giving cushion and silence to her tread. She didn't know where she was going, but when she looked into the sky to see the risen sun and the rising of the first moon, she felt certainty and so kept them in her sight until they'd reached overhead, and then she kept them to her back. Throughout the day, she saw no other people, but many times small animals scurried out of her way and, once, a large antlered stag leaped over a log and dashed away.

In the quiet and tranquility of the forest, her thoughts calmed, her panic faded, and she was able to think. It was true, she'd stayed too long at Meg's inn. She'd felt welcome and become complacent. She needed to keep moving, to find a place for her and her child farther from the manor where she was raised. Farther from Mikel and his soldiers. How far would she need to go? How far could she go? She was young and strong, but even now, after walking most of the day, her muscles ached and the weight in her belly pulled. Meg said her child would be here soon, but she knew there was still time. Time to find a place for them, a place where she could hole up and give birth. A place where, at least for a short time, they could be safe.

Staying on the path she'd set, feeling a pull within, she walked into the night. When the second moon rose almost at the setting of the first, she knew the night was almost over and the dawn would be approaching. Her exhaustion hung heavy on her frame. Now she kept her eyes open for a safe place to spend the daylight hours before she again began her trek.

Soon after, a small gathering of trees called to her. When she pushed her way into them, she found a small bed of grass—

possibly utilized by a deer. Amid the smell of the sod and soil was the earthier smell of the animal. She pulled the cloak's hood over her head and face and was soon asleep.

STILL HALF IN THE LAND of dreams, Sylvan shifted to lay her palm on the side of her swollen belly. Under her hand, she felt the child kick.

He's healthy, she thought and rubbed her skin with loving strokes.

Opening her eyes to the setting sun, she blinked slowly until her consciousness returned fully. Yes, she was in the forest—she remembered now. No hot kitchen to work in this day.

With a yawn and a stretch, she sat up and surveyed her surroundings. Taking a quick sip from a container of water she'd brought, she stood and silently made her way out of the immediate area to empty her bladder. Relieved, she returned to gather her belongings and begin her evening hike.

THROUGHOUT THE REST OF THE evening and the night, Sylvan kept from the roads, though she passed homesteads with dark windows. Once or twice, a dog barked in the distance, but as they never approached her, she was in no danger.

Each day she found a place to rest, and each night she continued her trek. When she stopped in the dead of night to pilfer from fields and gardens for food, she didn't feel guilty for the theft. Her need was great, and she never took more than a day's worth of food. Streams were plentiful, so fresh water was always at hand. For a time, alone and self-sufficient, she felt as if she could walk forever.

DAYS LATER, SYLVAN APPROACHED A darkened cabin. Across a field lay a lake, sparkling in the moonlight. The smell of the water drew her, and after approaching the edge, she kneeled to refill her flask. Holding herself still with a hand placed on the rocky beach, she peered over the calm water. It seemed to be a sheet of black glass, mysterious and unknown. Faint, almost imperceivably, the lapping of the water on the lake's edge was a steady pulse.

When an owl hooted, she blinked and broke her reverie. Leaning forward, she pushed to stand only to have her attention caught by something sparkling under the water's surface. It was out a foot or so, just out of her reach from the bank. Curious, she sat and pulled her boots from her feet and rolled off her hose. She grasped the back of her skirt and pulled it forward between her legs to tuck it in the waistline above her belly before she waded into the lake.

The bottom, muddy and cold, squished between her toes. She curled them to grip as the mud became slippery. When the water moved from her ankles to her knees, a small shiver snaked up her spine, her body cooling in the night chill.

When Sylvan reached the area where she had seen the sparkle, she pulled up her sleeve and reached into the water. Unerringly, her fingers touched an object. It was hard but smooth, almost the size of a peach pit. Closing her grip, she pulled it from its watery bath.

She opened her hand and studied what seemed to be a stone. In the dark of night, the only illumination the moons, it appeared black, shot through with starbursts of white light. Taking it in her other hand, Sylvan turned the stone and found markings. She ran her finger over them and recognized the three joined lines that had led her down this path.

She knew the discovery of this talisman was not mere chance. She had come to where she was supposed to be.

Splashing through the water back to the lake's edge, Sylvan kept her gaze on the rock. When her feet once again landed on firm soil, she took her view from the stone long enough to pull on her boots, sliding her hose within the tucked pocket of her skirt.

She stood for a bit longer, captivated by the stone, entranced by the glitter of white. Finally, lifting her gaze, she looked across the field to the cabin. She made her way through the darkened field, her sights on the lodging.

She found the garden area overgrown with weeds and the door to the cabin hanging ajar. This homestead was vacant. She'd walked many miles to find this place. In front of it, she spun in a slow circle. There was no evidence of civilization, except for this small building. No sounds came to her in the clear night air, and for as far as she could see, there was only darkness, forest, and the lake.

Thinking she'd found a good place to stay, the girl pushed on the jammed door and entered the dwelling. When she stepped inside, a warmth such as she'd never known filled her being, and for a moment, she was blind to the room. Overlaid on the darkness of the cabin, a tableau showed itself. Her older self stirred a meal within a pot hanging over the fire. Flowers peeked at the windows and a gentle breeze blew in from the open door.

With a blink, the night silhouettes of the room came back into view. She again stood in a darkened one-room cabin with a large cooking fireplace. Windows on two sides gaped into the night. The smell of small animals dominated, and with a wrinkle of her nose, she moved forward. The feeling of calm stayed with her, and she breathed a sigh. She'd followed the sign and it had led her here. She'd come home.

THE NEXT DAY, SYLVAN INVESTIGATED her new surroundings. The cabin would need some fixing up, but it was work she could accomplish.

Her innate magic, she knew, was the ability to mask herself, to entrance if necessary. She'd used it before. She tried not to think about the black swarm when the soldier had grabbed her—the mass of it. That was not magic. That was a curse.

Standing within the walls of the cabin, she closed her eyes and focused her mind. Held tight within her hand was the newly found amulet. She concentrated far into her psyche where the ember of magic burned. When she found it, she embraced it, breathing a greater life into it, blowing on its flame until it was blazing. With the fire strong, she began to push. Her fist closed ever tighter on the talisman. When her nails cut into her palm, causing a small welling of blood, she didn't notice.

In her mind's eye, she saw her magic as a bubble—

translucent but shiny and bright. She made the bubble larger until it surrounded her body, then the cabin, and then the valley. Farther and farther, she pushed out. Her dome of magic soon surrounded a large portion of her valley. When she could do no more, she dropped to her knees on the earthen floor of her cabin, her energy depleted.

After a time, she stood and stumbled to the cold fireplace. Reaching once more to feel the ember of her magic, her eyes opened wide. She reached again. Nothing.

It was gone.

18

NATHANIEL CREPT FROM THE BUILDING to slink along the exterior wall.

West, he'd heard Mikel tell his men, and west he would go. A sigh of frustration pushed past his lips as he thought of the long journey with no promise of finding Sylvan. If she'd been a better student and less prone to allowing her mind to roam, she'd have learned to control the power she was obviously using now. Her power, she didn't even realize, was exceptionally strong. With fear for her life driving her, he may never locate her whereabouts.

Moving away from the building and out the gate of the manor, Nathaniel didn't encounter anyone. Ever since the day of the massacre, there hadn't been any townspeople around. Only the soldiers and a few scared servants populated the mansion. The normal running of the home, deliveries from town, workmen, people coming and going, had halted that dark day.

The oppressive nature of the area cleared quickly after he

left the manor. Nathaniel moved easily through the undergrowth. Though intelligent and cunning, he was still a cat and possessed the physical attributes and abilities of all felines. With fluid motions, he shifted between shadows; not even the birds and small animals were aware of his passage. He would travel quickly, staying ahead of the complement of soldiers. With luck, he would find his girl and with her they would travel to safety.

19

THE PRISONER TROD HEAVILY BETWEEN the soldiers. His current capacity for rational thought a thing of the past, his instincts warned him of the coming of pain. Pain was either with him or coming. The only time he was allowed out of his hole was to once again endure the beatings and punishments. So far gone was his mind that to get some reaction, his jailer had resorted to amputating fingers. His left hand now had two stumps where his last two fingers used to be. For a time, he thought he'd die of blood loss or infection — he'd welcomed the indelibility of this, but fate was cruel, and he healed.

The footsteps of the soldiers' boots echoed before and behind them. The prisoner's boots had long ago been taken from him, and his dirty and scabbed feet made no sound on the stone floor of the dungeon.

When the soldiers turned to climb a set of stairs, the prisoner stopped. He'd never been taken this way, and for all the pain he knew was coming, at least it was a torture he knew.

The soldiers grabbed his chains and yanked him forward. When the three moved down a hall through a door and into a back alley, the prisoner cried out and flung his arms over his head. So long had it been since he'd been outside, the scent of fresh air and the great expanse of the sky caused the burn of panic to flare in his system.

The soldiers clubbed him to keep him moving. His forehead now trickled blood and his thoughts were even more confused, but the chained man shuffled forward without further complaints. Within moments they reached a back gate, and unchaining him, the soldiers pushed him outside the wall and retreated in, slamming the portal closed.

Standing in the quiet of the night, afraid to move, the prisoner looked out between the hanks of his filthy hair and waited to see what punishment would be coming. Tricks had been tried many times before, and it only took being punished for him to learn his lesson. Minutes passed and the only sound was the calling of distant night birds, hunters perhaps. Afraid to move, instinct telling him this was some test, he stood still and waited.

Time passed, and the moon moved overhead. No one came near the gate or the prisoner as he continued his vigil. Sweat ran down his temples and back, but still he didn't move. The only thought in his head was the memory of beatings. He was good. He would stay.

When the moons set and the sun began to lighten the sky, the prisoner chanced to look around. He didn't like the idea of being caught out in the light of day. The dark had afforded him some sense of security, but now he considered finding somewhere safer to be. Scanning the area once again, he knew he was alone. All alone for the first time in his memory.

Taking a step, he looked about and took another tentative step. Still no one called out a warning, no heavy fist came down on him, and no arrow pierced his heart. Step by slow step, he moved from the wall and gate. A moment later, he entered a stand of trees, and without a backward glance, he took off as fast as his legs would carry him.

20

MIKEL PAUSED. BENT OVER THE body of a soldier, his breathing hissed out. His clenched fist dropped back to his side.

When he released the collar of the soldier, the unconscious man slumped to the floor. Mikel's blank stare remained on him for a moment more, and then giving the body one last kick, he moved to his dais.

He'd been so certain. He thought they'd have the girl in no time, but now, somehow, she had evaded them once again. He was unsure where she'd disappeared to. Her damn cat must be with her, giving her aid. If she was alone, he was sure to locate her.

Turning, he saw a pair of servants standing next to him with water and cloths. He leaned forward and put his hands out, and they poured water from the urn over them to catch in a basin. Briskly, he rubbed them together to remove the blood that stained his knuckles. Taking a cloth from one of the servants, he dried his hands.

He gestured toward the body. "Get that out of here and send in the first of the petitioners."

Ruling, he found, wasn't something he enjoyed. Being in charge, that was another thing altogether, but settling disputes, listening to complaints—he just wanted to kill everyone. But his generals counseled that if he killed everyone, there would be no one to rule and no one to pay taxes.

"Bring me some wine."

As the servants rushed to do his bidding, soldiers led two men into the room. The men were dressed as merchants, and one man had a young girl trailing him. The three of them watched as the soldier's body was removed. Shock stained their faces, and they paused in the middle of the room. Looking from the body to Mikel, they didn't move.

With an impatient gesture, he ordered them forward.

The girl had his immediate attention. Young, not overly attractive, she had a lushness about her that had his heart beating in his ears.

His servant announced them, explaining the dispute, but all Mikel heard was the low roar of his desire. When no one spoke and all looked at him, he cleared his throat and sat up straighter in his chair.

"You sir." He realized his voice was much too loud in the quiet room, and clearing his throat again, he said, "You," with a gesture at the man with the girl. "Tell me in your own words what this dispute is all about."

The man swallowed with difficulty as he stepped forward. "M'lord," he began, "this here is my daughter. My neighbor" —

he gestured at the other man—"me and him had an agreement for them to wed."

Mikel looked from one man to the other, his eyes constantly drawn back to the girl. She stood silently, hands clasped in front of an ample bosom. Her gaze never strayed from a spot on the floor, which held some special interest.

"Do you have a written contract?"

"Um, well, no m'lord." The father of the girl fidgeted, wringing his hands and shooting glances at his neighbor.

"Was this agreement witnessed by an elder or councilor of the city?"

The father pushed his shoulders back and spoke in a clear voice. "No, m'lord. It were a gentlemen's agreement."

"Hm . . ." Mikel looked at the three. "To participate in a gentlemen's agreement, one must be a gentleman. That was your first mistake."

With a motion in the direction of the neighbor, Mikel said, "You, sir, are free to go." The neighbor man hurried from the room.

As the father began to protest, Mikel rose and walked toward him, causing him to quiet and back away to stand with his daughter. Now they both stood still, eyes diverted from him.

How lovely.

The stale reek of fear came from the duo. It pleased him.

"Now for you," he said and began a slow circuit of the pair. "The last thing we need is for a dispute to tear apart the harmony of this community." Coming to stand before them, he said, "Therefore, the girl will stay here, to work within the temple."

"But—" Her father looked up into Mikel's eyes and then dropped his gaze. The daughter, who until this moment hadn't moved, grasped her father's hand, her fingers turning white.

"She'll be well cared for, I assure you."

The father stepped forward again. "But, m'lord. She's needed at home."

"Not so much that you weren't willing to sell her to your neighbor." Mikel gestured over his shoulder to the guards waiting by the door. "Take her."

"But—"

"I'll hear no more from you. The girl stays."

When the guards advanced on the girl, her father attempted to step in front of her, but one of the guards easily pushed him away, causing him to trip and fall on the marble floor.

"Daddy!" the girl called and reached for her father. Before she could get to him, the guards grabbed her, each by one arm, and moved her toward the main door into the interior of the temple.

From the floor, the old man watched all of this, tears in his eyes. Wails, like those of an injured bird, could be heard coming from the girl as she was ushered out of the room.

Gazing down his nose at the merchant on the floor, Mikel pursed his lips and said, "You're free to go," and then he turned to follow the guards and the girl from the room. With him gone, the only sound was the soft sobbing coming from her father.

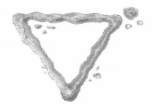

21

"COME IN," MIKEL CALLED IN response to the knock at his chamber door.

Without turning from the mirror, he continued to straighten his light cotton shirt and then pulled his tunic over it. Glancing in the reflection, he saw Orson enter his room. The balcony doors were open a crack, and with the second door ajar, a breeze whipped through, clearing some of the stale, heavy air. The small man stopped when the body flung upon the bed caught his undivided attention.

Mikel turned from admiring his image and watched the other man.

With hardly a glance in Mikel's direction, Orson approached the bed. His eyes seemed to glow, and the curves of his nostrils quivered with the scents rising from the bed.

The sheets were balled up, most of their length falling to the floor on the far side of the mattress. On the sheets, bloody and broken, lay the naked body of the girl from town. Once wholesome and alive, she now resembled a doll, limbs twisted grotesquely. Her neck sat at a peculiar angle, allowing the head to crane backward, cloudy eyes staring sightlessly out the window. Her skin, before a lovely pink, was now gray in color where it showed beneath the red. Pools of smeared and drying blood surrounded her, and in a small pile by her head was a finger and what appeared to be a tongue. On the sideboard near the bed, tools lay in disarray. Their serrated and sharp edges jelled with cooling body fluids.

A small smile played about Mikel's lips as memories of their time together filled his head. He'd been right—she'd been prime for his brand of play.

When Orson moved even closer, his eyes riveted on the sight before him, Mikel said, "Do you like her?"

Orson glanced in his direction, but his gaze was drawn back to the girl. Without breaking the contact, he muttered, "Yes."

"Well, she's yours then. I'm finished with her."

Orson didn't acknowledge the other man's words with more than a nod. He stepped so close as to bump the bed with his legs. Then he reached forward and, with a knuckle, gently rubbed a digit over one of the girl's nipples.

"Well, good then." Mikel clapped his hands. With a toothy grin on his face and a jaunt in his step, he left the room.

22

SYLVAN AWOKE, A GASP TRAPPED in the back of her throat. For a moment, she remained in the grip of slumber, lost in the image of a nightmarish creature with its talons buried deep into her body.

As another pain shot from her back to tighten the muscles of her abdomen, she came fully awake. Her time was upon her.

As soon as the pain subsided, fear tried to fill its place. She was alone and about to give birth. With an iron fist, she pushed the fear to the back of her mind and assured herself she could do this. She'd assisted in many births, been present for many more. Over the past few weeks, she'd prepared herself and the cabin the best she knew how.

I can do this. Everything will be all right.

Edging her legs over the side of her small bed, she stood and moved gingerly toward the fireplace. The embers glowed brightly, and when she added fresh fuel, the flames leaped to consume them. With a groan, she stood upright and filled a kettle with water before placing it near the fire to warm.

As another contraction moved through her frame, she gripped the mantel and bent forward. A groan pushed through her pinched lips, surprising her with its guttural tone. Her hair fell to cover her face, and sweat beaded on her brow to run and drip from her nose and chin. Panting like an animal, she wrapped her free arm under the bulge of her belly and applied pressure. Just as the pain began to wane, Sylvan felt a release deep within, and a flow of liquid ran down her leg to wet her nightgown.

"Oh." She breathed and stood straight, pulling the cloth away from her damp legs. Breathing in and out, centering her focus, she looked at her bed with desire. What she'd give to have a helping arm to lean on.

With a shuffling step, she made her way back to the bed. Like a snail, a trail of liquid followed in her wake. She stared for a moment at the bedding and then again lifted her damp gown from her legs. She grasped the fabric in her hands and slowly pulled it over her head. Balling it up, she pushed it between her legs before lying on the thin mattress.

The fire blazed and the room warmed as she lay back to relax. This was going to take some time, she knew, and for now, she needed to conserve her energy. With a deep breath, she prepared as her abdomen again tightened. The pain radiated out, causing her to gasp for air, and a fresh sensation of movement began.

SYLVAN DIDN'T KNOW HOW MUCH of the day had passed. The world beyond her windows had lightened some time ago, and she'd watched as the shadows lengthened and shifted across the floor. Now all she knew was the pain. It radiated from her back to fill her body. When the crest of the pain was upon her, she knew only a white light and the hollow sound of her breathing.

Now, as the pain ebbed, she collapsed onto her sheets, soiled with her sweat and other body fluids. Her mind grasped for the moments of peace and turned to memories of her first few weeks in the cabin.

Being heavy with child and alone, Sylvan had done the best she could to ready the cabin and herself for winter. During the first week, she traveled the distance to town twice to gather supplies. She bartered for some small items with medicinal pouches she'd made, and as luck would have it, the owner of the store believed in her honesty and allowed her to have items on credit. The owner, Mr. Bachmann, told her their healer had moved on some time ago and so her potions, pouches, and abilities would be in great need. He felt certain she would easily pay him back and even make a profit.

She wasn't surprised by the looks the townsfolk, especially the women, sent her way. She was a woman, all alone and obviously in the family way. Keeping her chin up, she gathered what she needed and didn't spend an undue amount of time in the small town of Roadstead. It, like other towns, had worked hard to become a community the citizens could be proud of. Along the way, many of them had lost their empathy and souls to bigotry and judgment.

Though her carpentry skills were wanting, she repaired the door hinges. The tough rawhide still clung to it, and with a few new nails and a borrowed hammer, her cabin was soon secure. Among the other items advanced to her on credit, she selected some fine but heavy ticking with the plan to make a mattress. Each day, on her treks, she gathered birds' feathers, soft mosses, and straws. In her home, she set aside a corner for storing her healing balms. Seeing them all organized and in rows gave her a sense of accomplishment and contentment.

When the first town dweller arrived on her step, it filled her with such well-being that for a moment she just smiled at him without speaking. She could do this. She could make a life here outside this community. Her healing ability would give her a commodity with which to barter and maybe even make a living.

The man was an easy fix. He had an aging wound on his shoulder that didn't want to heal. With a little lancing, poultice, and a prayer, she sent him on his way, happy and already feeling better. News traveled and soon after she had as much business as she could handle.

The town women continued to look down their noses at her, and she would often hear them whispering as she moved across the floor, but her condition didn't dissuade them or their men from seeking her services. Her mother before her was a talented healer, and she'd ensured her daughter would follow in her footsteps—though she never imagined where she'd be practicing the healing arts.

CRACKING HER EYES OPEN, SYLVAN scanned the room. She'd done well for herself in a small span of time. She was capable and she was proud of herself. Now to get through this next challenge.

When the pain hit again, she bent almost double, and unable to stop, she pushed as hard as she could, an animalistic grunt forced from her lips. When she felt a shift deep within her body, she stretched her arms to reach between her legs and feel the head of the infant emerging. Another pain and a contraction squeezed her abdomen, forcing the small body from hers. Guiding as gently as she could, Sylvan felt the baby slide, wet and slippery, onto the mattress of her bed. Leaning upward, she gazed between her legs to the limp shape of her child. The skin was cast in gray, flecked with a white substance and her blood. Her hand trembled as she reached out. Just before her fingers touched the chest of her child, it rose with a first-drawn breath—and it came out in a bellow.

She was transfixed to see a rosy hue flow through the small body. What was once gray, now turned pink. Small arms and hands balled into fists and waved in a frantic motion, bent on getting some attention.

"Hush, hush, my love," she whispered and slid her hands under the babe's arms, supporting the head with her fingertips as she lifted. Holding the small body aloft, Sylvan stared, and a smile creased her face.

"Maya."

* * * * *

WITH THE FIRST CRIES OF the babe, three heads came up, each registering a change in the flow of magic of the land. Cassandra, the cat, and the coercer. Each had their own concerns with the

coming of this change, each their own motives and plans — two
for bad, one for good.

Cassandra hunkered down in her castle, this birth one she'd
expected but was leery of just the same. What would this new
life bring to the game, and how could she turn this event to her
side? She'd tried for many days to read the omens in her
viewing bowl. She was confident the mother would be hers, but
what of the babe? The magic felt particularly strong. She
couldn't allow her brother to have this one. If she couldn't turn
her, she would have to kill her. With a muttered spell, she
touched the mind of her henchman.

The coercer, Mikel, giggled in mad glee for many seconds
and then, summoning his commander, sent a battalion of men
in the direction of the change in flow. For him there was no light,
no questioning of his faith or abilities — just an avarice hunger.
Happy for his mistress's call, he didn't know what set about this
change, but on the wind, he smelled Sylvan.

The cat set his sights on the glow of magic, for him like a
rising sun in the eastern sky. Its beacon short-lived, it allowed
him a moment of hope. He now had a destination, a route to
travel. Sooner or later he would find his girl.

* * * * *

TWO DAYS LATER, SYLVAN SAT nursing her daughter. She
hummed a small song her mother used to sing to her and rocked
her body. Her view never left her child's profile, and with each
draw of milk the baby took, her heart swelled.

She was in love. There wasn't another way, a better way, to describe it. She thought her heart full of her love for Eldred, and then she thought it broken with his death. Neither of these feelings was as pure and true as her love for her daughter. She felt as though she might burst—a shining, white light flowing from every crack to overtake the world.

When a soft knock sounded on the door to her cabin, her head came up and she scented the air like a she-wolf. Cradling Maya to her breast, she moved to crack open the door. Standing on her stoop were three women from town. They looked from her face to the babe and back to her face.

"Ahem, Miss Sylvan. We, the ladies of Roadstead, wish to offer you our assistance in your time of need." The woman shifted her gaze to include the duo behind her and then she turned back to Sylvan. Just as she opened her mouth to take a deep breath and continue, Sylvan softly shut the door.

For a moment, the town women stood and stared as the door closed in their faces, and then muttering among themselves, they turned and walked away from the little cabin.

23

THE ROBED MEN STOOD IN a loose circle around the body. They'd come upon it unexpectantly while moving through the forest. The first ones saw it was a man, though they thought he was dead—just one more victim of a band of robbers in the area. As more of them gathered, the body released a groan. The men nearest jumped back, but then a brave one reached down and shook the man by his shoulder. The only reaction they received was a flickering of his eyelids.

He was filthy. His body starved. His clothes hanging on him in tatters. A prisoner, they decided. But released or escaped?

"What should we do with him?"

The vote was split, some to aid him and some to leave him.

One outspoken individual offered, "If we'd have come up the other hill, we'd have passed right by him," to which some of the others nodded their agreement.

Brother Samet, who led these men, listened to the arguments. Lifting his hand, he nodded slowly as the men quieted.

"It is true as some of you say, we might have just as easily passed by this poor soul had we but taken a different road. The fact remains, however, that we did not pass by, and having found him, we cannot simply pretend we didn't. He is now our responsibility."

A rumble arose from the men. Some nodded in agreement and some shook heads in dissent, though no one spoke out against the leader's words.

"Make camp. We'll stay here for the night. We'll warm him and try to get some liquids down him. If he's still alive by morning, we'll decide then what to do with him."

When the camp was made, Samet had men bring the stranger to the warmth of a fire. They wrapped him in a blanket, got him to take a small amount of water, and left him to the hands of fate. Live or die, it was now up to him. Samet hoped, by morning, the man would wake.

* * * * *

WHEN THE PRISONER WOKE, HE lay perfectly still. His eyes remained closed, but his ears reached for every nuance of sound. Curiosity filled him at the noises. The buzz of many voices and the clank of pans. Opening his eyes and rolling onto his side, he scanned the camp.

Men, each clad in rough-spun brown robes, moved around, going about or completing tasks. Some carried water or cooked food, and some packed supplies. The last thing he remembered—and the memory was foggy—was wandering through the forest.

He stretched his body, catching himself as a spike of pain shot down his back. Freezing, he assessed the sensation and, with a small shift, determined nothing seemed broken, just strained. Slowly, he stretched his limbs, careful not to pull too hard or quick. Old wounds made themselves known.

At the sensation of being watched, the prisoner again scanned the encampment. Seeing he was of no immediate interest to the men, he rolled to his other side. Over the fire, he looked into the eyes of a man.

Neither spoke. Finally, the man approached the prisoner. The prisoner scooted backward until he came up against a pile of logs. Curled into himself, he watched the robed man, who squatted beside him and offered a container.

The prisoner waited for a hint as to his intentions. When the robed man didn't do anything, the prisoner took the container with a quick jerk. He sniffed the mouth of it and sipped, allowing the fluid to swirl over his tongue. Water. Cool water. Tipping the flask, he took a long pull and sighed as the water washed down his throat.

The robed man gestured behind him, and another man—a boy really—ran over with a platter of food and handed it to the prisoner. Looking from the food to the man, the prisoner hesitantly reached out and took the platter. On it was a thick porridge and a small loaf of bread. The man couldn't remember when he'd eaten so well. The gruel in the prison wouldn't allow a swine to live.

He stuffed the food into his mouth and took long swallows of water. Eyes squinted, he watched the man move to a seat across from him.

He couldn't trust anyone.

The prisoner sopped up the last of the porridge with what remained of his bread and stuffed it into his mouth. Keeping his eyes on the robed man, he licked the last of the porridge. He savored every bit and chewed slowly.

His gaze vigilant, the prisoner assessed the area for an avenue of escape. If need be, he would be swift.

When he'd swallowed the final bite and finished the water, he faced the man.

"Who are you? Why am I here?" he asked in a voice raspy from disuse.

For a moment, the prisoner didn't think he was going to get an answer, but then the man leaned forward and placed his elbows on his knees.

"We are the Brotherhood of Fate. I am Brother Samet."

The prisoner crinkled his brows, narrowing his gaze at the man, but didn't respond.

"Last eventide, we came upon you. You were unconscious. We could have left you, but that would have been against our beliefs. So, we camped. You woke this morning and here we are." After a moment of quiet, he continued, "So now a question for you. What is your name?"

The prisoner shook his head and looked down at his hands, taking in the stumps of two fingers. "I don't know."

His voice intense, the man said, "Do you know why you're

here, and in this condition?"

Again, the prisoner shook his head. He hoped the men would allow him to stay with them. He'd slept without harassment and they gave him a meal.

"No, I don't remember who I am or where I've come from." All the prisoner remembered was pain. Sitting straighter, he turned fully toward the other man. "Who is the Brotherhood of Fate?"

The man stood and gestured for the prisoner to follow him.

"Come. I'll show you where you can wash and get some clean clothes. We're heading toward the mountains, and you are welcome to come with us."

The prisoner pushed himself to his feet and hurried to follow the other man.

As they moved through the camp, the prisoner saw many men. They were packing up their camp and loading supplies. Cook fires blazed. The smells had the man's stomach growling even though he'd just eaten.

He scanned the area as they walked and saw all the men had on the same type of robe, brown and coarse. Their feet were shod in sandals.

Looking at his own clothing, he saw how battered he appeared to them.

When Brother Samet stopped and gathered fresh clothing and sandals from a bundle, the prisoner reached for them. Stopping, he stared again at his hand. As if not attached to his arm, he watched it. Then he wiggled the remaining fingers.

He had no memory of what had happened to him, though

it was obvious he'd been harshly used. He didn't know if he'd
ever remember, and a part of him hoped he wouldn't.

24

THE WOMAN WAS BEAUTIFUL, HER skin soft, her voice gentle. A warmth filled his heart as he reached for her, and she turned to him, a soft smile on her lips.

The man woke to stare into the starry night. He'd been with the brotherhood for weeks now. The occasional dream, or more often a nightmare, was all that remained of the man he used to be. It seemed at times he would be in this one place forever, never moving forward.

A large bird of prey flew silently over where he lay. If he hadn't been looking up, he would never know this hunter was on the prowl tonight. Soon after, he heard a far-off squeal and congratulated the predator for his success.

Who did he used to be? Was he a predator? The brothers said prisoners of state were kept at the keep. What had he done to warrant being in such a prison? And how did he get out? Was he released or did he escape? Did he deserve the treatment he had received? He didn't feel like a bad man. Wouldn't he know? Wouldn't he feel it within himself if there were a darkness that ruled?

Turning to his side, the man stared at the dying embers of the fire.

His time with the brothers had been welcome. His body, now mostly healed, felt strong. His wounds had healed with the aid of the healers within the ranks of the brotherhood, though scars marred his skin. Brother Samet told him they were visible evidence of his inner strength.

The man smiled sadly at this. One thing he could say about Brother Samet was he was terminally positive.

The man slowly blinked at the fading fire. He was tired. Tomorrow they would meet the main body of the brotherhood, and he would decide if staying with them was the path he wished. He trusted the brothers. They were good men, honest and happy in their lives. Maybe he shouldn't worry about not knowing his past. Maybe it wasn't a past anyone would want to know.

Relaxing into his blanket, the man tried to fall back to sleep. The warmth of the fire at his back and the fresh night air in his lungs lulled him. He was almost asleep. His body, near to slumber, gave a jerk and then settled. His breath heaved in, filling his lungs, and then with an audible rasp, it expelled from his body.

The moon crested, shining down on the encampment of men, each sleeping soundly. As a breeze picked up, ruffling through the man's red hair, he jerked again, his sleep now disturbed. A loud moan came from him a moment before he sat straight up, staring into the night.

"Sylvan."

25

"**M**AYA."

Behind her, Sylvan heard the child screech to a halt. Pursing her lips, the woman controlled a desire to smile and, with a stern look planted firmly on her face, she turned.

Her heart swelled, as always, at the vision of her child. Two braids of flaming red—just like her father's—fell to the front of a shirt stained with dirt from the morning's play. Smudges of the same dirt marred her rosy complexion. She stared at the ground, unwilling to meet her mother's gaze, hands clasped behind her back.

"What do you have?"

"Nothin'," the small voice answered, defiant in the way of a five-year-old.

Crouching to better face the child, Sylvan held out a steady hand. After a moment, the child looked up into the unbroken gaze of her mother. She hesitated as if considering her options, and then placed a small polished stone in the larger palm.

Sylvan glanced from the child to the stone and her brow furrowed. Turning it in her hand, she stared at the image of a beautiful leaf etched on the surface.

"Where did you get this?"

"The tree."

Sylvan's body flushed with the softly spoken words. She'd waited for this day, thinking it might never come and almost hoping it wouldn't. The magic running deep within the Singh bloodline would occasionally skip a generation or show evidence of its existence much later in life. Here was her daughter, barely five years old, and the magic was manifesting. "The tree," she'd said. Really, she wasn't surprised. Maya had always been one with the forest—as if she were an animal running free.

"Here, my love. Why don't we put your pretty stone on the shelf to keep it safe?"

Brightening, the small girl ran to the shelf by the bed she shared with her mother. She bounced on her toes as the woman set the stone in its place of honor next to two precious books, a small vase of wildflowers, and a beautiful blue gem.

Sylvan took a moment to study the stone she'd pulled from the lake. It too was etched. That night what she'd thought was black was actually a deep blue in color. Even years after finding it, the white lights still sparkled within the stone.

Turning around, she looked at her daughter.

"There, doesn't that look pretty?"

Nodding, braids shaking, the child gazed at the stone on the shelf.

"Okay. Run along and play."

26

ELDRED'S MIND RETURNED TO THE beginning of his time with the brotherhood. It had been many days before his memory began to resurface, and he remembered all that had happened, all that his brother had done to him and their families, before he came to be with the men of this sect.

Now he walked slowly beside another man. They were both clad in rough brown robes, sandals on their feet. In physicality, they were much the same, though one man was obviously the elder.

"Primary," Eldred began. He stumbled over his words, not sure what to say and how to say it. When the head of the brotherhood paused and turned toward him, Eldred decided to speak succinctly. "I have welcomed my time with the brotherhood. You and the other members have become my family."

The head of the order nodded his understanding, and as though assuming Eldred would follow, he again turned to stroll up the rise.

"We have enjoyed having you with us."

Heading up the hill after the leader of the brotherhood, Eldred's attention momentarily caught on a high-flying bird— an eagle or perhaps a large hawk. For some reason, his thoughts turned again to Sylvan. Always to Sylvan. His beloved. For long stretches of time, he wouldn't think of her at all, and then for no reason, he couldn't get her out of his mind.

"Thank you, Primary. I've appreciated everything you've done for me." With a quickened step, Eldred caught up to the other man and added, "I have the need to do more, however. I've been thinking about my family home and perhaps heading that way."

The Primary stopped and studied Eldred's features.

"I thought you told us your family was killed, all except for your brother."

"Yes." Eldred's gaze dropped to his feet. "My brother. The instigator of all this evil," he muttered under his breath.

"Yes, blood relations can be challenging."

Eldred blinked, the enormity of this understatement catching him by surprise. Then hurrying after, he began again. "Yes, so anyway, I feel the need to do something more with my time . . ."

Stopping and causing Eldred to pause, the Primary of the Brotherhood of Fate looked off into the distance, his face thoughtful.

"I have been planning on sending some of the brothers to a settlement closer to the city of Berth. It is there where they are keeping an eye on the corruptions of the peoples, infiltrating your brother Mikel's sect"—at the second reference to his brother, Eldred winced—"and recruiting to our cause." Moving forward, the men crested the hill and began down the far side. "I believe you would be a benefit to this enterprise." Turning to Eldred, the older man took his hand in his and asked, "What do you think, Brother Eldred? Would you partake in this new challenge?"

Eldred felt a shiver move down his spine and a slight light-headedness. This would be perfect. He'd become complacent and bored in the brotherhood's encampment. Perhaps this change would allow him to use his talents for the betterment of the order.

"Yes, Primary." A smile crossed his face and lit up his eyes. "I would like very much to be part of this excursion."

"Wonderful." The leader slapped Eldred on the shoulder and, turning, continued their walk.

27

T HE FIRE CRACKLED AND SPARKED, light reflecting off the odd assortment of collectibles displayed on the shelf next to the bed.

The woman and girl worked silently, each stitching a small square that would one day be part of a larger quilt. The girl, just a few months past her tenth Names Day, still had her bright red hair, which seemed to be part of the flames burning in the fireplace.

A cold wind howled outside the cabin, but inside the mother and child were warm and safe. The cabin, though small and quaint, had become more hospitable over the years with the woman's expertise. With her skill in the healing arts, she provided a valuable service for the people in the area. A service they paid her well for.

The cabin now had a large bed for the two to share, a small table, and serviceable chairs. The homemade braided rug not only kept the floor's chill from their feet, but its cheerful colors brightened the mood of the room. Not needing to work only from the light of the fire, Sylvan and Maya sat around the table, and on the table sat a lantern that threw enough light for their small stitches.

With a sigh, Sylvan straightened and stretched her back. She clenched and unclenched her hand. As the cramp passed, she moved her gaze from the hypnotic swirl of the flames in the fireplace, to the flames of her daughter's hair and her classic profile. The older Maya grew, the more the girl looked like her mother. Her features were all Singh, but that hair and those eyes, a bright and shining green, were all her father. An odd duality filled her—sorrow for Eldred and the life they should have had, and love for her daughter and the life they lived.

Her gaze shifted as her thoughts drifted and she glanced about the room—the home they'd made. As she looked past the door with a bow and quiver of arrows propped beside it, a smile of pride at her daughter's prowess with the weapon—even at ten years of age—crossed her face. Her ability allowed them the luxury of meat on their table year-round.

The bang of the wind knocking on their windows brought her eyes to the closed shutters, and pride filled her. She'd done well. She'd made a fine home for them here.

As her eyes shifted over the collection on the shelf, she paused and turned back to study it. Over the years, Maya had brought home an assortment of items. Among them, the rock with its frond etching, a brilliantly colored leaf that never dried, an intricate boat made from bark, and many others that she always claimed came from the forest—gifts from the trees. Other than these gifts, Sylvan never saw a manifestation of magic in her daughter. She supposed she was glad of that. Without the teachers and elders of her family, she didn't know how she'd mentor the child in its use.

Next to her daughter's treasures, the blue stone still rested. Its sparkling had never dulled. Nor had it ever become any of the wild imaginings Sylvan had dreamed of over the years, but it still filled her with the balm of peace. Focused her in times of stress.

Allowing her gaze to drift from the shelf, Sylvan studied her daughter again.

Seeming to sense it, Maya looked up, and the corners of her mouth turned up.

"What is it, Mother?"

"Nothing, my love," she answered and gestured toward the piece the girl worked on. "Your stitches are very fine. Soon you'll be better than me."

The girl chuckled at what she thought to be a joke, but it was the truth. The child had many talents. Sylvan ran her fingertips down the side of her head and ran her knuckle across her cheek. Feeling completeness she thought she never would again, the woman went back to her sewing.

28

"MAYA!" SYLVAN YELLED AS THE girl ran through the cabin, a small gray pup hot on her heels. She wondered when that child would learn not to run through the house.

With a whoop, the girl cleared the door, and she and the canine took off across the field. Sylvan released a loud sigh and watched them go. She pushed a piece of hair from her face with the back of her wrist and turned back to the fireplace where a slab of meat roasted. In the distance, she could hear the pup bark and the girl giggle.

She was growing so fast. Soon it would be her fourteenth Names Day. Sylvan remembered the excitement of being that age—so close to becoming a woman, so close to her sixteenth Names Day and the gifting of her pedagogue. What would happen with Maya? No one ever explained this type of situation. They were far from their family home and its traditions. Throughout her life, Maya hadn't exhibited the gift of magic. She still claimed the plants talked to her and, occasionally, she would bring home something else she said came from the trees, but nothing more tangible than that. Nothing Sylvan had witnessed. Without a mentor of her own — Nathaniel left behind years ago — she didn't know what to do with the coming of age of her daughter. Time would tell what would come.

And past even those concerns, Sylvan found herself thinking about the future more often. Maya's future.

She wished a normal life for her daughter. A home of her own. Someone to love her. Children. Would these things be available to her? Was Mikel still out there? Still looking for her? It had been years since she'd seen any of his soldiers. Years would pass without thoughts of him and the dangers he represented.

Would normal even be possible?

Sylvan continued to baste the chunk of meat on the spit. Her motions automatic, her thoughts elsewhere.

A future for Maya. A home. A husband. Children.

She would like to see grandchildren one day. Perhaps a grandson to carry on her father's name.

Standing and stretching, Sylvan moved to the doorway, her gaze homing in on her daughter and the pup racing after each other in the field. Taking another step out the door, Sylvan squinted in the bright sunlight.

When she was this age, she already loved Eldred. Already planned on marrying him. Did Maya have these thoughts? What young girl wouldn't?

Just then, Maya looked up from her wrestling with the pup

and waved. Sylvan waved back, a small smile curving her lips. She walked back into the cabin, her thoughts in turmoil.

29

MIKEL WOKE TO THE SOUND of dripping water. When he tried to move, to shift his body, a stab of pain shot down his spine and caused him to gasp.

It was cold. And dark.

His memory came quickly. He'd been summoned by his mistress. Now after a long night together, he was cold and stiff.

Had she fed from him?

He lifted a heavy arm and, barely able to control it, felt for the wound on his shoulder. His breath hissed when he touched the ragged edge of it. She, or something else perhaps, had torn into his skin, leaving a shredded and gooey mess. His fingers stuck to it, creating an audible sucking noise when he pulled them free. Blood and slime now coated his fingers.

Sitting in the total blackness, he listened. Small, scurrying shuffles close by. And still the dripping of water. He shivered in the damp air, naked to the elements.

He knew where he was. Her den. Her lair. At the thought, pure adoration and excitement filled him. This was where he longed to be, and where he so rarely found himself. No matter the pain, the degradation, he would stay until she threw him out.

When the fire ignited, he threw an arm up to cover his eyes, having grown relaxed in the darkness. He lowered it quickly, eager to see his mistress, but had to squint. He scanned the room, but she was nowhere to be seen.

"My lady," he called as he took to his feet. His voice reverberated from the recesses of the cave. He kept his eyes open, rapt in his attempt to locate her.

Stepping carefully on his bare feet, he approached the fire, taking comfort in the thought that she had started it for him. For now, he was still a weak man. Still in need of warmth and food. She had promised him this would not always be so. One day, she would make him more. He would continue to serve her and soon, all his wishes would come true.

Small animals moved around the room, seemingly afraid to come into the fire's light. Over the years, he had become used to the creatures that shared this domicile. Like nothing he'd seen anywhere else, they made him wonder where he was. This land of hers was different in almost every way from what he knew.

The fire flared, the flames jumping to heights over his head. The heat grew so intense, he had to step back or be burned.

When the flames once again sank to a manageable glow, across from him stood his mistress.

"My lady," he said, dropping to the ground to lay prostrate.

Unable to see her from this position, he listened, his hearing attuned to any shift in the atmosphere.

"Mikel."

A quiver moved through him to hear his name on her lips.

"My lady," he mumbled, his face to the dirt floor.

"Stand. I have need of you."

Rushing to his feet, Mikel stood ready to serve. Her eyes glowed as she approached him from around the fire. His heart rate increased; he was eager to be whatever she desired.

30

MAYA'S SIXTEENTH NAMES DAY DAWNED bright and clear. Sylvan spent the morning straightening up the otherwise-clean cabin, her head full of memories of her own sixteenth Names Day. All the hope and anticipation of the future with Eldred. She never would have thought in her wildest dreams she would end up where she now found herself.

This morning, Sylvan had taken two precious coins from a stash she kept and sent Maya to town for some foodstuffs to make her Names Day meal special. She expected her and her dog back soon, and then they'd cook the meal to commemorate Maya's coming of age.

This thought, the idea of her little girl becoming a woman, gave Sylvan pause. Where had the time gone? And the thought that plagued her the most—what would Maya do with her life? It always seemed as if they had plenty of time and now, here they were, on the cusp of a major change for them both.

Standing, Sylvan placed her hands on her lower back and stretched. Some days she felt so tired and old. Some days she could hardly remember the girl she was. Her life, here in the cabin with Maya, seemed to be the only life she'd truly lived. The life in her parents' manor, married to a man she loved, pampered and indulged, that world—that girl—seemed a million miles away. Now her back ached, and her hands were rough from gardening and milking a cow. She'd learned not only how to mother, but how to father her daughter as well. With a surge of pride, she admitted she'd been successful at it, too. They'd not only lived but thrived. Maya was strong, healthy, and intelligent, and their world was more than enough for Sylvan.

But the girl. She'd need a husband—a man, a home of her own, children. The Singh legacy was gone. Everyone but herself and her daughter dead. A new life begun in a new place.

SYLVAN HEARD THE DOG, RORY, bark a few moments before Maya and he blew in through the door. They were always traveling at a quick pace and causing the dirt to swirl about them. After depositing her purchases from town, Maya grabbed a basket to gather vegetables from the garden and then to milk the cow.

"Take the dog with you," Sylvan called to her as the girl ran out the door. Maya loved to be outdoors, and her affinity with the flora was evident by how well the garden flourished. Her abilities in the garden were the only sign of magic Sylvan saw. In years past, they had bartered the extra and got things they couldn't make or grow on their own.

Sylvan enjoyed the time spent in her cabin. The home she and Maya had created was warm and welcoming.

As DINNER NEARED COMPLETION—A large fish, a favorite of Maya's—Sylvan moved to the doorway to call her. Her voice caught in her throat when she heard the deep baritone of a man floating to her from around the corner of the cabin. She stood for a moment, her hearing attuned to every nuance of the voices. His, soft and cajoling—Maya's, hard and aggressive. Low and in the background, the dog occasionally issued a growl.

Sylvan stepped from around the corner of the cabin, prepared to do battle if need be, only to pull up short when she recognized the man who stood with her daughter. Teck, one of the young men from town. His body language spoke volumes as he leaned toward Maya, who stood on the opposite side of the corral holding a bow and quiver of arrows. Even from a distance, Sylvan could see the bow was a work of art.

She stepped toward the couple and caught their attention.

"Teck?"

"Ma'am," he said. Sylvan smothered a small smile when Teck stepped back from Maya, his skin a slight reddish hue.

"You're just in time for last meal. Please stay and help us begin our celebration of Maya's Names Day."

"Mother—" Maya started.

With a quick glance at the girl, he turned fully to Sylvan. "I'd love to."

A small sound came from her daughter, but Sylvan ignored her. Taking Teck's arm in hers, she turned him toward the cabin. She'd always thought of Teck as a nice young man. He came from one of the more affluent families in Roadstead—his parents owned the mill. Her thoughts moved along the lines from before, and she thought he would make a fine husband for her daughter.

A few moments after she and Teck entered the cabin, Maya sulked in behind them. She still had the bow and quiver in her hands but didn't look happy about their guest.

"Maya, put your gift away and set the table for last meal." Maya did as she was told, so she looked at Teck. "Would you like to sit, Teck? I bet you'd like a mug of cool water." He nodded and took a seat at the table. "Please, Teck. Tell us about the present you brought Maya. I had no idea you were so talented." Sylvan kept a half-eye on the couple, curious about their interaction. In her opinion, her daughter was putting too much energy into disliking the boy. He was obviously captivated, rarely taking his eyes off her. "Maya, come sit and visit with our guest."

When she saw Maya's entire body straighten as she sat, she looked from the girl to where she glared only to see Teck calmly petting Maya's dog. Rory sat with his head tilted up and his eyes closed, completely enjoying the attention. Throughout the meal, Teck grew more relaxed and Maya grew more tense.

When the meal ended, the relief was obvious in Maya. With a small smile, Sylvan told the couple, "Why don't you and Maya step outside. Maybe take a stroll, and she can show you her garden."

"Mother . . ." Maya began, but Sylvan cut her off.

"Go now and quit your complaining." She shooed them out the door and Rory slipped out to follow them. Watching the youngsters walk toward the edge of the property, Sylvan breathed in the cool night air. She would feel much better if she knew Maya's life had a direction and she had someone in it besides just herself.

31

NATHANIEL KNEW HE WAS IN a dream. Dirkcats were too old and wise to be confused by works of magic. What he didn't know was why.

He'd been on this path, tracking his girl, for a long time. Almost two decades had passed since Sylvan had fled from the massacre of her family.

In the dream, Sylvan's image came to him. It was indistinct, as if seen behind a gauzy drape. In her arms, she held a baby, its head covered with a red fuzz.

When the image changed, the child was older. Running to Sylvan, she wrapped her arms around her mother's legs in a fierce hug.

Then, both of them were women, one older than the other. The girl had long red hair and the beauty of her mother. They stood outside a small cabin, the front windows adorned with boxes bursting with flowers. Across a grassy field was an expanse of lake. On the far side of the lake, the rising sun crested.

In Nathaniel's mind, a beacon lit. He knew in which direction they resided.

NATHANIEL WOKE FROM THE DREAM, confusion filling his mind for the first few seconds of wakefulness, his mind still tied to the dream. He glanced around the hayloft and after a second glance, remembered where he was.

Every day's an adventure.

Ever since that fateful day about sixteen years ago, when he'd tasted the burst of magic, he'd been on the move. He knew that day his girl was alive, and nothing else mattered until he found her. The problem was, the silly chit had become quite adept at keeping herself hidden.

Now the dream. Nathaniel recognized it as assistance. Aid given from someone . . . or something.

Without moving, he stared out at the awakening day, and the significance of the timing rattled his brain. A burst of magic woke him sixteen years ago and started his search. Now magic filled his dreams. In his mind, he again saw the second girl in his dream. It was obvious who she was, and obvious where the two occurrences of magic had come from. The girl's arrival in this world, and now her maturation.

But if he could sense her, others could, too. He would need to hurry.

With a sinuous arch of his body, he stretched. As magical beings, dirkcats lived extremely long lives, but the last sixteen of Nathaniel's had tested his patience for such things. When he saw his girl, he was going to give her a piece of his mind — the least she could have done was take him with her.

But now, after almost two decades, his heart filled with hope. The dream of the night previous told him all he needed to know.

Nathaniel listened to the waking of the day for a moment more. Only normal sounds—various bird songs, lowing of the cattle below, and soft sounds of the family, whose barn he'd holed up in last night.

Padding down the stairs from the loft, he silently glided by the cows and slipped out as the farmer opened the barn door.

He moved across the cultivated field and toward the rising sun. In his years of searching, he'd been all over this land, and now, once again, he retraced his steps. With a lift of his head and swish of his tail, he headed out. Like a scent to a hound, the essence of magic drew him.

* * * * *

CALEB STRODE THROUGH HIS ESTATE, his destination the top of a far hillside.

Perhaps he shouldn't have interfered. Perhaps he shouldn't have gone into the cat's dreams—and even for an ancient, they had been strange dreams indeed.

He knew his sister used her abilities to influence the outcome of their game. She had her contacts in this world. Men of low morals, susceptible to her influence. He had used this knowledge to justify his own incursion. Just a nudge, he'd thought. Just a small bump to get an ally moving in the right direction. Really, what could it hurt.

The game was truly in motion now. Two of the Three in play.

All he could do was continue to monitor his sister and try to intercept her interventions.

She had good reason to believe she would win this game; she'd won all the others. What she didn't know, or didn't acknowledge, was he'd allowed her to win. His love for the being she used to be, the sister of old, made him weak concerning her desires.

Caleb stared across the land, seeing the beauty and uniqueness. He was right. It was time he changed his game plan. This time, this world and all its inhabitants would be more important than Cassandra.

* * * * *

HIGH ATOP THE PARAPETS OF her castle, Cassandra too perceived the ripening of magic.

Finally, she thought. *At last it begins in earnest.* A millennium of waiting and the time of triumph was at hand.

Cassandra flowed through the outer doors into the great room, a cold wind preceding her.

With a laugh that startled the small animals scurrying around the rushes on the floor, her step quickened to her scrying bowl. She would observe and see where she could aid her puppets toward her win.

* * * * *

MIKEL BATHSAR SAT STRAIGHT UP in bed, his spine tingling down to his fingertips.

"Orson," he bellowed and was gratified to hear rapidly approaching footsteps. A rat-like man nearly tripped over his feet rushing in.

"My master," came a wheezy whisper as he lay prostrate.

Mikel threw off his covers and slid out to the cold floor. "She's been unveiled."

Orson offered a jacket, but Mikel ignored him, thinking excitedly that at last he'd found her. He'd send his commanders west. They'd check every inn, every home. They'd find her and bring her to him. Squatting by the fireplace, Orson stirred the coals and laid new logs, which caught quickly.

"Get my clothes," Mikel barked, causing Orson to hustle into the wardrobe and begin pulling items out. Continuing to pace, Mikel rubbed his hands together, his face breaking into a large, toothy smile. "Finally. After almost two decades, she will be mine."

After being clothed, Mikel told him to send doves to his commanders. Orson hustled to do his lord's bidding, but Mikel reached out and grabbed him by the collar of his night coat.

"Quickly, Orson," Mikel whispered. "We must get her before she's able to flee again." With a final shake, Mikel Bathsar pushed him away. The firelight grew brighter and, in its glow, a monstrous shadow formed on the far wall. A shadow that moved with the man as he continued to pace.

32

ORSON STOOD IN THE COVE and watched as the messages he'd personally written were attached to doves. Each would be sent to a different commander of his master's forces around the land. Each commander would then move in a pincer-move toward the area Lord Bathsar said the woman resided in. Even if she managed to realize they were on to her and leave the area, they would be able to corner her and take her prisoner. Finally, his salvation was at hand.

As the dove marshal released each bird, Orson tracked it in the sky until the bird disappeared.

Everything depended on this. If he failed to bring the girl to bear this time, he knew, despite all his loyalty, his master would adorn the wall with his skin.

As the last bird took flight, Orson turned and walked toward the manor. He would pack his belongings and prepare to head out. As soon as they received word from one or more of the commanders, it would be his responsibility to retrieve the girl.

He'd never enjoyed sitting on a horse. Never enjoyed the hardships, smells, and discomforts of the trail. If he could, he would send another in his stead, but if anything happened— anything that got in the way of a perfect collection of what his master wanted—he would be blamed and punished. Unfortunately, he would have to be present to ensure success.

* * * * *

As the last of the doves gained height and caught the winds that would lead them to their destinations, a man watched from the hillside. With a slight motion of his arm he called someone forward. This man carried a bow already notched with an arrow. Both men tracked the dove as it neared the hillside and, with a quick motion, the arrow flew. Barely a sound issued from the courier as the arrow hit true. Wings askew, it plummeted to the ground, bounced, and lay still as the men approached. The first man, the leader, picked up the bird, and after giving the arrow back to the marksman, he detached the note from one leg.

"It's time," he whispered. "Tell the men we head west."

At his words, the second man's breath caught, and he touched his forehead with the fingertips of his right hand, muttering a small prayer. Nodding, he turned and headed down the hill to a stand of trees where man after man emerged. Each man was dressed as the first two—a dark green tunic and brown trousers covered them. Strange boots covered their feet and an amulet hung from a small cord strung around their throats. The amulets reflected in the morning light and revealed the image of a square encircled by amber.

33

T HE NEXT DAY BLOOMED BRIGHT and sunny. Sylvan smiled
as she watched her daughter and the dog run from the
house across the field. Then, as if a dark cloud passed
overhead, a foreboding from a night of troubled sleep caught
her in its grip.

"Be careful!" she yelled to the departing duo and heard
Maya respond with a fading platitude. She shook her head at
the daring of the young, then she turned back to planning her
day—straightening the cabin, fixing the meal, and since Maya
would be out most of the day, she would milk the cow and
check the garden for mature vegetables. After that, she would
work on stitching a new shirt for Maya. Maybe she'd have time
to work in her flowers, which grew in beds at the front of the
cabin.

WITH THE SUN WARM ON her back and filtering around the brim
of her hat, Sylvan plucked the dead heads off flowers and
stirred the soil around each plant. This was her favorite chore—

even calling it a chore was wrong. It was pure pleasure. The smell of the flowers and dirt, the warmth of the sunlight and the feeling of the cool breeze on her skin. Each sensation dove into her core and made her happiness spread.

She was humming a little song to herself and moving to the next planter when the whinny of a horse made her lift her head and look around. Before she thought to move or try to hide, men on horses came from all sides to fill the field between her cabin and the lake. Loud, even within the chaos of the men, was the rattle of a large wagon pulled by a team of four horses.

Momentarily blinded by the sun glinting off their tack and weapons, her breath caught in her lungs when their uniforms became clear.

After all this time. How have they found me?

All around her, the turmoil of horses and riders, the sounds and smells of many animals and men, and all she could do was stand frozen in fear, disbelief, and shock. The colors, the red and black. They were the same soldiers that were in her parents' courtyard that long-ago day. The same soldiers who caused her to run from Meg's little inn. She knew who they were. Mikel Bathsar's men. All the fear and confusion of those times came back to her threefold. It was some moments before one thought pushed its way in.

Maya.

Scanning around the men and over the field, she looked for a sign of her daughter. She hoped she would see nothing, that the girl would stay away. The sounds faded into the background and her body broke out in a sweat. She was so focused on looking to the tree line that she didn't at first notice the man who stepped in front of her. When her view became blocked, Sylvan focused on a young man's face. A helmet covered his hair, and a dark bushy beard covered the lower part of his face. His eyes, almost black, stared at her and, as if living her worst nightmare, she stared back.

"Ma'am." His voice came out in a whisper she almost missed as it mixed with the sounds of the men and horses.

He reached toward her. Grasping the handle of the basket she still held, he pulled it from her lax fist and placed it at their feet. Pausing just a moment, the man took her upper arm and directed her toward the waiting wagon. Sylvan floated alongside him, a fog distorting her vision. Part of her mind cried out for her to wake up, just wake up, but she couldn't shake the lethargy that had her in its grip.

As they moved through the men and closed in on the transport, the sun broke through the clouds and glinted off bars mounted on the vehicle's windows. A shaft of light caught her eye and she squinted, pulling her head back. Blinking rapidly, she became aware of the vise-like grip on her arm. A flush of adrenaline flowed through her system, pushing her to act, but it was too late. She was at the small steps leading to the inner realm of the carriage. The inside was dark—just small streaks of light penetrated through the bars for her to make out a wooden bench, and rushes on the floor. The smell, though not unpleasant, was musty and dry.

When the panic broke through everything else, Sylvan stepped back and her body came up against the officer who'd led her out. She pushed harder and tried to turn, but two large hands grabbed her by the waist and effortlessly lifted her into the wagon. She stumbled forward and landed hard on her knees. As she looked over her shoulder, the door slammed, and she heard a key turn in the lock.

"Wait," she yelled. Wrenching her skirt out of the way, she stumbled to her feet to face the closed door.

She couldn't stand fully in the small space. She grasped the bars in both fists and dropped again to her knees to stare out of her cell.

"Wait!" she cried again at the departing officer. He turned to look at her. He gave a gesture toward the wagon, and the driver obeyed, the carriage rolling forward. Sylvan heard the crack of a whip and the wagon quickly gained speed. The motion threw her to the side, but she pulled herself back to the door to peer out.

Her cheek laid against the bars, and she strained to keep an eye on her home. Just before her view was lost, she saw the officer take a torch from a solider and throw it into the cabin.

34

FOR HOURS, THE WAGON RACED. One hand was wrapped around the iron bars of a window, the other braced on the seat. With her booted feet planted firmly on the floor, Sylvan tried to control her body and keep it from sliding on the wooden seat. She'd forgotten when her limbs had ceased to scream in protest—their muscles drained. Now she lived in a fog of exhaustion. Neither her mind nor her body was able to function or object. Both locked into the realm of existing.

Once, hours ago, the carriage careened to a halt and the lathered, heaving horses were exchanged for waiting ones. With the crack of a whip, her moving cell lurched forward and again sped down the lane.

Though she didn't know where she was or where she was going, through her fatigue, her heart pounded with the fear that came from knowing Mikel waited at the end of this journey. So many years ago, she'd fled from him just to end up back within his clutches. Muscles tense, rocking with the wagon, she raised her head, chin thrust forward, eyes sharpening. No longer was she a young, innocent girl. In the almost two decades since she turned her back on everything she knew, she'd matured into a woman who took care of what was hers. She wouldn't be such an easy mark for Mikel's sadistic pleasure.

THE SUN WAS LOWERING IN the late afternoon sky when the carriage again came to a halt. The sounds of shouting men had her stretching her limbs and shifting to peer out the window. In front of the caravan, across a narrow spot on the trail, a large tree lay. The men gathered and appeared to be discussing how best to move the timber and be on their way.

At a sound like whistles, she looked to the sky with curiosity. On the tail of the sound, men began falling to the ground, arrows protruding from them like porcupine quills. When her driver's shadow passed overhead and she heard the impact of his body, she ducked back into the recesses of her cell.

Men shouted, and curiosity got the better of her as she snuck up and again peeked out her window. Bodies lay strewn about with blood pooling. Men ran, eyes scanning overhead to locate where the arrows came from. As they ran, they too became victim to the archers.

One soldier, grasping the bars of her cell, yelled for her to let him in. With a *thunk*, an arrow struck him in the throat. The look of amazement on his face had her scurrying back as he toppled to the side.

Sylvan's breath caught in her throat and then exploded from her lungs. She scrunched herself back against the carriage wall and sat still. A period of silence ensued, but before long male voices came to her—quiet and questioning. She pushed herself even harder against the wall. Barely breathing, she hoped these men would pass her by. Once she wanted out, but now, not knowing her enemy or the threat she faced, she hoped they'd miss her.

As the voices came nearer, it was not to be. A large hand gripped the bars from the outside and when it gave a shake, the whole carriage moved, eliciting a small squeak from her. A face peered between the bars and the eyes, a deep brown, locked on her form.

The face disappeared.

"Search the officers and the driver. Find me the key."

She leaned forward to track their movement, but when the man looked back into the carriage, Sylvan shrank into the wall again.

"Don't be afraid, my lady. We'll have you out in one moment."

My lady? Who are these men?

It wasn't more than a minute or two when a young man ran to the carriage. He and the man in charge spoke softly, and then with a squeak and a clank, the door to her cell slid open. Sylvan sat still as men's faces and bodies filled the opening. She looked from one to the other, her heart pounding in her ears and a fine sheen of sweat breaking out on her upper lip.

What was to become of her now?

Each man wore a dark green tunic belted at the waist. Seeing they each wore an amulet around their necks, she squinted to better see it in the sunlight. What appeared to be amber caught the light and shone with a warm vibrancy.

Moving the other men aside, the one in charge leaned in and offered her his hand.

"My lady, please come with us. We must be away from here."

Sylvan looked from his face to his extended hand and back to his face. She didn't know any of these men — their dress and manner unfamiliar — and pushing herself flat against the back of the cell, she mutely shook her head.

The man dropped his hand and head and gave a mighty sigh. Then he turned his gaze back to her. "Don't make me come in after you."

A chill snaked up her spine and heat exploded in her cheeks. She blinked rapidly, her mind spinning to find a solution to her dilemma. When he again extended his hand to her, she didn't see another option and leaned forward. She took his hand with her own shaking one.

When Sylvan moved from the doubtful safety of the wagon, she stood and faced row upon row of men. She swallowed hard but lifted her chin. She would face what came and try to do so with bravery.

The amulet each man wore caught her eye, but in the bright sunlight she couldn't make out a clear image. Her gaze panned from face to face just as the man who'd spoken to her turned toward her.

"My lady." The raspiness of his voice scratched over her already frayed nerves, but his greeting was deferential, and now, so was his tone. With an effort, she curtsied — a move she hadn't performed in almost two decades.

"Sir, can you kindly explain what is happening? Who are you and your men?"

With an answering nod and bow, he said, "We are the Bordermen. Let me assure you, we are here to give you aid and see you to safety."

She squinted, and her brows drew together. "I've never heard of you or your group. The Bordermen, you say?"

With another nod the man continued. "That isn't surprising, my lady. My name is Lamar, and you and I will talk more when we are away from here. Now we must be off."

Another man stepped from behind them. Crowded in, she moved away with the men.

35

NOT A BLADE OF GRASS was displaced as the cat made his way toward the burnt remnants of the cabin. The essence of his girl flowed strongly under the acrid scent of smoke. His girl and other things.

Dog, he thought with a sniff, *and another being.* Another being who smelled suspiciously like a version of his girl. His thoughts went back to the child in his dream, his suspicions confirmed. *Sneaky.* He always thought his girl was sneaky. To have kept something like this from him—and now he knew where the burst of magic had originated.

Nathaniel continued around the area, his nose wrinkling at the scents of men and horses. Many men.

Moving closer to the ruins, he stayed well back in the shadows, his eyes and ears open to any nuance of sights and sounds, but there was nothing. Whatever had happened here, had happened days ago. He circled the area twice before deciding the more vibrant trail of scent lay to the mountains. It wasn't his girl—it was the other and the dog. His brows pulled down with the thought of a canine. Stupid beasts. Always running about, slobbering all over everything and everyone. With another sniff of disdain, he decided he would be the bigger being and put up with a dog to meet the girl.

He broke into a trot and headed into the woods leading to the mountain pass. Now that the hunt for Sylvan had begun in earnest, his heart quickened. Soon he'd be face to face with her again. Soon they'd be sitting alongside one another, discussing issues and the workings of the world. Soon, everything would be as it should. The long wait would be over.

NATHANIEL'S CLAWS RELAXED ON THE tree branch, and he stilled his body. Hidden among the leaves, he observed those below. The three spoke in tones of mixed aggression and sarcasm. Their scents were of the cabin. The female of the group he knew to be Sylvan's child. Even if the wind weren't blowing her scent—a hint of Sylvan in its essence—just looking at her face would give it away. Her coloring was of her father, a more striking mix with her red hair and honeyed skin, and she was built taller as Sylvan had never reached a height of any proportion, but her features were all her mother. Beautiful.

Now, what was going on with the man and her? Was he friend or foe? She'd obviously been surprised to find him in her camp when she woke and didn't seem happy about it. But not threatened. Nathaniel watched them from above, his only movement the twitching of the tip of his tail, and an occasional flicker of his ear. A flying bug hovered over him, drawing his attention, but soon it flew off. When the girl began packing her belongings, Nathaniel scampered out of the tree to move down a trail. He would continue to watch and follow.

36

THE MEN TRAVELED FOR SEVERAL days with Sylvan in their midst. They rested rarely and when they did, it was for short bursts to eat and sleep. She became used to Lamar shaking her awake from the heap she'd dropped into upon stopping the previous night.

She didn't know how long this arduous pace would continue, and when she asked, no one gave her an answer.

A few days later, the trees parted and before them appeared a fine manor. The walls were a particular shade of golden brown like wheat ready for harvest. Broken by a gate in the front, a wall ran back and seemed to surround the entire property. The men didn't hesitate as they moved toward it and passed through the gates. Sylvan heaved a sigh of relief. It looked as if they'd arrived at their destination, wherever that might be.

The men dispersed, and she eyed them, her heartbeat speeding up as she stood alone, and no one approached her.

"My lady."

Her hand flew to her throat and she spun at the words.

Looking down at her was Brother Lamar. He extended an arm toward the manor.

"If you would follow me, I'll show you to your accommodations."

"Can you tell me, sir, where we are. I need to return to my home."

He turned from her toward the manor, saying over his shoulder, "Soon, my lady. We have a few items to deal with first and then we shall return you to your home."

She followed him through the manor door, and even through her nerves, she couldn't stop a small smile that lifted the corners of her mouth. The interior of the building was well cared for—clean and well-tended.

Through the building and up a flight of wide, marble stairs the duo walked. How long had it been since she'd even seen a home this fine? The art and tapestries brought memories of her childhood rushing back.

Partway down a central hallway, the brother stopped and pushed open a door, indicating his desire for Sylvan to precede him. As she moved into the room, her eyes scanned the area. A round table sat near the door, and a large bed occupied the center of the room. Along the wall a wooden bureau took up space. Next to a window she saw a fragile-looking table with a basin and vase upon it.

"My lady, this will be your quarters while you are with us."

Turning to look at him, she asked, "And how long will that be?"

Moving back into the hallway, he answered over his

shoulder, "As long as is necessary," and he shut the door quietly behind him.

Sylvan turned from the door to again study the room. When she heard a key turn in the lock, she spun and hurried to the exit. The knob wouldn't give.

"Lamar," she called, her mouth to the portal. She waited to hear an answer, as an insidious thought entered her mind. Could it be she'd gotten free from one captor simply to be confined by another? What could these men want from her?

"Lamar!" she called loudly and banged on the door.

She pulled on it, rattling the knob, but all she managed to do was make her hand sore. The door was locked tight and no one came to her calls.

Spinning to place her back to the door, her breath came in puffs, and her heartbeat sent a rush of blood pulsing in her ears. She hustled across the room and approached the window to turn the handle. The pane stayed closed when she yanked it. She shook it, pulled, and twisted. It rattled in its frame but didn't open. Out the window, in the distance, she could see a lovely, private garden. The view was broken up by thick metal pieces that checkerboarded the glass. Even if she broke the pane, she'd never fit out between the squares of metal.

The sound of a key turning had her swinging back toward the door. She rushed forward before it even cracked. Her momentum caused her to skid to a halt as the door swung open. Two men entered, followed closely by a small woman garbed in a drab dress and apron. A third man entered behind the woman carrying a tray of food.

The first two men kept a wary eye on her while they blocked the exit and the other two came into the room. She rose to her toes, swaying side to side, straining to see into the hall. With the big men blocking her, she saw just a touch of it. No one passed while the door was ajar.

The man set the tray on the small table, and as that brother left the room, the woman turned toward Sylvan.

"My lady, I am Marie. I'll be seeing to your needs while you stay here."

With a quick scan, Sylvan turned on the men. Advancing on them to stand toe to toe, her eyes shot sparks.

"Where is Lamar? What is happening here?"

The men looked down at her and didn't say a word. As one, they shifted their gazes to look over her head.

"Hey," Sylvan snapped. "Answer me." She thumped her finger against the nearest man's chest. He didn't react.

Behind her, Marie touched her arm. "Ma'am. If you would come this way . . . I have a light meal for you."

Throwing a look over her shoulder, Sylvan studied the maid from the top of her head to the toes of her leather shoes.

Is she insane? Doesn't she see what is happening here?

When she turned from the maid to again face the men, they were moving out of her room. Her protests meant no more to them than a gnat's buzzing.

Marie slid past her and out the door before the last man. Sylvan rushed forward only to be halted when the man put up a hand. Staring at her for a moment, he stepped back and silently pulled the door closed. The rasp of a key turning in the lock made her blink. When she stepped up to the door to try the knob, it was without surprise that it wouldn't turn. Once again, she was locked in.

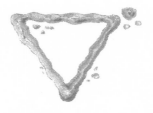

37

BROTHER LAMAR LOOKED AT THE assembly of men. In their eyes he saw acceptance and trust. These were his brothers, his family. Men who had desires and goals the same as his.

When they broke from the Brotherhood of Fate, they didn't know where their path would lead, but now they had the woman in their possession. She was the key to all their desires. With this bargaining chip, they could have anything they wished.

Lamar and his followers thought the Brotherhood of Fate to be idealistic and unrealistic. The brotherhood wanted a perfect world with no evil, no strife. Where men would live together in harmony.

Lamar gave a small shake of his head. That world could never be. But he knew that their little part of it could be better. They could live well. Their lives could be easier.

It all came down to Lord Mikel Bathsar. They could give him what he desired — and he could give them the same. Lamar was sure Mikel Bathsar could be reasoned with.

Word would be sent to him. Word that they had rescued the woman from a band of men. Men who had killed his soldiers and taken her prisoner. Men who planned to do awful things to her. She was safe. Safe for him, because of the actions of his Bordermen. For this, Lord Bathsar would reward them. He would bargain for all they desired.

A smile flitted across Lamar's face, and as he surveyed the room of men, his eyes shone with the imagining of his plan coming to fruition.

"You'll see, Samet," he muttered. "You'll see, I'm the one who will be leading."

38

ORSON STOOD AMID THE CARNAGE and surveyed the area.

His men were dead, the carriage abandoned, and the woman gone. He'd sent out trackers to locate a trail, but as of yet, nothing. His breath caught as he considered his master's reaction to the news of Sylvan's escape. It was quite possible he would not survive the telling.

"Sir."

Spinning to the approaching soldier, Orson recognized him as a young officer who'd been ordered to stay behind to destroy any evidence around the area of Sylvan's cabin.

"Sir." The soldier slid to a halt before Orson. Though Mikel's second-in-command was small, he was imposing. The men knew how harsh a leader he could be. Failure was dealt with quickly and severely.

With a pant, the soldier caught his breath.

Never one for patience, Orson raised an eyebrow. "Well?"

"Sir, I came directly to tell you . . ." Gasping again, the

soldier bent over and pulled in a breath, coughing.

Orson squinted and studied the soldier, contemplating his murder when the man caught a full breath, stood, and said, "The villagers, the villagers said the woman has a child."

Orson had just been turning away—planning on dealing with the soldier later—when his words sank in. He froze.

With a glance over his shoulder, he slowly turned to again face the soldier.

"A child? Are you certain?"

"Yes sir. A daughter. Maya. They said her name is Maya."

Orson paced slowly away, his mind working furiously.

A daughter. What could this mean for my master's plan? Where is the girl now?

He gestured to the soldier. The man hustled to Orson, his face pale.

"Take two trackers. Go back to the cabin and find the girl's trail. She must be around their home. Find her."

Nodding quickly, the soldier turned and ran to the camp.

Already moving on with his plans. Orson contemplated his master's reaction to this news. Would it be good or bad? If he found the child, it just might save his neck.

39

FOR SYLVAN, THE DAYS IN her new prison dragged on. She saw no one, save Marie or the silent men. The maid refused to talk to her, though whether due to fear of or loyalty to the Bordermen, she couldn't tell. She had no idea where she was or why she was here.

The maid brought in her meals twice daily and cleaned her room once a day. During this time Sylvan could visit an inner courtyard. The man, the same brother who always showed up to lead her to the yard, watched her closely as she wandered about in the sunshine. She'd attempted to talk with him, but he ignored her—looking over her head to stare out into the yard.

The next time she was taken to the courtyard, she turned on him.

"How long am I to be kept here?"

He didn't speak to her and simply looked over her head into the yard beyond.

"Hey! I'm speaking to you." She kicked him in the shin. "Ouch," she muttered, turning and limping away. Now, in addition to everything else, she might have broken her toe.

As she wandered around the courtyard, Sylvan kept an eye on the brother. He didn't trail her as he usually did.

She was across the yard from him, inspecting an apple tree, when another brother entered the garden and approached him. Their conversation soon became heated and, when a moment of inattentiveness gave her the opportunity, she stepped to the backside of the tree.

Her heart beating a staccato rhythm, she climbed the outer wall, sure to keep the large tree between her and the brothers. The wall was old, and although still solid, the years had provided many handholds and places for her feet.

When she reached the top, she peeked over the edge to scan the area beyond.

She didn't see any brothers in the vicinity, and to her delight, the tree line wasn't too far from the wall. If she could make the forest, she would have a better chance of escaping.

She risked a small glance over her shoulder, and then pushing herself to the top of the wall, she spun and started down the other side.

She was partway down when she heard the brother call from the yard. Adrenaline surged through her, for a moment making her feel faint. Clenching the wall with her fist, the burn of sharp rocks cutting into her skin pulled her focus back to the problem at hand. She looked toward the ground, judging the distance, and with a push, she dropped the remainder. Hitting solid on both feet, her injured toe screaming in protest, she limped toward the trees, glancing around in desperation.

Calls came from behind her, hastening her flight. When trees closed around her, the coolness of the forest filling her lungs, her lips curved in a smile. She might make it. For a few moments, she thought she was alone, thought her escape successful, but then the shouts began again. Men appeared at all avenues. She didn't see an opening.

Reminded of the night she fled the tunnel to the river, she wished for her magic. But she'd used it up protecting her home. Now she was on her own.

She stopped, desperate for a direction to run. She couldn't come to a decision. All she saw were green shirts.

She put her head down and rushed for the center of a man. She dug in her toes, pushing power into her limbs, and prayed.

When she hit the man, he stumbled back. She ended up on her back, dazed from the impact. In seconds, she was grabbed and hauled to her feet. Rushed back, pushed and shoved, and painful grips on her forearms, she had no option but to go with them.

Through the gate, in the manor, and up the stairs they hauled her.

Once again, she was a prisoner, but the sweet taste of her brief freedom had whetted her appetite for more. Even as they pushed her back in her room and slammed the door, the key rasping in the lock, she was thinking of her next attempt.

NO MATTER HOW OFTEN, OR in what form Sylvan strove to win her freedom, the brothers always found her out. She had become so quick to run, that for a time, she wasn't allowed out of the security of her room.

To get some fresh air and sunshine, she resorted to promising to be good. She wouldn't run, she wouldn't hide. They allowed her back into the courtyard, though now she was accompanied by two brothers. She kept her eyes open for her escape, her words of promise a lie.

Out of boredom and desperation during her confinement with the Bordermen, Sylvan again began practicing her magic and that of Nathaniel. She remembered when she'd cast her final spell to protect and hide the valley she and Maya lived in, she'd felt the glow and heat of her magic leave. She'd felt empty, hollowed out until Maya had filled her with love again. She didn't know, but she hoped that with practice she might once again find the magic within her.

Over the years in the valley, she'd rarely thought of the magic she'd been born with. Her life with Maya was reward enough. She had no desires other than those for her child to be healthy and happy. More often, when thoughts of her past had risen, she'd thought of Nathaniel and wondered where he'd ended up. The thought of him brought guilt—she'd left without any consideration for him. Her concern had been her child and that was all she'd planned for.

Each day with the brothers, Sylvan concentrated on finding her magic, but the flame remained elusive. She'd never heard of a Singh losing their ability, though to the best of her knowledge, no Singh had faced the perils she had.

She'd never thought her magic was very strong and to her this proved it.

If she'd had something else to do, hadn't exhausted all avenues of escape, she might have given up, but the forced inactivity drove her forward. She'd stop multiple times daily and concentrate—looking inward, searching for the spark, and when faced with the maid or the man, she attempted to mesmerize them. Always, day after day, she failed.

A FEW WEEKS IN, THE day dawned sunny and bright. As Sylvan opened her eyes to the light filtering in through her window, she felt different.

She tried to identify the feeling. Finally, she decided, she felt expectant, as if something was going to happen. Sitting and throwing her legs over the side of her bed, she heaved a heavy sigh. After weeks of nothing, perhaps this was just wishful thinking.

The day progressed, but through it all, the meals and her walk with a stoic brother, she kept checking over her shoulder, looking to the horizon—always there was the feeling of something coming. A storm rolling in off the far mountains. Electricity seemed to fill the air.

When her door opened to admit Marie, Sylvan looked up from the stitching she was busying herself with. Her eyes shifted as she caught a small movement not created by the maid. It appeared out of the side of her eye, and when she looked straight on, it was gone. Before the maid turned to her, she scanned the room.

A small smile caught at the corners of her mouth, and relief drooped her shoulders, expelling a sigh. She dropped her head lest the maid see her features before she could school them. Never had she imagined he would find her here.

When Marie turned and left without speaking, Sylvan waited a moment and then said, "Hello, Nathaniel. I've missed you, old friend."

A shimmering began across the room and intensified in brightness. In the next moment, as if from the very air, a large, striped cat jumped onto the bed with her. Laughing, a sob caught in her throat as he walked around her, bumping her with his head and arching along her body. She buried her face in his nape. His purr vibrated loudly, and she wrapped her arms around him and kissed his head. Falling back on the bed, she pulled him with her, his large body wrapped tightly in her arms.

Some moments later, they lay staring at each other. His eyes large, a luminous yellow, and hers overflowing with tears she didn't even attempt to halt.

"I'm sorry, Nathaniel." Salty tears fell over her lips. "I know our separation has been hard on you, also."

The cat continued to stare at her and then he blinked slowly. "Your child is amazing."

"Maya—you've seen her? Is she all right?"

Nathaniel pulled from her embrace and leaped gracefully to the floor.

"We need to leave this place."

"I've tried over and over again."

"Yes." His tail curled around his front legs. "But you didn't have me."

40

"**I** AM TRYING," SYLVAN HISSED between her teeth.

Throwing her a look over his shoulder, Nathaniel gave a swoosh of his tail. Approaching her, he said, "Not hard enough." With a paw at her chest, he blinked. "The magic is in here."

"Nathaniel," she drawled.

"Don't, 'Nathaniel' me. You need to try harder." He walked away to curl up in a far corner.

"Damn cat." Stomping to the other side of the room, Sylvan thought back to the last few weeks since Nathaniel had arrived. He was on her, almost constantly, to find her magic. They would sit together, and he'd tell her to concentrate.

"Look inside. Find the spark, fan it, and allow it to grow."

He insisted her magic was still there, just dormant. When she disagreed, he told her no magic disappeared. It was always there—even after she had ceased to be, her magic would exist.

She didn't believe him though. She'd felt it leave. She tried to explain that to him. How it had felt. Her belief was that the final spell had been so big, it had taken everything she had with it. And she feared for Maya. How strong must her daughter's magic be for it to have broken through the spell? To have allowed others to find them, to sense her daughter's magic.

At least Maya wasn't alone. Nathaniel told her the last time he saw her, she was with Teck. He said they were searching for her. It was imperative she get out of here and find Maya. What if Mikel still searched for her? She was sure the soldiers at her cabin were from him. What would he do if he found Maya? The girl was ill-prepared to face such evil. The closer Maya got to her, the closer Mikel would get to them both.

And Maya's magic. A power that strong would require her to have someone to stand with her. Someone she could learn from and lean on. Someone to help her control the magic, to answer her questions. She was only sixteen—just a child.

Heaving a sigh, Sylvan stood and walked toward Nathaniel.

"Okay. I'm ready to try again."

IN THE DARK RECESSES OF her mind, Sylvan moved. She didn't know exactly where she was—shadows shifted, and hollow sounds echoed—but she moved forward. The soft tones of Nathaniel's voice helped to keep her focused and grounded.

"Search for the spark."

In her mind's eye, she pushed forward. It seemed in the haze of darkness, a light, no matter how small, would stand out. She imagined she walked through a large mansion. A mansion with many rooms. She moved down hallways, opened doors, and searched rooms. Over and over they searched, but all that was there was the darkness. Dusty, cluttered, and difficult to move through.

She knew what it felt like, the memory clear in her head, but nothing seemed familiar. The farther she went, the denser her mind became, as if it were a cloak covering her. Pushing it aside, she moved forward.

She came to a set of stairs and started down. When they opened into a cavernous cellar, a shiver of apprehension moved up her spine. She told herself she was being silly, that this was, after all, her own mind, and she moved forward.

"Nathaniel, I don't feel anything. Nothing familiar."

"What do you see?"

"Darkness."

Sylvan scanned the area. Dark muted walls faced her. Seeing what appeared to be a painting hanging on a wall in the distance, she moved to it. When she neared it, she realized it was a mirror. She studied it—and the reflection stared back at her.

The mirror was large, reaching almost from floor to ceiling. The frame around it was copper—the metal patinaed with age but intricate with swirls.

She stared for many minutes at herself. Her image within was altered somehow, but she couldn't put her finger on how. Darker. Something floated across the mirror. As she watched, it clarified.

Nav-lys.

Sylvan read the word. Was it a name?

* * * * *

SITTING ON THE BED NEXT to Sylvan, it was clear to Nathaniel she was exhausted. Her shoulders slumped and there were dark circles under her eyes. She'd done well — quit fighting him — but they still hadn't found anything. How was it alluding them? And why?

The cat shook his head and his own shoulders slumped. "Come back, Sylvan. Come back. You need some rest."

* * * * *

SYLVAN HEARD THE CAT, BUT her attention was caught by the image in the mirror and the name. It looked familiar. Where had she seen it before?

When her dream-self reached out to touch the mirror, the reverse image did, too. Laying her hand upon the glass, she stared into her own eyes.

Exhausted, willing to give up for now, her hand dropped to her side. With a start, she saw that the hand in the opposite image remained pressed to the glass.

The glass began to bulge where the hand touched.

Gaze jumping from the reflection's hand to its face, she stepped back when the eyes swirled with a black mass.

ON THE BED SYLVAN'S EYES moved behind her lids, her breathing coming fast. Nathaniel watched her, his concern growing. After a moment, he reached out and placed a paw on her arm.

"Sylvan." He gave her a shake.

Her breath hitched again, and he shook her harder.

When her eyes popped open, he didn't think she knew him or where she was. Fear filled her gaze.

"What?" he asked. "What did you find?"

Sylvan bent at the waist, leaning from the bed, taking great gulps of air. With a hand on her chest, she tried to talk.

"I—"

Nathaniel moved closer on the bed, worry evident on his face. He didn't push her, though, allowing her the time she needed to get herself under control. When she tried again, she was able to tell him.

"A mirror. There was a mirror with a reflection of me. But it wasn't me." She stood to pace to the door and then back to where he sat on the bed. "And it tried to get me."

"My dear," the cat began. "You're tired, perhaps confused."

"No. No I know what I saw." Approaching the bed, she flopped down next to the cat, her head on one of the pillows. Nathaniel curled up next to her, his purr comforting and calming her.

Sleep pulled at Sylvan, exhaustion washing over her. Fear kept her awake for a time, but like a wave, she soon slipped under. Just before succumbing to its pull, she muttered, "Do you know what *Nav-lys* means?"

The cat lifted his head to look at her, but seeing she now slept, he lay down and joined her.

* * * * *

THE DOOR BURST OPEN WITH a crash as it hit the wall and bounced back. Lamar—who Sylvan hadn't seen since arriving—rushed in followed by a group of men.

Sylvan sat straight up in bed, her eyes wide, her breath caught in her throat. She pushed herself to the headboard to avoid Lamar's outstretched hand. She could have saved herself the moment of panic, however, when his hand came away gripping an angry cat.

Nathaniel spit and hissed. His claws flayed, hind legs kicking and front legs grasping, but before he could do much damage, a burlap bag was produced, and he was unceremoniously dropped into it.

"I knew you were up to something," Lamar said with a finger jabbed in her direction. "Voices, they said. They heard voices coming from your room."

He shook the bag, causing a screeching yowl to issue forth.

"What is this animal? How did it come to be in your room?"

"Give him back!" she yelled, launching herself at the man. Before she could do any damage, he had her by the throat. Gasping, unable to draw a normal breath, Sylvan clawed at his hand. With a sound of disgust, Lamar flung her back to the mattress. She stared at the man and the bag he held aloft.

Crawling to the center of the bed, Sylvan moved to her knees, her gaze focused on the bag.

"Please. Please don't hurt him," she pleaded in a whisper.

Lamar swung the bag against the wall, causing the

screeching to stop mid cry.

"No!" Sylvan yelled, gaining her feet.

"You will tell me, or I'll beat this animal until it's nothing but pieces." He swung the bag again.

When Sylvan heard a crunch come from the bag, her mind blanked.

"No!" she shouted again, but the sound coming from her was deeper as if spoken from the depth of a well. Lamar and the other brothers swiveled as one to stare at her.

Standing on the bed, arms outstretched, hair and nightgown buffeted by a mysterious wind, she turned eyes that had gone black as the darkest night on the assemblage of men.

"No," she said again, but this time it came out as a whisper. As the word ended, her body arched, head thrown back. A fog of black erupted from her, seeming to pour from her skin. For a moment, it swirled before the staring assembly, and then quicker than the eye could catch, it had Lamar encased.

The bag containing the cat dropped to the floor, spilling the feline's body partway out. The group of men stepped back from their leader, eyes wide. No one ran, held spellbound by the image before them. The black mass swirled around him, tighter and tighter, lifting him from the marble floor. With a final hiss, like gas releasing from a fissure, it squeezed, and Lamar exploded into bits of crushed flesh and blood. The explosion of shattered parts rained on the gathering of men and fell well into the room.

Gasping and muttering, the men stumbled back from the carnage. Some of them grasped their amulets and, falling to their knees, prayed, throwing panic-filled looks at Sylvan. She still stood on the bed, seeming to levitate as the blackness roiled about her.

Turning her head to the men with her obsidian eyes, she made a small gesture and the mist moved again, this time to swarm them. Surrounded, they struggled for a moment before they dropped silently to the floor, dead as Lamar.

When the last man hit the floor, the black mass retreated into her body. As if in a trance, she stepped barefoot from the bed and walked to the bag. Nathaniel's upper body lay out of the burlap, his front legs bent in an unnatural angle. His eyes, large and luminous, stared, and after a second, he slowly blinked. Kneeling beside him, the edge of her nightgown trailing in the blood that covered the floor, she scooped up the cat and tenderly held him to her breast.

Step by step she moved out of her prison—through the door of her room, down the hall and stairway, she exited the manor. Along the way, servants moved back from her into the shadows of adjoining rooms. The maid, Marie, peered out from a room but didn't venture forth, as though afraid to step forward and incur the woman's wrath.

When Sylvan left the manor and the lands surrounding it, no one stopped her. She walked, the cat cradled in her arms. Her trance was so complete, she didn't notice the stones and thistles she trod on or when her feet began to bleed.

It was sometime later when the woman sat against the trunk of an old tree, sheltered by the leafy canopy. The cat, either sleeping or unconscious, didn't move as she shifted him to lay on her lap. With a hand on his head, she closed her stormy eyes, and once again the mist seeped from her skin to encase the duo in a mass of swirling gases.

In the woman's mind, in an empty mansion, down in the lowest reaches was a mirror.

It used to be a thing of beauty, but now it was old and aged—and the glass was cracked.

41

PATRICK RAISED HIS HEAD AT the end of the prayer and glanced around. He was surrounded by men of the Brotherhood of Fate. He knew these men. He'd been with the brotherhood for many years, and he'd only recently come to realize why.

Some nights, lying in his cot, listening to the sounds of his chamber mates breathing, he tried to remember what the exact feelings, the exact words had been that had brought him here. Even the face of the man, whose directive he served, would suffice.

While the other brothers chanted out loud to their deity, Patrick's prayers were silent. He prayed constantly for guidance.

As a youth, living off the refuse of others, wandering the streets, he'd thought his world was over that fateful day he'd woke to a man sitting beside him. Fear and the sickening weakness of inevitability had filled him. Unable to even move, he'd lain and waited with the thought that his fate was upon him. Others, those stronger, who lived on the streets would always prey on the weak, and now it was his turn. He hadn't been fast enough. He hadn't been crafty enough.

But the man had begun to speak to him, his voice deep and pleasant. As he talked, Patrick's fear left him, and wonder took hold. The man invited him to walk with him. He told Patrick of his destiny. He gave Patrick a name.

The man, Caleb, explained to him an age-old foretelling. A coming together of peoples. Three, and then Three — and they would become One. In becoming, they would be strong enough to defeat an ultimate evil.

Patrick had a part to play. A part in the war to come. And Caleb had directed him here, to the brotherhood. Here he would be safe. Here he would grow and learn. And here, he would be ready when he was called.

Now, decades later, Patrick no longer struggled with his goal. For years, he'd thought perhaps he'd imagined the man who'd talked with him. Maybe he'd been a fantasy contrived by the mind of a lonely child. As time passed, the more likely it became that the mind of a lost, unimportant orphan boy had created a situation where he was important. Where his life had a destiny. A grand destiny to save the world. He had battled his yearnings for years. But no longer.

Caleb had returned to him.

It was just yesterday. He'd been praying with the other brothers. Reverently. Silently.

When he'd opened his eyes, he'd no longer been in the home of the brotherhood. No longer surrounded by his brothers.

When he heard the crash of surf, he'd swung around, and a marvelous vista opened up before him. With a hesitant step he approached the edge of a high cliff, the surf pounding far below. His eyes took in the bluest ocean there could ever be. Just to see it made his eyes burn. Great birds swooped over the waves, catching fish in their hooked talons.

"Patrick."

He spun to face the other direction, the ocean now at his back. There before him was the man from his youth.

"Caleb?" He truly had gone insane. His mind had fabricated this delusion.

"No, Patrick. I'm no dream."

Patrick studied the man. He hadn't changed since Patrick saw him so long ago. How could that be?

"Come, walk with me and we will talk." The man extended a hand to him with a smile and then turned to move away from the cliff face. Patrick hesitated a moment and then stepped to follow him.

As they walked beside each other, the man glanced at him. With another small smile, Caleb said, "What would you ask of me?"

"Are you real?" Without waiting for an answer, he added, "How can you be unchanged?"

"You knew the day we met that I was not like you. Why do you ask these questions when they are not what is really on your mind?" Caleb stopped and faced Patrick.

"What am I to do?"

"There is the question that has been plaguing your mind." With a hand on Patrick's shoulder, Caleb led him up the hillside to a spot under some trees. Birdsong filled the air, and light filtered through the branches to fall like raindrops on the grass.

"Sit with me," Caleb said. "Sit and we'll talk."

Through the hours that followed, Patrick learned all he was to know about the coming battle for the world. Some he would need to find on his own. He learned information of who the main players were—the Three and Three—and when he would meet them. One, who he would assist in saving, would be the child of someone he already knew. A couple, he would not know for some time. Caleb counseled him to be patient. All things would come. Caleb said he was the right man for the job.

When Caleb stood, Patrick jumped up to stand alongside him.

"You must be ready to act when called upon."

Nodding vigorously, Patrick assured him he would be ready.

"Close your eyes for a moment, Patrick. Close your eyes and relax." Caleb placed a hand on Patrick's head. Bowing his head, as if in prayer, Patrick closed his eyes.

When he opened them, he was again in the prayer room of the Brotherhood of Fate. The sounds of the brothers' prayers filled the air. Nothing had changed except the knowledge Patrick now had for the future.

42

SYLVAN'S BROW FURROWED MOMENTS BEFORE she woke. She scanned the area with eyes of the purest blue, and looking down to her lap, she placed a hand on the sleeping cat. His fur was warm, and under her hand, his body rose and fell with his breaths.

What happened?

A small shiver moved through her, and it was only then that she became aware she wore only her nightgown. The morning's brisk air mixed with the night's moisture to create a chill in her frame. Only the heat from the cat kept her from being truly cold.

A small movement had her glancing down to look at Nathaniel again. In the next moment, he lifted his head and peered at her.

"My lady Sylvan. I thank you for saving my life."

Nodding slowly, Sylvan stared out. "How did we get here? I don't remember what happened."

"I believe it is safe to say you found your magic, though we can be certain it has changed over time. It's something I'll have to consider." Standing, he stepped from her lap and arched his back to stretch his muscles, which had tightened from sleep. "I think, first, we need to find you adequate clothing for our journey."

SQUATTING BEHIND THE SHED, SYLVAN and Nathaniel watched the homestead. After traveling most of the morning, they'd come upon the buildings in the woods. They'd been there for almost an hour, watching, and hadn't seen anyone.

"Should we go in? Maybe we can find clothes for myself and some supplies."

There was no answer from Nathaniel. He watched the house, and she waited for him to speak.

"Well?" she prodded. "What do you think we should do?"

With a low sigh he walked around her. "Wait here. I'll check it out." He moved like a wraith through the tall grasses toward the home. A slight breeze picked up, and far off a bird called, but here, everything was silent.

Nathaniel disappeared into the knot of grasses that covered that side of the farm property. Sylvan sat quietly, tapping her finger on her knee. Every minute or so, she'd peek around the edge of the shed, expecting to see the large multi-hued cat.

When Nathaniel didn't return after a time, Sylvan became impatient and stepped from the screen. The grasses weren't a good cover for her, but staying crouched, her night dress bunched in one hand, she moved carefully through their tangled growth.

She wasn't quite at the back of the house when a faded

curtain flapped through the partially open window. Ducking into the grasses, she watched the movement, eyes and ears alert for any danger. The area was quiet, the gradually slowing beat of her heart the only sound in her ears. The hot sun baked down, the cracked ground a testimony to the heat, and she knew she needed to move.

When the curtain continued its innocent flapping, Sylvan stepped to the back wall of the house, her senses attuned to any changes. With the window to her side, she looked left and right, not sure where to go.

The wind picked up for a moment, snapping the curtain, when the scent hit her. Something, or someone, was dead in the house.

Just as she decided to slip around the corner and look for Nathaniel, he slinked to her, his serpentine body against the wall. Squatting, she waited for him to reach her.

"The building is empty . . . at least of the living . . ."

"What happened?"

Looking her over, he said, "The world is a different one now than before you disappeared. After the massacre of your family, Mikel, his men, and others like him have run amok over the land. This maliciousness is allowing others to rise. All around us are gatherings of men and women living in their destructive natures. The light is fading, and the darkness is growing. Mikel is becoming ever stronger."

"He was always an evil child." Thinking about the man she'd been promised to, a shiver passed through her.

The cat moved from the wall to stand in front of her. Sitting, his tail curled, he stared into her eyes.

"We need to go into the house. There are things we need for our journey—clothes, packs, and maybe even some food—but you must prepare."

Sylvan felt another shiver snake up her spine at his tone.

"The inhabitants are dead. Unspeakable things were done. The men, soldiers who follow Mikel or others, are the beasts men become when no laws, ethics, or morals govern them."

Leaning into him, she said, "I'm not a child, Nathaniel. I've seen awful things before." She stood to move around to the front of the home.

With a small raise of his eyebrow, the cat allowed her to precede him. He stopped at the entrance, sat, and waited. He didn't have to wait long.

A crash sounded from inside, and Sylvan flew back out through the door. She stumbled to the side and, with a hand firm to the wall, bent and retched onto the dry, cracked ground. Sucking in a breath, she expelled it in a sob.

The cat watched. With a final gag, Sylvan straightened. Long, shaky breaths followed before she wiped the spittle from her mouth and the tears from her cheeks.

"By the gods . . ." She gasped for another breath then turned to Nathaniel. "I don't understand. Are you sure these people were killed by men?"

At his nod, she walked away. Turning back toward him, she neared but kept throwing furtive glances at the door.

"How can people do this to one another?"

"As I said, darkness now rules the land."

"Mikel?"

"Mikel is but an instrument. The darkness goes deeper than him, deeper than his soldiers."

"Well, it must be stopped."

"Yes." He nodded. "Yes, it must be stopped."

She continued to pace and collect herself. Finally, she stopped in front of him, her eyes clouded.

"Ready?" he asked.

"No. Not really."

Turning from her, he moved to the doorway and, without a backward glance, disappeared. With a deep, shaky breath, Sylvan followed.

The first thing to hit her, even before entering the building, was the smell. Bile rose in her throat at the reminder of her recent visit. The inhabitants hadn't been dead more than a day or two, but in the heat, the scent of decomposition was intense. The smell was so powerful, she tried to breathe through her mouth, but then she could taste it. Taking the lesser of two evils, she curled her arm around her face and breathed through the sleeve of her nightgown, shallowly.

Sylvan kept her eyes on the cat, sheer will the only thing that controlled her impulse to look around the room, already knowing what lay beyond her view.

"Here." Stopping at the back of the building, Nathaniel opened a drawer of an old, broken dresser. "Look through here for some clothing. We need to get outfitted and move on. We've been here too long as it is."

Sylvan moved forward and reached around the feline to

pull open another drawer. Nathaniel moved on to the cooking area of the home.

The first drawer was full of rough linens. When Sylvan moved them, she discovered a swatch of lace. She spread it upon her hand. It was beautiful. The woman of the house probably valued this little piece of delicate femininity in a life otherwise full of hard work and long hours. With a gentle touch, she folded it and placed it back in the drawer.

The next two drawers had shirts of various sizes. After pulling one out, Sylvan determined it would work and moved on to the next drawer, which contained a few pairs of pants and skirts. All were too large, but by cinching in the waist with a piece of rope from the wall, she was soon clad in serviceable clothing.

Nathaniel pushed a pair of boots to her, and Sylvan opened a chest set next to the drawers in search of stockings.

With a shriek, she stumbled back as a dark shape sprang out. The cat arched and hissed, launching his body to the side. Trying not to step on the cat, she put her foot on something soft and squishy. It slid out from under her foot and caused her to lose her balance and land hard on her tailbone.

Air exploded from her, and a door to a rudimentary closet slammed shut. Catching herself, she yanked her hands back when they landed in something sticky. Now smeared with a blackish, smelly goo, she shuddered and held them out from her, looking at Nathaniel.

"What," she panted, "was that?"

His back still in an arch, Nathaniel moved around her.

Standing erect, he grabbed one of the linens she'd recently moved and tossed it in her direction. She caught it and frantically wiped her hands.

With a gesture toward the other side of the room, he whispered, "Come with me."

He moved toward the closet in the corner. Sylvan rose to her feet, still rubbing her hands on the cloth.

"In there." He gestured with a paw. "Slowly."

Cracking the door, Sylvan peered inside. Staring back at her, eyes bright, was a boy of about six. A ragged, dirty boy. For a moment, she froze. What was she supposed to do now?

"It's all right," she whispered. Squatting to his level, she put a hand up, palm out. "It's okay. You're safe now."

The boy moaned and pushed himself into the corner. When she reached toward him, he wailed low and kicked out at her. Pulling back, she glanced at the cat, who sat and watched. When she caught his eye, he raised a brow.

"Leave him. We don't have time for this. He'll do just as well on his own."

"I will not leave a traumatized child to fend for himself."

Padding from her, he threw over his shoulder, "We leave in a few minutes."

She tossed him a look and sat in front of the closet. To limit the boy's view of the room beyond, she pulled the door partway closed. Speaking in a low voice, she told him about herself and her hope for him to accompany them. When he showed signs of relaxing, leaning back to the wall, his head swiveling on his shoulders, she whispered, "My name is Sylvan." His eyes rolled toward her, glistening in the half light. She hoped he was listening to what she said.

"What is your name?"

Almost lower than she could hear, he muttered, "Wyliam."

"Wyliam. Why don't you come with me and Nathaniel? There's nothing for you here."

He peered over her shoulder, scanning the room but saying nothing.

There was a slight bump on her arm and Nathaniel sat next to her, staring at the boy. She looked from the cat to the boy and back. With a small tip of her head toward the cat she said, "This is Nathaniel. He's a close friend of mine."

The boy watched the cat, curious, but not showing any signs of fear.

"Nathaniel, this is Wyliam. I've invited him to travel with us."

"Hmph," the cat said and turned to walk away. "We need to leave."

Sylvan gave the child a crooked smile and held out a hand to him. Tentatively, he reached for her palm. She helped him get to his feet and put an arm around him, drawing him into her body. With her other hand covering his face to spare him the horror of the room, she walked him from the building.

Once they'd reached the bright sunlight, she maneuvered him to a fallen tree across the front yard and sat him there.

"Stay here for a moment. I need to get a few things and then we'll be away from here."

When the boy stared at the house, she placed a hand on his

shoulder and gave him a slight shake. He blinked twice and looked up at her.

"All right? You'll stay here and wait for me? I'll be right back."

He gave her a small nod, then his gaze returned to the house. She hoped he would be there when she returned.

Approaching the entrance, she took a fortifying breath, squared her shoulders, and once again stepped inside. She blocked most of the devastation from her view and searched out the cat. He was stuffing a loaf of bread in a knapsack with his back to her.

Hustling across the room, she once again pulled open drawers searching for stockings. Finding a pair, though they were too big, she yanked them on and the boots over them. Nathaniel waited for her by the door. She didn't need any further incentive to vacate the building and, after grabbing two cloaks from a hook beside the door, she stepped into the welcoming sunlight.

The boy sat where she'd left him.

"Are you certain it's wise to bring him with us?" Nathaniel said.

"I told you, I can't leave him to fend for himself. He may add to our responsibilities and maybe even our hardships, but we'll have to deal with that. The world might be going the way of the darkness, but we don't have to follow." She moved away from the feline and toward the boy.

As she approached, the boy's eyes shifted to her. Surprised, she stopped for a moment. His eyes were the deepest gray she'd ever seen.

"Come on, Wyliam. Let's leave this place." When he stood, she put an arm around him and turned him on their path.

43

ON THE STREET, ORSON WATCHED the young girl from behind the screen of men. Her fear excited him. He wished she was for him but knew this one would be taken to his master.

She'd led them on a merry chase. Luckily, he knew something about people and what motivated them. Giving the barmaid a coin to proposition the man in front of her had worked perfectly. The girl had bolted and, once alone, became easy pickings.

He watched for a moment more, enjoying the tension of his men. Their sounds and smells. The promise of violence.

If only she weren't so important. He would enjoy turning them loose on her. In some situations, watching was as much fun as doing.

He withdrew his own desires and again faced what must happen. The girl must be delivered unharmed to his master. She wasn't one of many, easily used and disposed of. This one was special.

He hadn't been made privy to all she was to be, but his master continued to mumble about his mistress and the coming of the Three, whatever that meant.

Orson knew his goal tonight was to obey his orders, retrieve the girl, and be rewarded for his efforts.

"Halt!" he ordered in a loud voice. "Back. Step back," he shouted. When he shifted through the men, they stepped aside and allowed him access to the girl. The look of fear in her eyes almost got the better of him, but with a steely hand, he held himself back from the violence in his heart.

"Maya," he said and stepped to her. "At long last we meet."

44

SYLVAN, NATHANIEL, AND WYLIAM MADE good time the first day. The boy, after getting away from the home, seemed to shrug off the trauma he'd experienced. Sylvan kept a close eye on him, but he wasn't apt to wander.

That evening, after their meal, she coaxed the child into a small stream to bathe. Scrubbing him with sand, her breath caught at the color of his hair once free of the dirt that coated it.

Even wet, the light color was evident, and it shone like the sun when it dried. Sylvan didn't think she'd ever seen hair that color. It had her thinking of a tree full of Alderfruit. Golden and delicious. With his large gray eyes, he was an extremely unusual yet attractive boy.

By the end of the first day, the cat seemed to take this addition to their party in stride. Once, while they slept, she woke to find Nathaniel sitting near the boy. He stared at Wyliam, but with the soft breeze in the trees and the flickering of their campfire, she soon dropped back to sleep. The next morning, nothing was said, and the cat behaved as normal.

On the third day, Wyliam began earning his keep. To avoid detection, they'd wandered off the trail but kept it in sight. Sylvan gathered roots, berries, and other wild fruit to add to the foodstuffs they'd taken from the farmhouse. She and the boy walked together, Nathaniel having wandered farther on.

When Wyliam froze in his tracks, Sylvan froze, too. It was more instinctive as her eyes scanned the area to determine what he'd seen.

Bending slowly, he retrieved a medium stone from the ground and launched it into the brush before them. A great squawking erupted, and hens flew from their cover. Rushing the brush, Wyliam grabbed the bird he'd hit and wrung its neck. Turning to look at her, he held the body aloft, smiling for the first time since leaving the cabin.

Sylvan couldn't help but respond to the beauty of his smile and clapped her hands.

"Wonderful, Wyliam. It looks like we'll have fresh meat for our dinner."

Glowing in her praise, the boy's stride had a bounce to it for the remainder of the day.

Sylvan talked to Wyliam, but other than saying his name days ago, he hadn't uttered a word. She wondered if the shock of seeing his family slaughtered had made him mute, or if he never had talked. She continued to try to get him to interact and kept up a steady prattle of nonsense. Although he kept an ear tuned to her, he didn't add anything to the conversation.

As the days passed, he wandered a bit farther from her and always came back with fresh game for their dinner. She grew used to his presence, and since she was a woman used to being a mother, her heart grew for this small, damaged child.

THAT EVENING, SITTING AROUND THEIR fire, she discussed their destination with Nathaniel.

"So, Maya and Teck were heading to Berth?"

"The last I saw them, they were nearing it. She was searching for a priest." The cat spoke but didn't look at Sylvan. His eyes reflected the flames, and he seemed to view a different scene.

Sylvan sat beside the sleepy child, her fingers running through his hair where his head rested in her lap. Her actions made them both feel a long-lost peace.

"Do you know any more?" she asked. "The name of the priest? Where to find him? Why she was seeking him out?"

"No. Just that they were heading to Berth."

"It's a large city. Full of danger. Maya's never been anywhere like it." She stated these facts, not expecting an answer from the cat but needing to voice her concerns. "I'm glad she has Teck with her. He'll keep her safe."

Nathaniel wandered toward her from around the fire. He sat for a moment, watching her ministrations on the boy, and then after butting her leg with his head, he lay down beside the two of them and was soon fast asleep.

45

THE WALLS OF BERTH ROSE before the trio.

Once, Sylvan's parents brought her to Berth for the Spring Festival. It had been, and still was, the largest city she'd ever seen. At the time, her manor home and its adjoining land seemed large, but this city was something else entirely. Clearing the outer walls, the buildings began and went until reaching the seawall. They stretched for miles. Some were modest, some opulent, and many in between. The sounds — the babble of many voices, the bray of mules, and the clang of moving wagons, and the scents — dust, food frying, and animals of the city — made her heart squeeze with memories and longing for her parents. The knowledge that they were gone forever caused her breath to catch in her chest.

The last time she'd spoken to them, it had been casual good nights at the end of the day. Had she known her life would be altered so irrevocably, she would have held them and told them how much she loved them.

Sylvan ran her hand down the child's sunburst hair, finding

comfort in the silky feeling and warmth. He turned his face up to glance at her, a question in his eyes. Giving him a small smile, she shook her head. He returned his gaze to the wonders of the city.

He was an amazing child, she thought, having rebounded from the tragedy at his home to act as normal as anyone. Though, other than telling her his name, he'd yet to speak.

Looking beyond the boy, Sylvan watched Nathaniel pace beside them. For all appearances, he was a normal cat, though larger and with peculiar coloring. He created no interest in the citizens around them—everyone focused on moving into the city.

Once within the walls, shops spread out on either side of the main road, their wares spilling into the street. Sylvan kept a steady watch on the boy who, lately, was prone to wander when something caught his eye.

The farther into the city they moved, the more the crowds dissipated. Each fork from the main road allowed people to filter off. Soon, the street they traveled on had large stretches of path where they walked alone.

Sylvan turned toward a small side street and the two followed. She needed to speak with Nathaniel and didn't want a passerby to hear the cat talk.

Stopping at the corner, she squatted.

"Well, now we're here. How do you propose we find the priest?"

The cat gave a small shrug. "There must be a church around here somewhere."

Sylvan put her head in her hands, for the first time truly feeling the enormity of their task. "But one particular priest in this whole city? How are we to locate the proper one?"

"Perhaps he'll find us."

"And, and how are we to eat. Where are we to stay?"

"A fine time for you to consider these things." Reaching into the pack beside her, Nathaniel dragged out a small cinched bag. When he shook it, it jangled. With a flick of his wrist, the cat tossed it in her direction.

Sylvan jerked back and caught the bag.

"While you were gathering the boy, I was gathering supplies."

Sending him a dubious look, Sylvan loosened the knot and opened the bag. She upended the bag and dumped coins into her hand.

"Where did you find these?"

"I have a nose for finding what will benefit me." With a sniff, he turned from her.

"Nathaniel." Her voice calmed and she gave him a small grin. "You're the best. You know that, right?"

Glancing over his shoulder, he looked her up and down, and with another sniff, he said, "Of course I know that. I'm a cat, aren't I?"

He started down the back lane. With a small chuckle, Sylvan put the coins back in the bag, sealed it, and returned it to her knapsack. She took Wyliam's hand and followed the cat.

A few streets more, and in the distance, they heard people. A tavern came into view.

People moved in and out, and as they neared, the scent of food caught them in its snare. Wyliam pulled her toward the building, his big gray eyes pleading.

The sun had begun to fall as they'd wandered the streets, and now, with the scents of food, her stomach grumbled. She was as hungry as the boy.

"This place will do." She looked at Nathaniel, resisting Wyliam's pull. "Don't you think this place will do?"

She caught his nod, and as she turned and allowed Wyliam to pull her along, she heard Nathaniel add, "Before the boy pulls your arm off."

Sylvan kept a firm hand on the child as she moved through the crowd of people at the tavern's entrance, trusting the cat to keep up. Slipping sideways, she moved toward the front counter to see if they had a room available. After getting settled, they would come back down and get a bite to eat.

"Ayah?" The proprietor looked her up and down. He didn't need to say anything more. From his look she knew that once again she was being judged for being a woman traveling without a man.

Giving a sigh, resigned to the prejudices of society, Sylvan moved forward.

"I need a room. For me and ..." With a pause, she looked down at Wyliam. She smiled and turned back to the innkeeper, a hand on his head. "For me and my son."

"You got coin? Ain't got no time for female wiles."

Lips pursed and brows drawn, Sylvan stepped even closer. Her voice barely above a whisper, she said, "Yes, I have coin, and you're insulting to insinuate I might pay in any other way." Even though it wasn't the truth, Sylvan used a threat to get them a room. "When my husband meets us in two days' time, I'll be sure to have him discuss this with you."

The man stepped back, putting hands up to halt her words. Hands, Sylvan noticed, that had nails caked with dirt. If possible, she was even more disgusted by him.

"Now, ma'am. There ain't no call for that. How was I to know—woman and a boy traveling alone."

"It's wrong of you to assume." With a step back, she shifted the pack on her shoulder. "As I said, we require a room."

"Yes, ma'am. Of course. I have a very nice room just up the stairs."

BY THE TIME HE FINISHED and they had a key to their room, all three of them were ready for quiet.

"I wonder if they'd bring our meal to our room," Sylvan muttered as they trudged up the stairs.

"That innkeeper is a boob," she heard Nathaniel breathe behind her.

Turning the key in the lock, Sylvan allowed Wyliam and the cat to precede her. She pushed the door shut and locked it behind her, sighing and surveying the room. Clean and airy.

Taking Wyliam's hand, she led him to the bed.

"Sit, Wyliam. Let's take off your boots and you can relax for a bit."

With his boots off, the boy crawled onto the bed and Sylvan swore he fell asleep before he laid his head down. Her insides battled between the sweetness of the child and her hunger.

"I guess we'll take some downtime and get food later."

46

WHEN SHE CRACKED HER EYES open, Sylvan saw a figure standing before her. The light in the room was low, and it took her a second to identify the figure as Wyliam. Blinking rapidly, she sat up straight in the chair. The child stood, silent and watchful.

"Hi, honey." She gestured him forward as she scanned the room. Nathaniel lay curled on the bed, almost invisible on the patchwork quilt.

"Are you hungry?"

He nodded, and his large gray eyes pleaded with her.

"Okay. Let's see if Nathaniel wants to get up and go with us."

Taking his hand, she stood, stretching her back to alleviate the muscles that had tensed during sleep. As she neared the bed, Nathaniel's breathing remained deep and even.

She kneeled and helped Wyliam to put his boots on. "Let's leave Nathaniel," she whispered. "We'll bring him back something."

Once again shod, Sylvan and the boy headed out and locked the door. As they traversed the hall and neared the stairs, the noise level increased drastically. It had grown late while they slept, and the patrons at this hour where long into their cups.

The babble of voices became distinct conversations when they entered the main hall, and they moved into the crowd toward the kitchen. Scanning the area to find a place to sit, Sylvan watched waitresses move among the patrons. They slipped in and out of pockets of people like quicksilver fish.

Beer splashed on the hardwood floor as two men jostled, and Sylvan pulled Wyliam back from the burgeoning conflict. The entire crowd flowed from the area and then back as the men came to a cordial, drunken agreement.

Seeing a table near the back of the room, Sylvan led the boy through the people.

"You'll be needing a seat for you and the boy, ma'am?"

Sylvan glanced over and saw a small woman watching her, her eyebrows arched.

"Yes, please. We'll be needing to have a bite to eat."

With a nod, the girl led them through the seating and, upon reaching the same table Sylvan spotted, she put her arm out to indicate where they were to sit. She disappeared into the crowd after taking their order.

Sylvan and Wyliam watched people. Due to Wyliam's silence, their conversation lagged, but the food arrived quickly. It consisted of a hearty stew and a coarse, dark bread. The waitress poured them a weak ale then moved to another table after pocketing Sylvan's proffered coins.

After her initial hunger was satisfied, Sylvan nibbled on her bread and watched the boy. He consumed his stew with a single-mindedness she had to admire. Her lips turned up as she brushed a hand over his head and down his back. Her thoughts flew back to Maya at this age, and the smile that had lit her face faded.

Where is my girl?

Thoughts of Maya pulled at her heart and she dropped her gaze, blinking rapidly as tears gathered.

Her hand still on the boy's shoulder, her attention caught when he stopped eating and turned his face to her. Swiping a tear under her eye, she gave him a bright smile.

"Do you like your stew?"

Nodding vigorously, he turned back to finish.

"Eat your bread, too, Wyliam."

The boy grabbed the loaf and soaked it in the remnants of his stew. With another gentle smile, Sylvan watched him until her mind again wandered.

If Maya was within the walls of Berth, what steps would they have to take to locate her? Would she still be with Teck? She'd forgotten the size of this city. The enormity of their task had her emotions on a ride of highs and lows.

These thoughts and others flowed through her mind.

When another fight broke out across the room, she blinked. She sat taller to scan the room between the patrons to see what was happening, but the gathered bodies proved too dense. She turned to Wyliam only to realize she was alone at their table.

Her heart beat a hard thump in her chest, and she peered left and right looking for the boy. Bending over, she scanned the area under the table, but he wasn't there either.

"Wyliam!" she called.

She moved off the bench and, rising to her toes, she looked around. She didn't see the boy anywhere.

"Wyliam!" she raised her voice to be heard over the immediate crowd.

She didn't want to leave the table in case he came back looking for her, but she was beginning to feel the stirrings of fear.

Just as she was preparing to scream his name and push people aside, the boy slipped effortlessly through the throng. He smiled up at her, and although Sylvan's first impulse was to grab him, shake him, and insist he tell her where he'd been—forgetting in her panic that he didn't speak—what she did do was grab him in a fierce hug.

The boy stood still, his arms at his sides neither rejecting nor participating in the show of affection.

Releasing him, she squatted and asked, "Where were you?"

With a half turn, the boy pointed back the way he'd come.

"Well, don't wander away again. Let's get some food for Nathaniel and return to our room."

* * * * *

WITH HIS HAND CLASPED IN hers, the boy, Wyliam, walked down the hallway toward the room. Memories of his past life were already fading from his young mind.

When he glanced up at the woman, he felt the first emotion other than fear that he'd felt for days.

Fear had colored much of his memory and, after that, only numbness. Now, a warmth filled him. The woman, Sylvan, carried a covered plate with one hand and had his hand in the other. Every few moments, her thumb would rub his skin—he didn't think she even knew she was doing it.

Nearing their door, Sylvan stopped and turned toward him.

"Hold this for me, will you please, Wyliam?" She handed the plate of food to him. With her hands free, she dug in her pocket. The smell of warm stew came to him, and although he'd just eaten, his stomach growled. When Sylvan pulled a large key from her pocket, she smiled and held it up for him to see.

"Nathaniel will be excited to have something to eat," she informed him before turning the key in the lock and opening the door.

Light from the hallway spilled into the room, illuminating it down the middle to leave darkness in the outreaches. The cat lay on the bed, just as they'd left him. As they moved into the room, Sylvan locked the door behind them.

"Stand here a moment, dear. Let me get the light." The woman moved across the room. A flame flared, and she lit a lantern by the bed. Motion and a small noise drew his attention to the cat, now stretching on the bed.

With a mighty yawn, Nathaniel eyed them both. He squinted in the light, and when he caught sight of the plate still in Wyliam's hands, his nose twitched.

"Is that food I smell?" The cat moved across the bed toward the boy.

Wyliam met him at the edge of the bed, pulled off the covering, and set the plate down.

"Come here, Wyliam." Sylvan directed him to the other side of the bed. "It's late and we've had a long day. Let's get some sleep." She assisted him in getting ready for bed and then lay down with him. Before the cat had finished his meal, the two of them were sound asleep.

47

SYLVAN LOOKED DOWN THE STREET at the large church with its aged and scarred wood door. This must be the location of the priest. They'd been all over Berth in the last two days, with no luck. Other than the large temple in the center of the city, this church was the final place to search for the priest. Nathaniel had drifted away on private business. She'd waited most of the morning for him until she couldn't wait any longer.

Drifting toward the large door, she heard the melodic chanting of male voices. Their sound seemed to float above the noise of commerce on the street and it tugged at her—but not in a good way. If she had any other plan or another place to look, she'd walk away from this building and all it contained. Something about it—a color, a scent—had her animal impulse rearing up and pulling her back. It was only the maternal instinct in her, stronger than any other, that had her moving forward. She must find Maya.

Placing her hand on the boy's shoulder, she looked down at him. Should she leave him to wait for her? She couldn't put a finger on why, but she was certain danger resided inside the shrine. But she couldn't be sure Wyliam wouldn't be in as much, if not more, danger alone on the street.

With a sigh, she ran her hand through his mop of hair.

"Come on, Wyliam. Let's see if we can get in."

Sylvan and the child moved across the street where they hesitated before nearing the door.

"Psst."

Sylvan couldn't detect where the noise came from.

"Psst!"

Louder now, she realized it came from the side of the building. Taking the boy's hand, she moved slowly to the corner, into the shade of the alley, where she found Nathaniel. Sylvan rushed forward and dropped to her knees.

"Where have you been?" Her harsh whisper struck him. "We looked all over for you and then figured we'd better just head here."

"I've been surveilling the area. This is our last location to look, and I was hoping to overhear some information that may be of value." With a furtive glance around the corner, the cat turned back to her. "I don't know though. This church seems far different from the others we've visited. Feels different in some way."

Sylvan understood his hesitation. She'd felt the same foreboding.

"I'll go up and around and see if I can enter from the other side. You and the boy go in like worshipers, look around, and see what you can learn."

Sylvan was still unsure about taking Wyliam in with her, but with a small nod and a look over her shoulder, she agreed. "All right. Wyliam and I will go in and see what we can. We'll be out before midday. This entire place gives me the creeps." Taking the boy's hand, she wandered back around the corner and approached the front steps. At the top, in front of the door, waited an old woman in a full-length robe.

With a tightened grip on Wyliam's hand, Sylvan swallowed a lump in her throat and mounted the stairs.

48

ELDRED STARED AT THE GIRL—he couldn't help it. Her hair might be the flame-red his once was, but her face was all her mother. For a moment, he'd thought she was Sylvan. His heart had flipped in his chest and the air refused to move in his lungs.

Now, sitting with her and the man who came with her, he ate slowly. He didn't like the man, this Teck. His attentions were too familiar, too proprietary with his daughter. It didn't matter to Eldred that he'd just come to know she existed. Now that he knew, he felt it his job to protect her. A father's responsibility to protect a daughter's virtue. Body and soul, she was now his. He knew, in his head, that his dislike of the boy only drove her to him more, but in his heart, he couldn't stop himself.

A LOUD BANGING WOKE ELDRED from his sound sleep. The dying embers in his hearth sputtered and popped before the banging began again.

Who in the name of the gods is banging on my door?

"My lord."

He heard and recognized the voice, muted by the heavy door. Father Patrick. His heart skipped a beat—Maya. Only something happening with Maya would bring the priest to his door at this time of night.

Leaping from his bed, Eldred hurried to the door and wrenched it open.

"My lord." The priest leaned into Eldred, a whisper in his voice. "Your daughter has disappeared." With these words, he looked at Teck, drawing Eldred's eyes. Teck watched them with a scowl. The priest leaned out of the doorway and looked down the hall. A light illuminated in the distance.

Exiting the room, Eldred grabbed the priest's arm and hurried toward the light at the end. After a moment, he heard footsteps behind them. Glancing over his shoulder, he saw that Teck followed.

His footsteps faltered when he rounded a corner only to be confronted by the light. It pulsed and shone so brightly, he, Patrick, and Teck lifted their arms to shield their eyes. Eldred's memories stirred and had him recalling the fright of that day with Sylvan.

When she'd disappeared into the light, he'd thought he'd never see her again. Jumping to his feet, he'd started forward to where he last saw her only to have Lord Singh grab his shoulder and hold him back.

"Wait, Eldred. Everything will be well."

Looking at Sylvan's father, he hadn't believed him, and it must have shown on his face for her father didn't release his hold—if anything, it tightened. He remembered seeing the light reflecting off Lord Singh's eyes, their color distorting in the radiance. Pulling himself away from the hypnotic effect, he again looked at the growing ball of light on the dais.

He loved Sylvan, but then, staring into the light, he couldn't break the paralysis that had him in its grip. Would she be safe? Would she return to him the same girl who went up the stairs? All his fears filled his head and heart.

Now, looking down the hall he saw the same light—more than bright, blinding in its intensity. And the pulse of it, like a living thing—he felt the same inability to act, the same overriding fear.

"Maya," he muttered, eying the glowing doorway.

Teck moved past him into the room and Eldred grappled for him, but Teck eluded his grasp. He followed the younger man, the priest right behind them. Eldred squinted against the light and spotted Maya at the other end of the room.

"Maya!" the younger man yelled and started forward. Eldred stopped him.

"Wait." But the boy threw his hand off. Eldred's gaze shifted back to his daughter. Just as Teck took a step toward her, Maya shifted and lifted the object that was emitting the light. A moment later there was a mighty explosion, and all three men were knocked off their feet. Dirt and debris rained down, and Eldred's ears rang as he tried to sit up and locate his daughter in the dust-filled room. When he saw her, it was with a lack of surprise to see a man standing with her.

HOURS LATER, ELDRED STARED AT the stranger.

They—he, Maya, Teck, and Patrick—had been discussing the warrior, this Sentinel, but now he and the other two men were being unceremoniously kicked out of the room. Maya insisted she needed a moment with the warrior. Shaking his head, he ruminated over what an odd week this had been.

First to find he had a daughter. And then such a monumental happening while they were together. He looked over his shoulder to again study the stranger. He knew exactly what, if not who, he was. A pedagogue. He remembered from his childhood. He knew what this man would be to Maya just as the cat had been to Sylvan. He took in Teck's face, the high color and glaring eyes leaving nothing to the imagination of what he was feeling. For once, Eldred felt empathetic toward the younger man. He understood exactly how he felt. Hadn't he lost a part of Sylvan when Nathaniel had come into her life? Now, even after explaining to Maya and Teck what had happened, and who this warrior was, Teck fought it.

Eldred shook his head and, for a moment, looked at his boots. *Poor bastard.*

And now they were banished into the hallway while his daughter questioned the warrior. What was going on between the two of them? Why had the priest been allowed to stay while he was asked to leave?

Teck gave a loud sigh and was just turning to pace down the hallway when the door opened. Maya looked at them both but slid by before Eldred could reach her.

"Maya!" Teck yelled after her as she ran toward the exterior door. He followed her, and Eldred followed them. When they raced outside, he waited just inside to make sure she was okay. While he stood within the hidden doorway, Patrick walked up and stood with him.

"What happened in there?" he asked the priest. Maya had been upset when she came out, not willing to talk or even look at either of the men. The priest simply shook his head at Maya's father. Eldred glared at the priest, planning on questioning him further, but he heard footsteps from the entrance and turned to see Teck—and only Teck—enter. Eldred stretched his neck to look beyond him, waiting for his daughter to appear. When it became obvious Teck was alone, Eldred turned on Teck.

"Where is she?" He concentrated hard on keeping his tone civil, knowing from past exchanges with the boy that fighting wouldn't get him anywhere.

Teck continued walking but threw over his shoulder, "She needed some time alone."

Eldred caught up to him at the entry to the main hall. Forgetting his kinder, gentler thoughts from the moment before, he grabbed Teck's arm and wrenched him around. Teck wrenched his limb out of Bathsar's grip as his face became a hard mask.

"Do you really think alone and in the forest is the safest place for her to be? You can't be that dense." The two men stood toe to toe, neither willing to give an inch.

Patrick stepped up beside the men and, with gentle hands and words, got them to step back from each other.

"My lord. We'll go out and find her. Perhaps we could give

her a moment to clear her head. The information she's been given is a lot for her to take in, I'm sure."

After a moment, Eldred nodded in agreement. Looking around them, a new shock hardened his features. "Where is he? Where is the warrior?"

The three men whipped around, only to realize Sentinel had disappeared. Patrick stepped forward. "I'm sure he's gone to find Maya. His only desire is to protect her."

Turning toward the door, Teck started to leave again.

"Wait, Teck." Patrick touched his arm. "Allow them some time."

With a pause, Teck looked at the priest. "Time? I don't want him anywhere near her."

Nodding, Patrick looked down at the ground. "I know that. You're going to have to get used to his presence." With his arm out, he gestured toward the main dining hall. "Come, let's sit and have something to eat. They'll be back soon."

Moving toward the main hall as if taking for granted that the other two men would follow him, Patrick entered the room without looking back. He took a seat, and within a moment, he was joined by Teck and Eldred.

ELDRED FINISHED HIS MEAL AND stood from the table. His daughter still hadn't returned. He was glad Sentinel was with her, but despite that, he was beginning to worry.

"I'll see you men later. When Maya returns, inform the rest of us." The table of men nodded their agreement, and he headed toward the exit of the room. The sound of raised voices caught his attention. He slowed and looked around the doorjamb.

Men clothed in red and black capes swarmed through the hidden opening and over the bodies of two of the brothers.

With a firm grip on the hilt of his sword, Eldred pulled it from the scabbard on his hip. He yelled a warning to the men behind him and advanced on the intruders.

49

SYLVAN LOOKED BACK OVER HER shoulder, firming her grip on Wyliam's hand. The woman at the entrance stood still, only her eyes moving as she watched them walk into the building. She didn't stop them as Sylvan thought she would. The woman scrutinized them with an unblinking stare. It seemed wrong, somehow, for her to let them enter without challenge or welcome. Her mind filled with an image of lambs going to the slaughter. Perhaps this wasn't such a good idea.

As they moved through the corridor, they passed doors to rooms spaced randomly on each side. Some had closed doors and some, no doors at all. She craned her neck to peer in the doorless ones as they passed. The rooms appeared empty. Sylvan heard sounds behind some doors — faint — and something about the quality of it made her body flush and her breath come hard. It took her a few moments of this to realize it was fear that filled her blood. Her brows furrowed. What was happening behind those doors?

The hall was empty but so silent even a small thing like their footsteps echoed. She shifted to place her hand on the child's shoulder, to pull him near. This was not only to keep him close but to afford herself some measure of comfort.

Somewhere along the hallway, a door or window must have been opened since a fresh breath of air whistled past them. Sylvan's skirts flapped once, and her hair blew across her face to block her view. As soon as it came, it was gone, and they went back to breathing the musty, aged air of before. Only then did she realize the air, not only musty, had a peculiar scent to it that she couldn't place. Almost sweet, it filled her lungs.

"Hello," she called, but only the silence answered her.

After a time, the hall they traveled had straight, stone walls, unbroken by doors and doorways. They continued down the hall, their eyes starving for a change to the never-ending walls of stone.

Sylvan saw the shape of a door in the wall to one side. As they neared it, she slowed, angling closer. She didn't plan on being in this building very long. She needed to find someone to ask about a certain priest, and then they were out of here.

Glancing up and down the hall, she decided to try the door. They hadn't seen anyone since entering this church. Maybe the doorway would lead them to someone. She grasped the knob only to find it wouldn't turn.

She lifted her hand, fingers curled in a fist to knock, but paused when a small sound beyond the portal stopped her short. She laid her ear to the wood—every muscle tensed. The small sound came again, and something in the quality of the sound sent a chill up her spine, making her pull the boy back with her.

Eyes large, she scanned the portal and then looked back the way they'd come. Nothing but more of the same.

She needed to find this priest. He was her only lead to Maya. The only person who might know where her girl was.

"Don't be a baby, Sylvan," she whispered, her voice sounding scared even to her ears.

Glancing at Wyliam, she ran her palm over his head and offered a small smile of reassurance. She again took his hand and walked them farther into the building.

She was being silly, she thought. The sound wasn't even identifiable. It was nothing. Imagination was going to get the better of her.

Once again, she glanced at Wyliam to gauge his impressions, but she only saw a portion of his face as he looked forward, his hand tight in hers.

The priest, she thought. *Find someone to ask, find the priest, and find Maya.*

The corridor never changed. Certain the building hadn't been this large, Sylvan found herself second-guessing the direction in which they traveled.

She stopped in the center of the hall and made a complete circle, her gaze searching every nuance of the hall. Had they gotten turned around? Were they even now heading back the way they'd come? There were no identifying marks to indicate which way they should go, or which way they'd come.

"Hello," she called.

A warmth crept over her, and sweat broke out on her upper

lip. How could they be lost in a straight hallway? It made no sense. They should turn back, she thought. But afraid to make the wrong choice, she continued.

Just when Sylvan was coming to a halt, deciding she needed to quit moving, that they were getting more and more lost, that they needed to find where they were, a breath of fresh air blew over them again.

She glanced down at Wyliam then looked back down the hall in the direction of the breeze.

"Hello?" she yelled, craning her neck to see farther.

Her voice echoed. Breaths coming faster now, Sylvan moved to the side of the corridor. She placed her back to one of the stone walls and slid Wyliam partially behind her. Something was wrong. Something was coming. She could feel it.

She kept thinking her nerves were going to calm and that the edge of panic would leave. She'd call herself a baby again and get on with finding the priest, but the tension in the air didn't let up. The oppressive feeling was heavy. Even telling herself it was all in her imagination didn't work. Breathing was hard, her heart was pounding, and she felt hot and flushed.

When she realized her hand was numb, she looked down at the boy—she'd been so far into her own head, she'd almost forgotten he was with her. He had a two-handed grip on her. He was smashed into her body, his face hidden in the folds of her skirt.

Maybe it's not all in my mind. Wyliam is feeling something.

A spike of adrenaline hit her, and with a jerk, she grabbed

Wyliam and fled back the way they'd come.

A crash sounded behind them, and Sylvan spun when a door appeared on the wall right in front of them. Not thinking, only reacting, she grabbed the knob and it turned. She knocked her hip into it and pulled the boy through. Throwing her weight against the door, she slammed it shut behind them. Her cheek to the wood, she held her breath and listened. A single bump came from the opposite side, causing the door to vibrate. Wyliam moaned low in response, and she pulled him into her.

She waited for more, but nothing happened. All was silent.

When nothing occurred after another moment, she turned away from the door, breathed a sigh, and put her back to the wood and calmed herself.

Sylvan looked out from the wall to see where they were, and her breath caught. This room, this passageway, was just another corridor—exactly like the first. Across and down from them, closed doors cut randomly into the walls.

Wyliam slid down to sit, his back against the door.

"Wyliam?" She squatted next to him and put a hand on his shoulder. "Honey. Are you all right?"

He stared up at her, his soft gray eyes wide, but as usual, he was silent.

"I know. We'll get out of here soon." She patted him on the shoulder.

After giving him this assurance that she wasn't certain she could keep, she stood and moved to the center of the corridor. Scanning back and forth, nothing caught her attention. The hall was empty.

When she made her way back to Wyliam, he stared up at her, watching her every move.

"Okay, kid, let's get back to where we at least know where we were." She reached for the knob of the door they'd come through only to pause. When she stepped closer, she laid an ear against the wood, but there were no sounds on the other side.

She grasped the knob but it wouldn't turn. Now it was locked.

Grasping it in a firmer grip, she tried again, but it still wouldn't turn. She gave it a shake, but the door was solid and didn't move.

Sylvan stepped back, hands on her hips. For a moment she just stood there, and then with a ragged breath, her head dropped into her hands. A small sob escaped, and her shoulders shook. What had she gotten them into? They were trapped in this labyrinth.

A small sound came from the boy as he leaped to his feet to fling himself at the woman. Gripping her skirt, he buried his face in it, pressing himself against her leg.

"Mama," he whispered.

Sylvan dropped her hands, one of them finding his tousled hair. She dropped to her knees and pulled him into a fierce embrace. Rocking him, she drew comfort from his small body.

"Hush now, Wyliam, hush. We're going to be just fine," she soothed. "I know it's scary, but you and I, we're tough, and we're going to get out of here." She lifted her head, and once again scanning the hall, she gave him a final pat.

"Okay, kiddo." She wiped his cheeks with the edge of her

sleeve. "You and I are going to find an exit from this place. I just know Nathaniel is worried sick by now."

He stared at her, hope warring with fear in his eyes.

"And hey . . ." she said as though just remembering. "Did you say something?"

He nodded at her, his expression softening.

"Well, I liked it. You keep that up, and when we see that old cat, you can tell him all about our adventure." With that, she stood and took his hand in hers. Turning them back the other way, she again walked down a hallway.

SYLVAN SAW WHAT APPEARED TO be flat darkness in the corridor in front of them. As if the passageway were blocked. She slowed. When they got closer, the hallway ended abruptly. No windows or doors marred this perfect barrier—it was a solid stone wall.

Sylvan released the boy's hand and stepped up to it. She placed her palms flat against its cool surface and pushed. Nothing. It stood as solid as it appeared.

"Are you kidding me?"

Turning from it, she faced the boy and the long hallway they'd just traveled.

She'd been trying, for the boy's sake and for her own, to keep her head up—her chin forward. But now she just didn't know what to do. For the first time, her mind was blank. No ideas, no fear, no anything. She stood, her back to the end of the hallway, and stared into nothing.

When she felt a small hand push against hers, she met

Wyliam's gaze. She didn't know how long she had stood still and mute.

A sense of nervousness and fear filled her at his trusting expression. His life was in her hands. What was she to do? Where were they to go?

"Oh, Wyliam. Do you have any ideas, kiddo?" When his expression didn't change, she heaved a heavy sigh and tore her gaze from him.

"Okay," she muttered. "We can't go forward, though I don't know if we can truly go back either." She ruffled the boy's hair with her free hand, and bending to him, moved his bangs aside and gave his forehead a soft kiss.

Standing, she squared her shoulders and moved them back down the corridor, stopping to try each door they came to. They were all locked.

Sylvan could not comprehend how much time had passed if any at all, but finally she and Wyliam came to a door different from the others. Sylvan's brows furrowed, and she searched her brain for any remnant of a memory where this portal existed. She and the boy had walked by this very area—their footprints marring the dust on the floor gave testimony to this fact—but she could not remember ever seeing this door before.

Instead of a plain wooden access, this one sported gilding and what looked to be small jewels. There was no way she could have missed this door. Had she been walking in a stupor? What else might she have passed without seeing?

She reached with a shaking hand to grasp the lion's head knob, which protruded from the door. It turned easily, and with little effort, she pushed the barrier open.

She didn't move through the gap but bent forward to peer into the new area. There, on the other side, was a well-lit room. The sounds of birds came from an open window on the far side, and in addition to a large bed covered with a thick quilt and a high-backed chair in front of a fireplace, there was a table laden with food and drink. The smell of the former finally had her moving. How long had it been since she and the boy had eaten or drank anything?

She pushed the door completely open and, with Wyliam's hand in hers, stepped into the beautifully appointed room. Mesmerized by the tantalizing smells, she didn't notice when the door closed behind them.

50

WYLIAM WOKE SLOWLY. WHEN HE rolled to the side and opened his eyes, it was to see the woman lying beside him on the large bed. Allowing his eyes to drift, he scanned the room. He couldn't remember how they'd gotten here, or how long they'd been here.

He sat up slowly, his body stiff and achy.

When he slid from the silken comforter, his bare feet hit the cool floor. He noticed a stain on his skin and under his toenails. He picked up a foot and brought it closer to his face to peer at the discoloration then pulled his foot closer and took a sniff. Nothing. With a small shrug, Wyliam dropped his foot back to the floor.

The scent of food brought his head around. Slowly, he plodded toward the table. Trays of food adorned it, steaming and inviting. He glanced back at the woman on the bed, but when she continued to sleep, the boy climbed on one of the padded chairs and began to eat.

The more he consumed, the fewer thoughts filled his brain.

Where once he might have questioned where they were, or if a certain cat was missing them, as his stomach filled, he thought only of the food. The aroma drew him in, making him want to inhale it as much as eat it. He didn't think he would ever have his fill and continued to gorge while the woman slept.

51

THE WORLD OUTSIDE THE WINDOW sparkled in the late afternoon rain. Sylvan watched the drops fall, her mind a fog. She had memories, snippets of moments in the last few days, but then her thoughts became flooded again. The memories sank without a whimper submerged in the black mist of her mind.

The table was once again laden with fare, and the food beckoned. She reached for a roll. Its lush scent filled her nose as if still warm from the oven. With a hiss, she pulled back before she was able to grasp the bread, a pain flaring in her arm. Rolling up her sleeve, she gingerly touched a bruise that marred her pale flesh. Sylvan stared at it, her eyebrows drawing together. Where had she gotten such a bruise? Its color was almost purple with a fading around the edges. *When* had she gotten such a bruise? Fear knocked at her mind, but the scent of the food wound itself around her, pulling her in. Seducing her. Beckoning her.

Again, she reached for the bread. Just before touching it, a small sound had her whipping around. Seeing a boy on the bed, she stared for a moment. Who was this child?

When she stepped away from the table, the enticing scents almost drew her back, but she pushed past them to approach the bed. Gazing down at the boy, she ran her fingers through his hair and down his cheek.

Fear again filled her, her breath catching. Who was this child? Why did the touch of him bring her such confusion?

When she sat beside him on the bed, he shifted and stretched. Rolling onto his back, his eyes slowly blinked open. The most beautiful gray they were, and she felt as though she should remember them.

He sat up, looking toward the table filled with delicious treats. When she reached out again to touch him, to run her hand down his arm, he shrank back.

His large eyes peered at her, and his body tensed as if waiting to see what she would do. When she didn't move again, the boy rolled from her across the surface of the bed to drop to the floor on the other side. Keeping a watchful eye on her, he made his way slowly toward the table and what it offered. Her head and shoulders turned as they watched each other.

When he got to the table, he climbed onto a chair on the far side, putting the furniture between them. Still monitoring her, he ate. The more he consumed, the less concerned with her he appeared to become. Soon, his every attention was on what else he might eat.

Sylvan stood and headed back to the window seat. Though the rain continued to fall outside, she couldn't hear it. The silence drew her in. Shouldn't she be able to hear the rain?

Glancing from the vista outside their window, she again regarded the boy. Utter silence reigned inside, too. Neither she nor the boy had spoken.

No sound came to her as she made her way to the table, to the boy. As she neared, his head came up, and he watched her out of the corner of his eye. She stopped. What might have happened to make him wary of her in this manner?

Her heart pounded in her chest until she could feel it in her throat. She had no memory of any interaction with this child. Nothing came to her since she opened her eyes to the rain outside the window. The nothingness had her stomach churning.

When she reached for the back of one of the wooden dining chairs, the boy's gaze sharpened on her. She seated herself, careful to make all her actions slow and nonaggressive, but still he looked ready to flee.

"Wha—" With a grumble, she cleared her throat, surprised not only by her inability to speak but also the pain that accompanied her effort. How long had it been since she'd spoken? With a wince at the burn that followed her attempt, she pushed the words out.

"What is your name?" Though the words came out somewhat garbled and raspy, she thought the boy could understand her.

He didn't answer her, just stared for a moment and then went back to eating.

"What is this place?"

This time, he barely glanced at her.

She pushed back from the table, the chair making no sound on the wood floor, and stood. Moving toward the door, she passed a small ornate table with a fancy tea service upon it. A wisp of steam rising from the pot smelled heavenly of citrus and warm herbs.

Sylvan blinked and looked about. Her view had changed in an instant. Instead of standing beside the small table, she was now seated in the plush chair before it, a cup of tea halfway to her lips.

She gave a startled cry and threw the cup to the floor, shattering the fine china. She jumped to her feet, just sidestepping the puddle of tea and the shards of porcelain. With a hurried step, she headed toward the door. As she moved around the chair with its side table, her bare foot came down on a large unseen piece of crockery, cutting into her skin and wedging itself deep. Thick blood flowed from her onto the already wet floor, and with the pain and the sight of blood came a memory.

DARK. SHE WAS IN THE dark. A damp place saturated with the smells of mold and long-dead things. In the distance are the moans and screams of people.

When she tried to move, she heard the rattle of the chains that anchored her ankles and wrists to the wall. She was bound so tightly she could barely separate her body from the cold bricks that made this cell. Their frigid touch chilled her body and caused her to shudder.

A clang of an opening door echoed from the distance. Instantly, the fervor of the voices increased to deafening levels. Someone shouted above the voices and something was banged, as if against bars of a cage. The volume lowered, but the moans don't stop completely.

Within moments, the sounds of footfalls approached her cell. Her breath increased and a cold sweat broke out across her body.

They're back.

SYLVAN REMEMBERED, BUT SHE DIDN'T want to. She wanted to forget, to have the oblivion she knew before this memory came to her. Leaning into the chair, she lifted her foot, only then realizing, maybe for the first time truly seeing, the filth she was covered in. Her feet were caked black, and now the blood added another layer. She pulled the shard from her skin, throwing it across the room where it clattered in a corner.

What is going on here?

Her heartbeat pounded a rhythm in her throat, and she felt dizzy, lightheaded. She had a plan to run and bang on the door. Pushing to stand, she glanced back at the boy where he'd fallen asleep at the table, his hand wrapped around a crust of bread. Only now, the bread in his dirty grip was moldy and, as she watched in disgust, a small worm made its way from the loaf to fall to the table. All around the boy were broken pots leaking their crusty innards onto the filthy surface. Eyes wide, she scanned the room, but now it was not light and airy, a clean rain falling outside. There was no window, no beautiful draperies or plush bed. She and the boy were in a dank cell, dirty and airless, a bare pallet against the wall.

The air was strangely sweet.

Pulling her gaze from where she once sat watching the rain, she again looked toward the boy, head resting on a beautiful table.

The tableau stopped her. And in that instant, a tendril of scent wrapped around her senses.

What had she been thinking?

What a lovely room. What lovely food.

Walking toward the table—her limp and the blood she left on the floor no longer noticed, she sat at the meal, filled her plate, and began to eat.

THEY'RE BACK.

When Sylvan opened her eyes this time, she was back in the torture chamber. No longer did the beautiful room and heavenly scents bewitch her. She saw clearly. She had been here before, many times. What they wanted from her, she didn't know, and they wouldn't tell her. They just kept at it—kept at the torments. The punishments. She tried to withstand it, tried to be brave and give them nothing, but always, they broke her. Always she was reduced to a whimpering mass. Someone she didn't recognize. And even beyond that—beyond the pain and fear, was the loss of time. And then she was back in this dungeon, back among the tormented souls. In the recess of her mind, almost touched, was a memory—a beautiful memory. When she reached for it, it slipped from her grasp, leaving only the smell of warm bread.

Her head wrenched about as the door of her cell gave an almost human groan. Three men stepped through. A scream pushed against the back of her throat, though they hadn't touched her yet. Still, she couldn't stop the panic.

The men watched, leaning into each other to discuss her in a language she didn't recognize. What did they want? Why didn't they leave her alone?

When one placed a large pair of pincers in the fire at the brazier, her mind blanked; she could only stare at the fire.

The tip glowed red-hot when pulled from the pyre. Her breath slowed until she barely breathed at all and her vision became sharper. Her inner self, the woman she'd known all her life, drew inward until she was small in her mind. She took up so little room that the vacuum of her consciousness filled with something else. Something that had been there all along, with her, though mostly dormant her entire life. It had come before, but she'd always been able to control it. Now though—now the woman Sylvan was lost to oblivion—lost to fear so intense, she stepped out of herself. In her place, filling all the emptiness left behind, was the madness.

Nav-lys.

* * * * *

WHEN THE WOMAN STRAIGHTENED, NO longer leaning against the wall, the man stopped and said something over his shoulder to his cohorts. He took another step closer to her, close enough to touch her with the fiery brand. Instead of the fear or the scream he expected, the reaction he wanted, she lifted her head. Her features were almost obscured by the mass of dirty brown hair that covered her face, but in the light of the fire, her eyes glinted with mesmerizing black swirls.

The man's arms dropped, the pincers falling to the floor. His friends called out to him, but he was already moving to the woman. Before they reached him, he had his hands on her cuffs, first her ankles and then her wrists, releasing her. As he took his hands from her, a black inky substance flowed from her skin to his. On him it expanded, soon taking up his arms.

The woman never took her eyes from the man. He saw the foreign substance on his arms and hands, only now lifting them to peer at it. His partners saw it, too.

When he howled and his arms disintegrated and his howls became screams, they turned to flee what had always been their playpen.

Now it was hers.

The heavy cell door that they'd left open slammed shut before they could escape. The first man slowly disappeared into the black ooze, consumed by her hate, her madness. His legs buckled under the insidious force of the black mass. His body was a black, slithering ball with a howling head. As the goo moved against gravity, moving up his neck to the features of his face, his screams became garbled, then cut off as he was enveloped in the product of her hate.

The two remaining men threw themselves against the door. When it wouldn't budge, they slowly turned to face her. If she weren't mad already, seeing herself thus would make her so.

She was clothed in mere rags, the remnants of a once-warm and serviceable dress. Her physical self was filthy, bedraggled. Ratted hair covered her head and face to hang down her back. Her hands were caked with a myriad of substances, her nails dirty and cracked, colored black. She moved in a stoop, bent and creeping like a wild thing, pulling a wounded foot along the filthy floor.

Her only thought, the only idea in her head, was to make these men suffer.

As she neared them, they threw themselves back as far from her as possible. One turned to a corner of the cell. The other man ran into what was left of their friend, a lump barely recognizable as something that was once alive. He fell, sliding his leg through the remnants and getting some of the black substance on him. Afraid and repulsed, he tried to wipe it off, but it reached his hand. And it spread.

* * * * *

IN HER CASTLE, CASSANDRA STOOD over the water in her viewing bowl. Throwing back her head, she shrieked until her voice warbled out, leaving a silence so intense, it had weight.

Into the silence, a low sound began. Slowly it built until it was recognizable as a laugh. One full of madness and malice.

Spinning from her bowl, she continued to cackle, clapping her hands in glee.

"At last!" she screamed. "At long last."

52

ELDRED, PATRICK, AND A GROUP of men fled from the catacombs where the rebels had their encampment. Their routing by Mikel's forces had come as a complete surprise, and many had lost their lives. These few were lucky to get away with theirs.

When Eldred left behind many of his men, he felt the loss like an appendage, but he didn't know what else to do. Mikel's forces were many, and they overwhelmed the small community. Most of those with Eldred were wounded, some mortally. He didn't know where they should head. He needed reinforcements but didn't want to lead the enemy back to the main body of the Brothers of Fate.

As they ran, making their way through the deeply forested woods, he thought back to leaving. Making the decision to leave without Maya.

Patrick and some of the other men had to pull him from the makeshift barracks, his desire so strong to locate his daughter. In her quarters, he'd found her belongings. Among them her backpack, bow, and quiver of arrows. He'd seen the value she placed on the bow and arrows and, not wanting her to lose them, he had grabbed them up and taken them with him as he continued to search for her in the tunnels.

When a small force of his men found him, it was only Patrick's words, his calm logic, that prevailed and allowed him to leave the caverns.

He lay on the ground, held there by a group of the brothers, lest he return to the caves. "My lord, you saw her leave. How would she have returned with the soldiers so soon within the barracks?" Patrick had dropped to his knees beside him. "My lord," he intoned. "Think, she is not within these walls. And we should not be either." When he stood and held out a hand, Eldred had grasped it and allowed himself to be pulled to his feet. "You are best able to aid her by not becoming a prisoner of Mikel's."

He had seen the wisdom in Patrick's words. Fear continued to pull at him, but hope filled his chest that she was not within the boundaries of the brotherhood's community. Sentinel was with her the last he knew, and with him, she would be safe.

He would put out the word. They would continue to look for her until she was located. He wouldn't give up. He vowed to himself, he would not lose her again.

THE CLAMOR OF FOOTSTEPS AND armor woke Eldred. Men were running all around him, grabbing belongings. They were in a panic, fleeing into the trees around their campsite.

Eldred leaped to his feet, his head swinging left and right.

What was going on?

When a man ran by him, he grabbed the brother by the arm. "What is happening?"

"My lord," the brother gasped, pointing. "Riders. Riders approach from the hillside."

Eldred released the man and, turning, saw the mounted men coming at a gallop. They'd be upon them in no time. Thrusting his feet into his boots, he grabbed his sword. The riders' red and black uniforms glinted in the early morning light. Eldred calculated which direction would likely take him to safety.

He turned from the direction most of the men had chosen, and, heading back toward the advancing army, he entered the dense tree line and threw himself under a bramble of fallen logs. It was wet in the undergrowth, and slimy mud covered him, but instead of pulling back in revulsion at the feeling and stench of the bog, he burrowed in even further.

The ground shook with the pounding of hoofbeats as the riders got closer. Eldred froze in his hiding spot, afraid to even breathe. He hoped the logs and bramble would direct the horses around and not on top of him. Wind and leaves flew around him as horses shifted and some even jumped the wood he hid beneath.

When they'd passed, he waited for a few more moments, ears attuned to any sound of soldiers bringing up the rear. In the distance, he could hear men shout and the cries of the dying.

Fear shook him—fear and overwhelming cowardice. If only he could jump up and run to the rescue of his men. If only his one sword would make a difference.

Shame filled him. He held himself down, silent tears coursing hot tracks down his muddy cheeks to drop into the bog. For a moment, the guilt almost got the better of him, his desire to maintain his own life falling under the blanket of it. He pushed to his hands and knees, the mud making a loud sucking sound as it released him. He would go and do what he could even if it was only to die alongside his men.

Exhaustion overwhelmed him, and he again sank to his knees. His head turned tightly on his shoulders. Fear again held him in its grip, but the need to see, to witness what was happening, also controlled him.

All around the far hills he saw men run. Some of them were being cut down, run under the horses of their pursuers, but many of them appeared to be getting away. Hope sprang again within his chest. He would get away, too. He would get his men back together, and they would go on. Sacrifice was not the right answer. Survival was.

THREE WEEKS LATER, ELDRED AND his remaining men were exhausted from their continuous flight from the soldiers in Mikel's service. Just when they'd thought themselves safe, having at last lost their pursuers, the soldiers would turn up to hound them. Luck still followed the survivors, those men able to find each other and continue.

More of his loyal men had died. Those with debilitating wounds slipped from them, there being no time to stop and bind them and rest. Now it was just the fittest of them who continued to run. And even they were flagging, lack of proper food, water, and rest taking its toll. How much longer they could continue at this rate, Eldred didn't know.

He'd made the decision, just this morn, to head to the main body of the Brothers of Fate. Knowing he risked all with this choice, he had to get his remaining men to safety. Until they lost the soldiers, he would be unable to turn his attention to locating Maya. She could be anywhere by now. Each hour, each day made his finding her less and less likely. Desperation filled him. But with the desperation, hope rode. Hope that she would be found healthy and well.

He always kept her bow and quiver with him. It had become something of a talisman. He felt, if he kept it, he would one day be able to return it to her.

"Maya will be fine, my lord."

Eldred stopped in his tracks, swinging his eyes to the priest, Patrick.

"Am I that obvious?"

The priest shook his head. "No, but I know you, and I know thoughts of your daughter have plagued your mind these past few weeks."

The two men continued their trek, now side by side. Conversation halted as they climbed a rough hillside.

"I've decided to head to the city. From there we can contact the Primary of the Brotherhood of Fate."

Patrick nodded as if in understanding, if not agreement, and continued to walk beside Eldred.

"You don't agree?" Eldred stopped and faced the priest.

"It's not that, my lord. I understand the need to do something. This continued running is getting us nowhere." He turned and moved with the rest of the band of men. "I don't know what the answer is. Where do you think we might locate your daughter?"

With a deep sigh, Eldred followed him, his answer a mumbled reply. "I don't know. I only know I must try."

"Yes, my lord. So, we return to Berth?"

"Yes." Eldred hurried to tell the rest of his men the plan.

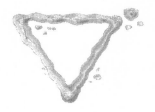

53

NAV-LYS STROLLED AROUND THE SMALL cell. Her bare feet sloshed through puddles that used to be her tormentors.

She inhaled. Drawing in the stale, musty, free air. With her head thrown back, she stretched. For so long she had strived to be free of the Other. Over many years, she had pushed and prodded for supremacy. Now she had it. In a moment of weakness, the Other had relinquished her hold, and Nav-lys had stepped in. Now Nav-lys had control of the body, and the Other was contained.

Nav-lys stopped her pacing and turned her attention inward. She could feel the Other. She only slept. But Nav-lys would do anything to keep the light.

She had always known of the Other. Always known they were two. This knowledge gave her proof of her superiority.

Of course, being in charge wouldn't stop her from poking at her new prisoner. Making her scared and unhappy was so rewarding. A sly smile crossed her face.

Turning her attention to the door of her cell, she decided it was time to venture forth.

SURVEYING HER NEW WORLD, NAV-LYS watched the bedraggled, filthy people wandering the area. None of them engaged her or even acknowledged her as their savior.

When she'd left the cell, she'd reaped destruction on the guards who had tried to stop her. After that, she'd freed the others from their cells. It wasn't altruism that motivated her — more the creation of a buffer from the world until she could prepare herself.

She'd watched as Sylvan lived her life, got in a punch now and then—like the death of the bird when she was a girl. Even though she knew quite a bit, it behooved her to study and plan. Like any good invader, she required allies. Strong allies.

54

ORSON STEPPED OUT OF THE temple. The girl was gone, and he didn't know where to begin looking for her. He thought he had been so smart. He'd located their hideout. And they had routed the resistance who'd been tucked in that little hidey-hole. But no girl and no Eldred. He had thought to bring his master both of them. Already, he'd been planning his triumphant return to the city. Instead, he'd missed her.

In his mind, he saw her again, fleeing the tunnels. Running alone into the forest. He should have gone after her himself. That very instant. But he'd been overconfident. He'd had a whole unit of men with him. How could she possibly get away?

He'd snuck back into the city. Him. Sneaking. But he knew his life depended on locating her and bringing her to his master.

The sun, blocked behind a bank of clouds, made the day dark and dreary. Staring for a moment at the sky, he thought it perfectly mirrored his mood.

"Saddle my horse," he mumbled to the servant who stood

next to him.

He waited, looking out into the city. The thought of getting back in a saddle had him tensing up and wishing for his whip. How had it all come to this?

When a man slinked up the stairs toward him, he almost lashed out and knocked him back, but at the last moment, the sun illuminated a tattoo on his neck. Orson recognized the mark of the Ring, a sadistic order that flourished within the city walls. Mikel knew of them and allowed them to continue their habits. He and Orson had even attended a ceremony or two, their practices something that interested them. Now he watched the man approached him.

"Master Orson," the man began, inching his way closer.

Orson gave a curt nod, keeping his eyes locked on the man. He didn't trust him for one moment. As powerful as he was in this city, he wouldn't put it past the Ring to attempt to put him in one of their cages. It was rumored, some of them even had magic. That they could make one yearn for torture.

"What do you want?" he asked, his manner and tone gruff.

"Whisperings tell that you are looking for a woman . . ." Saying this low and next to Orson's ear, the man looked around as if to ensure their conversation wasn't heard.

Orson turned more fully toward the man and looked him up and down. The man stepped back cautiously but then closed the distance again.

"I might know the location of such a woman."

Orson studied his nails. "There are many women in a city this size."

"Yes, yes of course. They are easy pickings for one such as you." Sidling up even closer, the man almost placed his lips to Orson's ear as he hissed, "But this one, she has magic."

Orson looked fully at the man. A spike of excitement shot through his veins at the words, but he cautioned himself to be wary. Magic, this man said, but did he even know what magic was? Perhaps his idea of magic was not true magic.

"What do you mean?" he uttered. "Magic, you say. What magic can she do?"

The man reached out as if to grasp Orson's sleeve, but at the last moment he remembered himself and pulled back. "She can change herself . . . and she can kill." At the final word, the man's voice shook, and he swallowed. "I have seen it. I have seen many men die."

"Why would you come to me with this?"

The man looked away, now seeming unwilling to face him.

"Come now," Orson blared at him. "You're taking up my time. Give me an answer or get away from me before I have you dragged into the temple."

The man cringed but didn't leave. He crept up and whispered, "We cannot control her. Many men have we lost. My leader, he bid me come and get you." The man stepped back. When Orson didn't say anything, the man took the step back to him. "He said, she is yours. No charge, no charge. Our gift, to you."

Orson squinted. Now his interest was piqued. Perhaps he could look at this woman. Maybe she would keep his master happy, and his own head on his shoulders, until the other ones could be found.

When the servant ran around the side of the building, the small man's horse in tow, Orson instructed him to take the horse back and bring him his carriage.

In no time at all Orson and the man were in his carriage and heading to the edge of the city. Orson followed the man's directions, but he knew where they were heading. He had fond memories of his time spent in this location. Anything the heart desired or the mind could imagine could be obtained within these walls. Many a homeless person had entered, never seen again.

The anticipation of his visit rode hard on him. When they arrived at the central home of the Ring, Orson calmed himself. He would like to run, to hurry the other man, but he knew what was expected of him. As they moved through the door of the large building, the guard at the entrance watched closely. Orson swelled with excitement. He couldn't stop his lips from curving.

55

ELDRED AND THE MEN OF the brotherhood walked boldly through the gates of the city.

He would meet with the elders of Berth. They must formulate a plan for the future of the brotherhood. But beyond that, his more immediate need was to locate Maya.

When they pushed open the door at the Boar's Head Inn, he scanned the room. It was dim, hazy with the cook fire smoke and tobacco, and full of men. When they stepped inside, some of the men turned to look at them, and Eldred raised his chin in greeting when he recognized a few.

Two men left their places at the bar to come to him.

"Lord Bathsar, it is good to see you after so long."

Eldred shook the proffered hand and clasped the other man on the shoulder.

"And you, Paulson. It is good to be back among trusted friends. My men could use some food and rest."

Leading them to the back of the tavern, the second man said, "And you, my lord. It is plain you have lost much weight on your journeys." The man gestured to the barkeep, and soon a serving girl had full trenchers of stew and bread set before the men. Tankards of ale came next, and with the warmth of the fire and good conversation, Eldred relaxed and enjoyed the comforts of the city. It was good to be out of the wilderness, among friends, and for the first time in a long time, he didn't feel hunted.

"My lord," Paulson said, looking down the table. "I would be happy to set up a meeting for you with the elders of the city."

"Thank you." Eldred gave a slight bow of his head. "I have much to discuss with them." He shifted his seat to more fully face Paulson and leaned forward. "A particularly pressing need I have is to locate my daughter—"

"Your daughter?" the man interrupted. "I was not aware you had a daughter."

"Nor was I," Eldred said. "She came to my notice recently, and during the battle with Mikel's men, we became separated. It is imperative I locate her."

"Is she within the city?"

"I don't know." At his words, the other man gave a sigh and his fingers tapped on his leg. His eyes on the other's actions, Lord Bathsar leaped to interject his thoughts. To convince the man to help him. "I understand it may be a great task to find her, but I have no choice. Find her I must." At the other's nod, Eldred continued. "She may come to the city. I know not. I require that the word be sent out far and wide. Your men must be on the lookout for her."

"Yes, my lord. I understand your concern, and we will do

all we can to aid you in this search."

"Thank you, Paulson. You are a good man." The edge off his worry, Eldred leaned back in his chair. "She should be traveling with a dark-skinned man, and possibly a large man with black hair."

"And her name? What should we call her if, and when, we find her?"

"Maya. Her name is Maya. Also, she has bright red hair. If seen, she shouldn't be hard to identify." The more information Eldred gave the other man, the surer he became of her being located.

"My lord?" Patrick entered the conversation.

Shifting his body to more fully face the priest, Eldred said, "Yes?"

"With all your daughter has been through, do you think she will come willingly to men she doesn't know?" Patrick's brows drew together as he voiced his concerns. "She may flee and then we would never find her."

"You are correct. She's been through many trials and will not assume anyone she doesn't know are her friends." Eldred leaned back again into the chair, and his vision was caught by the flames in the fireplace. "Perhaps I should give your men something to tell her . . . something that will let her know they are acting on my behalf."

Nodding, Paulson leaned forward. "Yes. That would be a good idea. It would eliminate having to force her to accompany them."

Eldred thought for a moment more, his lips pursed as he

considered and disposed of each idea. Finally, he nodded and, looking first from one man to the other, he said, "Tell her, 'We search for Sylvan.'"

"Who is this Sylvan?" Paulson asked.

The chair squeaked as Eldred pushed back and stood. "Sylvan is my wife."

56

A WOMAN TOOK HER HAND and they became one. Power like she'd never known flowed through her veins. Nav-lys knew she was in a dream. Knew the promises from the woman, Cassandra, could be truth. She could be free of the Other. Free in a way she'd never imagined.

She was given an image of the man. This man was her route to freedom. This man was her avenue to Cassandra.

THE CLANG OF AN OUTER door closing reverberated down the halls to dissipate within the cells. Now, all the cells in this hall were empty. The open doorways led into filth housed only by vermin and the rodents that crawled among the waste.

Nav-lys woke when the door closed. The displacing of air as the men walked down the corridor had her interest piqued and the corners of her mouth tightening.

Now, who would dare to venture in?

When the footfalls stopped at the portal of her room, Nav-lys peered between the crusted strands of her hair. Her eyes shone, no longer with black pools, but still they waited.

A face gazed back at her from the barred window, and she had a sense of recognition. Perhaps of like seeing like. The face was pasty white and hairless and seemed to float above the edge of the door. She stared, and it stared back, neither looking away. The longer she stared, the more the sense of knowing slipped from her misty mind. This was not the face from her dream.

When the face disappeared from the other side of her door, Nav-lys studied the floor. Patterns of dried blood held her attention until the mumble of voices from beyond her cell drew her back into the now. Their changes in tone and volume spoke to her of dark dealings on a dark night, but she couldn't make out the words.

* * * * *

"ALL I SEE IS A dirty female huddled in the middle of a room."

"Master Orson." The man who brought him here leaned in to whisper, "The woman is crafty—and deadly." He gestured to one of the jailers. "Bring one to give to her."

At his words, the man scuttled off down the hall. His guide turned back to him. "Not all of the prisoners were released by the woman. Many we still have. Killers, mean. She will not be happy to have one such as this in her area. When you see what the woman can do, you will want her for your own." Daring to peek within the cell, the man stood on tiptoes and glanced within. When he caught his breath and dropped below the line of the window, he glanced around furtively.

The small man didn't say anything to this claim. He paced in the hallway.

Deep breaths.

Orson counseled himself to stay calm, but it was difficult. When he'd peered into the cell, and the woman had met his eye, the air had fairly crackled with electricity. He didn't know what or who she was, but he was already certain he wanted her. Patience, he told himself. Patience was always a winning proposition. No matter what in life he was dealing with, holding his patience always made things come out on his side. Let others flail about and rush into decisions; he would know the whys and whens of everything.

Cries and grunts came from down the hall before he saw the jailer heading in their direction. With him was a man—half-starved and filthy—and he still fought the guard. As they neared the door, Orson stepped back to allow the jailer access.

His guide slid a large key from his coat jacket. With the key in the lock and a grip on the handle of the door, he looked over his shoulder at the two struggling men. The jailer gave a nod, the guide turned the key and pulled open the door, and the jailer shoved the prisoner into the room with the woman. He'd barely cleared the doorway when it was pushed closed and locked.

Orson stood in his position to the side of all the commotion, humor in his expression at the extreme measures the men were going to in their fear of what lay beyond the portal.

The jailer hurried back down the hallway, glancing over his shoulder in a furtive motion every so often. With him gone, the small man's guide turned to Orson and indicated the closed door. "Take a look. Tell me if that don't make your blood run cold."

Orson moved past the man. What a coward, he thought. How did someone with so little gumption ever gain a position with this type of organization?

Moving to the door, Orson placed his hands upon it and, rising to his toes, peered in.

* * * * *

WHEN THE DOOR BEGAN TO open, Nav-lys was already on her feet. She was moving and almost at the entry when a man was thrust in and the door snapped closed. For a moment, she stared at the door, but then the man's movements drew her attention.

"What you lookin' at, bitch?" He hissed at her, all bravado.

Still as a statue, she stared at him. This wasn't the man she waited for. She didn't know who or what he was, but she didn't like him in her space.

When he turned from her to wander the room, she always kept him in view.

From the far side of the room, the man turned and looked her up and down. Giving a little sniff, he moved toward her. He sucked his teeth, put one hand on his hip, and flicked the other through a long strand of her hair. "Looks like this is my house now. And everything in it is mine, too."

Nav-lys glanced at the door, again seeing faces looking back at her. This was not unusual; often had they observed her interaction with others.

She turned, her head cocked, to face this new threat. Even the stench of the man had her eyes turning black. When he reached for her again, she stepped into him and the mist erupted from her.

57

E YES ROUND WITH ASTONISHMENT, TONGUE mute, Orson stared. What had he just witnessed? Where had the dark mist come from? The woman didn't utter a spell, didn't call a power to her—it was just there.

A small giggle escaped his lips before he could silence it.

How exciting.

The woman again looked toward the door. She tilted her head to meet his eyes. After a moment, she broke the contact and resumed her spot in the center of the room. With her body squatted and her head bent, she seemed defenseless.

After a moment, Orson dropped to the flat of his feet but continued to face the door as his mind worked furiously. It was obvious to him that the guards of the Ring were in over their heads with this one. They were looking to get rid of the woman who had become a problem.

He turned from the door to face his guide.

"Where did this woman come from?" he asked.

"She came to us. Through the south entrance."

Orson knew the underlying message in this statement. The south entrance was like a trap for insects. There was one way in, but without assistance, no way out. They set it up—the church-like appearance—as a lure. Inevitably, it caught fish.

Orson nodded. "Was she alone?"

"No." The guide stepped forward, seemingly eager to share this additional information. "She traveled with a child."

At the word *child*, Orson's ears perked. Visions of the red-haired girl who got away filled his thoughts.

"Child?" he asked and was pleased he kept a tremble of excitement from his voice. "What child?"

"A young boy. White-haired and fair."

Orson's chest sank, but he knew it had been a long shot.

"I'm not interested in the boy," he muttered. "Sell him to the brothels if you wish."

Quick to jump on his first statement, the man asked, "But you are interested in the woman?"

The small man kicked himself for giving so much away and hurried to repair his slip. It wouldn't benefit him for the Ring to think him eager to acquire the woman. Even as a gift, it would be best if they thought he had done them a favor, not the other way around.

"Possibly," he uttered, turning from the guide to wander down the hall, periodically peering into other cells.

The man trailed after him to look in each cell after Orson moved on.

With a slow turn to head back the way he'd come, Orson asked, "How many have you given to the woman?"

"With this man, she has killed twelve. Three were her initial instructors."

Orson nodded. He knew the Ring referred to their torturers as instructors as if they were teaching their victims and not ending their lives. It was a title steeped in arrogance. They considered people to be theirs for the taking. This attitude was one that Orson shared, but as it related to him, not others.

"And what of the others in the room with her? Why hasn't she attacked them?"

"They are no threat. She seems to know the difference."

Orson took one final look into the cell and then stepped back. So it appeared as if the woman would only harm those who were a threat to her. This was good to know. He could be a friend. Respect her, but use her, as he would any weapon. Ultimately, give her as a gift to his master. Perhaps, he would become so entranced with owning this magic wielder, he would forget about the other girl and the fact that Orson was the one who lost her.

Deep in thought, Orson headed up the hallway.

"Um," he heard behind him and turned in surprise for he had forgotten the other man was there. "What do you think, Master Orson? Would you still like the woman?"

Orson nodded and continued down the hallway, the other man hurrying to catch him.

"Yes. Speak with whomever you must. I'll be back for her." Orson could think of little else.

58

THE WIND WHISTLED DOWN THE back alley to ruffle the white-blond hair. When the wind picked up, more of the body was revealed—reeking garbage blew down the corridor and a gray jacket flapped with its force.

It was the sound of the jacket cracking that drew the cat's attention. He'd been by this place for days, multiple times a day, and nothing. He'd attempted to get inside the church, but each time, the guard at the entrance had chased him away.

Now, he paced by the mouth of the alley for what seemed like the hundredth time. Only this time there was a change. The flapping of the clothing. Such a small thing, but it drew him in.

He turned into the alley. The closer he got, the slower he walked, afraid of what he might find at the end. When he saw the outline of the body and the color of the hair, his mouth went dry. In his mind, he told himself he'd never liked the child in the first place, never thought they should have taken him along, that his fear was for his girl. But standing over the body, the size that of a small child, his heart fell.

When a moan sounded, low and painful, he thought he imagined it. Just wishful thinking, he told himself. But then, it came again—the ache of a moan.

He rushed forward, pushing the remaining garbage off and turning the child. It was the boy, Wyliam. He had a gash on his forehead that seeped thick blood. It colored the hair around it dark, almost black.

"Wyliam," he whispered. Nathaniel started a bit at the sound of his own voice. The desperation. Swallowing deeply, steeling himself, he tried again. "Wyliam." And this time he didn't hear the warble that had hit to the heart of his fear.

One of the boy's hands rose, heading for the gash on his brow, but then dropped as if he didn't have even that amount of energy.

Nathaniel cradled the lad's head, touching his skin, sure to keep his claws retracted. When the eyes opened, a soft gray with all the familiar edges of intelligence, Nathaniel finally released his breath.

"Nathaniel?"

The cat just stared at the boy. In all the weeks of traveling together, he'd only once heard the child speak. That first day, in the abattoir of a cabin, surrounded by what was left of his family, the boy had said his own name. Now he said the cat's.

"Yes, Wyliam. It is me, Nathaniel." His voice broke at the end. Overcome with the emotion of the last few weeks, day after day of not knowing where either of them had disappeared to, now it released, and Nathaniel felt a tear roll down his cheek. The bead ran down a whisker, where it hovered before dropping onto the boy.

Once again, the child lifted a hand, this time to touch the cat. He petted him, starting at the back of his head, down his neck, and ending with his foreleg.

Nathaniel pulled himself together, knowing he had to get the boy out of this garbage-strewn alley and somewhere warm. When he sat the child up, Wyliam wobbled for a moment before righting himself. With the cat's assistance, he got to his feet and straightened to his full six-year-old height.

Needing to help the boy but still full of desperation, Nathaniel asked, "Sylvan. Do you know where Sylvan is?"

When the boy just shook his head, his whole being looking ready to drop, the cat said, "Come along, boy. Let's get you somewhere where you will be warm and dry."

Nathaniel kept his paw on the child and led him to the alley entrance. He paused there, knowing a cat walking upright was sure to cause a commotion. He looked left and right, unsure of where to go.

When Sylvan and the boy hadn't returned, they had forfeited the room they'd paid for. Though they didn't have many belongings, that too had been lost. But now, he had no room to take them to.

"Follow me," he told the boy and dropped to all fours to move out into the street. A few days ago, he'd seen a warehouse full of bales of wool. It was near the water and had seemed deserted. If they could get in there, they would be able to stay warm and dry. He'd get Wyliam settled and then head out to find something for them to eat and drink.

As he moved down the street, he kept to a slow, steady pace so he didn't lose the boy. Each time he glanced back, Wyliam had his eyes locked on the cat, trailing him obediently.

It wasn't too much longer before they came within sight of the warehouse. No one was around, but Nathaniel didn't want to take any chances of getting caught breaking in. If they had to flee, he was sure to lose the boy.

When he stopped, observing the area, the boy stood, head bowed, mute.

"Wait here for me, Wyliam. I will return shortly." He waited for the boy to give a short nod of agreement before moving away.

When he skirted the outside of the building, he almost ran into a man unloading a barge. Large bales of wool took up most of the room on the ramp and some remained in the boat, but the sun was dipping quickly toward the horizon, and Nathaniel hoped the day's work would be ending.

Using patience he didn't have, the cat waited while the man transported two additional bales. Then closing and locking the door to the warehouse, the man returned to his barge and set off down the river.

When he was gone, Nathaniel made his way to the door. He studied the lock. It wasn't very impressive, and he was sure he would be able to pick it. He glanced around and, after another moment, found a small spike of metal—just what he needed. He had the lock picked in no time but left it hanging so the door, if not inspected too closely, appeared to be secure.

Wyliam was where he'd left him, standing as if in a trance.

"Wyliam," the cat said before touching his arm. He didn't want to startle the boy, who seemed to be worse for wear. "Come with me, lad. I have a shelter for us—for the night, at least."

His eyes glazed, the child followed the cat without comment.

When they reached the corner of the building, Nathaniel peeked around the edge before leading the boy to the door. He herded the child in and shut the door. With a small inner shrug, the cat figured he'd done what he could to make the door seem locked.

He snuck into the building, aware of every sound. The boy trailed him with scuffing feet.

When he paused to listen, Wyliam stepped on his paw, causing the cat to leap in the air and bellow an ear-splitting yowl. Nathaniel landed on all fours, his back in a hump, and his tail bristled and straight in the air. His breath heavy, he surveyed the area. He could have just given them up if anyone was about.

Only silence came to him.

When he looked at the boy, Wyliam stared at him, but now the corners of his mouth were slightly upturned.

"What's so funny?" Nathaniel hissed, but the boy remained mute.

"Come on, let's find a place to sleep."

Deciding it would be safer to be off street level, Nathaniel led the boy to a set of stairs deep within the building and headed up, Wyliam close on his heels. When they got to the second story, they exited the stairs, and Nathaniel made a nest for the boy among the bales.

"Stay here and rest. I'll be back with food and water."

The boy nodded and lay on some spilled wool. He scrunched down into its softness and was soon fast asleep. For a moment, the cat watched the child, his heart in his throat and a question on his mind.

What has happened to my girl?

With the boy injured, he would need to find a safe place to leave him before he returned to his search for Sylvan. His mind full of what he would need to do next, he headed into the city.

59

PATRICK WATCHED THE MEN IN the small room at the inn. The issues they discussed had little to do with the bigger picture. They squabbled over property when the world was at stake.

For years now, it had seemed like he had questioned whether he remembered the man from his youth correctly. *If* he heard him correctly. Was it all just a figment of his feverish child's imagination? He had spent the better part of his life following something he couldn't guarantee was the truth.

Then Caleb had come back to him, just when he needed him. When he needed the assurance of the truth. And shortly after, he'd helped rescue Maya. Now, Maya was missing again. Such a large piece of the puzzle, and he didn't know how to locate her. And the other two? If Maya was one of the Three, when would he find the other two? How would he locate them? Would Caleb come back to aid him? It was as though he were walking in circles in a dark room.

With a small mental shake, Patrick gave his attention to the discussion surrounding him. The rebellion was making plans for ending Mikel's reign of terror. The main meeting hall of the tavern was full of men. There were the elders of Berth— powerful men, rich in both money and property, the men of the brotherhood, and himself. How was he to help reach their goal?

The problem with these men all in one room, these men who were used to leading, was that they didn't know how to follow.

When an argument broke out shortly after that, Patrick knew very little planning would come from this meeting. Rising, he moved toward the rear of the room. Perhaps there was something he could do. He was one of the very few who had been within the walls of the temple. Maybe, that could come in handy.

60

ORSON PEERED INTO THE ROOM, once again rising to his toes. The woman was in her usual spot, head down. The only thing visible was the part of her hair and her ragged gown.

He needed to get inside. He needed her to know him as a friend. But just how did he ensure she would realize this before she killed him? If he couldn't create a bridge to a relationship with her, he'd never move her from this cell.

Entering the room was a chance he was going to have to take. He couldn't observe her forever. And who said she couldn't send her magic outside of her room; perhaps they were all in jeopardy even now.

With an inner nod, he dropped to the flat of his feet and moved back from the door. The guard stood to the side, eyeing him silently.

"Unlock the door," he said, but the guard didn't move.

Was the man deaf?

"I said, unlock the door."

This time the guard moved forward, but not toward the door. He stopped directly in front of the small man.

"Now, sir," he stumbled. "You're not wantin' to be doin' that. That one . . . she's evil, sir."

Nodding, Orson said, "You just let me deal with that. You, unlock the door. *Now.*"

The man turned toward the cell, and with one final look back at Orson, he slipped the key into the lock. He didn't turn it though. Leaving it in the hole, he glanced over his shoulder where Orson waited and then bolted down the hallway.

"Wait!" Orson yelled. "What the . . ."

When the guard turned the corner and kept going, Orson stepped to the door.

"Just have to do it myself," he muttered.

As he thought he should have brought her an offering, his hand stopped on the key.

Yes, food or a clean gown.

He stepped back from the door but recognized the thought for what it was. A delaying tactic. A weakness. If he left now, he wasn't certain he would ever return. He'd continue to come up with excuses not to enter this cell. And really, what was the worst that could happen? His death? A painful death? He would soon die at the hands of Mikel Bathsar anyway, and he was certain it would not be pain-free. The girl had disappeared, and without her, he couldn't possibly please his master.

Unless this magic wielder could fulfill his need. This woman was his chance. A chance he had to take.

With a deep breath, he placed his hand on the key and

turned it within the lock. The mechanism's release was loud in the small hall, and for a moment he froze. He pulled the door and stepped within.

61

NAV-LYS WATCHED AS THE DOOR to her domain opened to allow entrance to a man. This was the face she'd seen looking at her.

He stepped in, pulled the door closed behind him, and faced her.

She inhaled deeply and caught a whiff of fear, underlying and buried deep. Her eyelids closed partially, heavy with pleasure. The scent coming off him was good. Fear was good.

For now, the others in the room were dormant. They'd dropped along the sides of the cell, perhaps sleeping. She didn't know and didn't care.

Standing, she paced toward him. Even at her diminutive height, they stood eye-to-eye. What could he possibly want from her?

She stalked nearer, ever vigilant. He kept his eyes on her, not submissively, but not aggressively, either. When she circled him, he turned to keep her within his sight.

A small smile turned the corners of her lips when he

squared his shoulders and raised his chin. Unless he was much more than he seemed, this little man was no challenge to her.

When he held out a hand, palm up, she stepped back, lest he try to touch her, but he didn't reach for her. She stared at his outstretched hand, wonder and curiosity filling her as to what he might want.

"My name is Orson." She raised her eyes to his. When she reached to place her hand in his, a spike of fear shot from him. She saw nothing, only knowing the fear by scent.

"Nav-lys," she said, her voice raspy.

"Nav-lys," he repeated, and although testing himself, he tightened his grip for a moment.

Curiosity filled her. The touch felt unusual. Unexpected. Her interest piqued, she released his hand and moved into the room. The man followed her.

What would this strange little man do?

She looked up again as the man moved toward her. Within her, the mist rose in defense, but it didn't act. The mist, its power, felt good, welcome. Pure.

The man made no offensive movements, just sat next to her.

"Would you like anything?" he asked in a low tone. "Some food, perhaps?"

She didn't answer him. She felt no need to make conversation, but her mist pulled back, and she relaxed.

NAV-LYS WOKE FROM A DREAM. Once again, it had been filled with a voice and the image of a man.

When she scanned the room, her gaze came to rest on the

form of the small man. He slept. His face was not the one in her dream.

She recalled the voice. Cassandra. She was full of power and fury. She made promises to Nav-lys. Promises of what she could obtain—who she could be—if only she did what Cassandra wanted. Nav-lys was promised a man. Another man.

A noise drew her attention to the man in her area. He lay close to her. Too close.

She moved away from him, but this movement woke him, and he opened his eyes. After a moment, the man stood, stretching his back. As he made his way to the door, she watched his every move.

When he knocked on it and she heard movement beyond, the mist rose again within her. It was a good feeling—a familiar feeling—and it relaxed her. She had nothing to fear from this man or the others.

When the lock sounded and the man pushed the door open, she caught a glimpse of the guard. He gave a quick glance in and then dropped from sight.

The man gestured toward the open portal. "Come. We're leaving this place."

Nav-lys glanced from the small man and then to the open door. She didn't know what was beyond.

When she shifted her gaze again, the man reached an open hand to her and, with a flick of his fingers, gestured for her to take it.

Nav-lys took his hand. Sliding her fingers along his palm, she felt every ridge on his soft skin. His hand trembled and she knew, he knew, she could kill him. When she caught his eye, she realized it wasn't trust that motivated him but desire. But not a desire of the flesh. His desire was her power.

When she laid her palm flat in his, he gripped her hand. He helped her to her feet.

She released his hand, and he turned and indicated the door.

Outside, all remained quiet, but as she neared the opening, she sensed the guard cowering between the door and the wall. She could hear him, his breathing spiking as she neared, and the scent of him. His fear was sweet, overflowing the sour smell of his body.

She ignored him and stepped into the hall, her head up and shoulders back. The small man followed her out and when she paused, he stepped around her.

"Come, my lady." And again, he indicated the direction.

When he turned to walk away, sure to check over his shoulder, she trailed him.

The hall was long and dark. Small lamps mounted at intervals on the wall threw sparse illumination, but each pool of light died before the next began.

She moved through these expanses of darkness, her crusty hem scraping the floor.

When they came to another door, she studied it. Two doors met in the middle for a large opening. When the small man turned a knob and pushed, it opened easily. He stepped out and she followed him, suddenly eager to be rid of this place. It was night, and she welcomed it. The darkness called to her. The scent of it, the feeling of the coolness on her skin. She wanted to revel in it, roll around in it until it covered her.

A carriage waited on the street with two horses strapped to it. In the upper front seat, a man held the reins. One of the horses shied at their arrival and stomped a hoof.

The small man opened the door to the carriage and again held an open palm to her.

"Nav-lys," he said as though tasting her name on his tongue.

She took his hand and climbed aboard. When he joined her, the carriage leaned to one side, a loud squeak breaking the silence, and then righted.

With a rap on the roof, the carriage pulled away into the night.

62

PATRICK'S AWARENESS CAME TO HIM in intervals.

First came the moans and the clanking chains. The soft squeaking of rodents as they moved along the walls. If he lay here long enough, he was certain they would dine on him.

The scent of the cell—blood, sweat, feces, and the sour stench of decomposition—came to him. He tried to keep his breathing shallow, to better filter the fetor air, but as his fear built, so did the speed of his inhalation.

Lifting his head from his spread-eagle position on the floor, he scanned the room in the defused light leaking in from outside the cell. His pulse beat out a rhythm in the split on his lip, and the blood rushing forward made it feel fat as an apple. When he licked his lips, feeling the swollen and torn flesh, the taste of blood—coppery and crisp—made his brain sharpen.

His wrists, ankles, and waist were immobile. Glancing at his frame, he saw the straps that ran across the bare skin of his body and bolted to the floor. His skin was covered in whip marks, cuts, and burns. Each more painful than he would ever have thought. Things crawled onto him from the floor.

He pulled on his arms and legs. Shifted his body. There was no slack in the straps, and moving only made the leather cut into his flesh. Warmth flowed from the new cut and made him lie still. How much blood could he have left?

When would they be back?

He had to keep his wits about him. To only give them enough that they thought he was broke, that they believed he was their creature. But he must not reveal the true secrets. Not all the information he'd been entrusted with.

They'd taken him suddenly. How arrogant he'd been, sure he could go back to the temple, that no one would question him. He didn't even hear them. Only the flash of pain in his skull. When he woke, he was here. Stripped and strapped down. Awaiting a form of punishment was diabolical in its ingenuity.

In the darkness, in the fear, his past flew through his mind. No one could know of the information he had. The things he had been told of the future. He didn't know whether they knew of his true calling or they just thought him another soldier of the resistance. He could only hope it was the latter.

As Caleb's man, he knew what had been and all the possibilities of what could yet be. He had been entrusted with the task of ensuring the coming of the Three. The coming was the only way the growing evil in this land could be thwarted. The only thing powerful enough. The only way they could all be saved.

He dropped his head back to the floor. He should have

given more thought before he attempted to reenter Mikel's temple. That had been his mistake. He thought they'd think he was just another of the monks. He didn't realize he'd been seen fleeing in the company of Eldred and his men. As bad luck would have it, a group of soldiers had just come in from the wilderness and one of them recognized him.

He'd already spent time with the head torturer. He knew they weren't done with him yet.

Caleb. Please make me strong for what is to come.

On the heels of that thought, the door opened, bringing in the pure, unmuffled moans of the other prisoners.

He wrenched his head around, trying to see what was coming, but they had him bound too tightly.

Footfalls approached, and a large shadow blocked out the meager light of the torches.

"So, this is our little bird . . ."

That voice—he knew that voice but never thought he'd be this close to the owner of it.

When the speaker stepped to the side and moved parallel with his view, he looked up into the grinning face of Mikel Bathsar.

63

SYLVAN TRIED TO MOVE HER body, but some force held her in place. The space she found herself in was too small to allow motion. Even her arms and legs were forced against her frame.

She lay in a fetal position, in an area too dark to see her own appendages. Her breaths came in small puffs, but no scents came to her. She was neither cold nor hot—just a tepid in-between.

"Hello."

Before she'd finished saying the word, it echoed back at her. Did that mean the space was tiny? But if small, would it echo at all?

"Hello?" she tried again, only to hear her voice bounce.

Where could she be? What had happened?

The last thing she remembered was the torture cell in the prison. Just the thought of it had her breaking out in a cold sweat. The men coming through the door. Then nothing. Was this another of their tortures? Losing time had become commonplace for her.

She pushed again, straining her legs to unfold, her arms to widen. Even lifting her head was impossible. She strained harder, emitting a small grunt—and her little finger moved.

Putting all her concentration into it, she again moved her finger. Sweat dripped from her forehead to run into the hair at her temple.

She continued to struggle. After a time, she was able to straighten her head. Unable to move her head from side to side, she glanced around in the darkness, her eyes moving furiously.

When she thought the inky blackness that surrounded her had lightened, her gaze stopped, her chest rising with the pants of exertion.

Was she right? Or was it just wishful thinking?

Moments later, she was able to move her entire hand. She arched the wrist and pushed against her calf. Reaching for her knee, intent on forcing the leg to straighten, her arm shifted away from her body.

A small smile curved her lips. She was going to make it.

When she shifted to grab her knee, she could see her hand reaching for her leg. Her prison *was* lightening.

Once again, she scanned the area. There was nothing to see, but instead of solid blackness, the air around her was gray. Dark gray, but there were no silhouettes of furniture, doors, or windows.

She stopped her struggles, giving herself a moment to rest, and attuned her senses to the immediate area. No smells. No sounds. She couldn't even tell what she was lying on.

"Hello?" she again yelled into the void.

Purpose filled her. She would find an escape. She had people who needed her. She needed to find her daughter. Where was Wyliam? Nathaniel must be worried sick.

These thoughts filled her mind, and she struggled again in earnest.

64

NAV-LYS'S BACK ARCHED, AND SHE stretched her arms
wide. With a smile, she ran her hands down the body
she possessed.

She was right to step in and push the Other back. Now this
body was hers. Hers to play with. Hers to use to play with
others.

It had been so simple. So easy to slide in. Now the body—
and the magic inherent to it—was hers. She could do what she
wished. Play with these men and women as she wished. And
play with the Other, too.

The woman who was once Sylvan Singh, and was now
Nav-lys, sat in a chair in the corner of a room. When the door
opened to emit the small man, she didn't move. Not a shift of
her gaze, not an increase in her inhalation, not a twitch of a
finger. She watched and waited. Cassandra had promised, and
Nav-lys would see the fulfillment of that promise.

* * * * *

ORSON LOOKED AT THE WOMAN from across the room. They'd managed to get her cleaned and redressed in a new gown without any loss of life. She'd allowed the maids to move her about like a doll and never once came across as threatening.

What was he to do with her now?

He did so enjoy looking at her.

When he'd gotten her to his house, he'd snuck her in the back way. One never knew when Mikel was watching or having others watch.

In the quarters he'd given her, he'd stood and watched the maids bring in bucket after bucket of hot water to fill a large brass tub. He didn't speak after directing the staff, and as of yet, all she'd said was to utter that odd word. Nav-lys. Her name.

When the bath was ready and the maids stripped her, it was to reveal marks of her imprisonment. Watching from beside the door, out of the reach of the light, he'd become excited.

In soft pants, his breath seemed to be pulled from his lungs, and sweat broke out on his body. Her skin, so beautiful and white, now marred by the red scars of the whip. And the still-festering marks of burns.

He wished he'd been the one to place these blemishes upon her. Though he knew, if he had, he'd be dead, just as her former jailers were. Somehow, the thought of that—the deadly threat—made him even more excited.

When he stepped from the shadows, she caught his eye, and he knew that he knew. She knew everything. She wasn't an ignorant beast, someone broken by the Ring.

His gaze slid over her as the maids washed her, and when he again looked to her face, a small smile curved her lips. Oh yes, she was aware.

NOW, ENTERING THE ROOM AND approaching her in the chair, her gaze swung to him, and he stopped in his tracks. Yes, he thought again, she might seem to be oblivious, lost within herself, but in truth, she was very aware of him and her surroundings.

When he took another step forward, she only watched. He sat in another chair across from her and waited to see if she would do anything, say anything. When she again turned her gaze to the room in general, he also glanced about. Food adorned the table, but it didn't appear as if she had eaten. He'd need to ask the maids if she ate. Perhaps she didn't need to.

When his gaze swung back to her, he gave a small jump. She was staring, expressionless, almost as if she were a beautiful, inanimate doll.

Now that he had her, he didn't know what to do with her. He'd thought at one time to keep her for himself, but now he was leaning toward his original plan of making her a gift for his master, Mikel Bathsar.

They'd been on the outs since the girl's disappearance. Their relationship had yet to recover from his lack of success where she was concerned. He was sure this woman would get him back in his master's good graces. He wondered how best she could benefit him. But how to make the gift a surprise, give him the best advantage, and grab Mikel's attention—would it be best to do it in private or at a social occasion? How could he ensure he could control the woman?

When he stood to leave the room, he didn't again look at her, his mind occupied with thoughts of his return to Mikel's inner circle.

65

NATHANIEL AND WYLIAM MOVED DAY to day, never staying in the same location twice. It seemed there was always an empty warehouse or vacant hovel for them to hole up in for the night. The cat was good at keeping them fed since most people didn't look twice at a stray feline — even one of his unusual size.

Nathaniel had no idea what had become of Sylvan, and Wyliam could tell him nothing.

For a week, he kept them within sight of the church and the alley where Wyliam had been found, hoping to locate his girl. After the first few days, when it became obvious she would not be showing up on the boy's heels, they moved farther into the city. Each day took them farther from the temple and closer to the outskirts of civilization.

This morning, sitting on the edge of the road, Nathaniel pondered what they should do while they ate on a roll of bread.

"Perhaps we should leave the city."

The boy looked his way, but as usual, he was silent.

"Really, Wyliam. You're going to have to learn to talk. How are we to decide on the remainder of our lives if we can't even converse?"

With a small shrug, the boy turned from the cat to again watch the foot traffic. He held his half of the roll loosely.

"Oh, come now. I didn't mean to hurt your feelings."

The cat sat for a moment, and when the boy didn't react or eat his bread, he heaved a sigh and touched the boy's arm.

"Wyliam. Don't be angry."

The boy glanced his way, gave a small smile, and went back to chewing on the roll.

"I know I heard you speak. In the cabin . . ."

The boy's eyes flickered with recognition.

Nathaniel cleared his throat. "In the cabin, with Sylvan, I heard you say your name. In the alley when I found you, you may not remember it, but you said my name. I know you can speak. You just have to want to."

The boy continued to eat his bread, now almost finished. He didn't look at the cat or give any indication he was listening to him.

"So?" Nathaniel continued. "What do you think? Do you want to give it a try?"

Wyliam shoved the last morsel of bread into his mouth, chewed it slowly, and, with a hard swallow, forced it down. He took another glance out at the street, which was becoming more crowded. Finally, he looked at the cat, pointed to his bread, and said, "Can I have that?"

For a moment Nathaniel didn't move. Recovering his wits,

he handed the roll to the boy, who took it and began to eat.

"Well," Nathaniel said almost to himself, "I guess one problem is solved."

66

PATRICK MOVED THROUGH THE CITY. He walked slowly, and when he forgot to concentrate, he limped.

They had released him from the prison. They wanted him to bring them information about the rebellion. They thought they had broken him. He would play this role, this part of betrayer. The pain—physical and mental—was foretold long ago. They were a sacrifice he was ready to give. His loyalty to the people of this land, and to Caleb, absolute.

Yes, Mikel Bathsar was an evil man, but his evil was a power given by something far greater than himself. When he'd first met Caleb—that day in the alley—he'd talked of his sister, Cassandra. She was the evil that filled the lands, an evil that rotted men's hearts—turned brother against brother and sister against sister. She was an evil that must be stopped. Caleb told him what must be. The revelation would be fulfilled. He was committed to doing what was necessary to see this to the end.

Even then, it would take all of them to end her tyranny. She had continued to grow in power millennium after millennium.

Caleb hadn't realized by allowing her to win their game, he was making her stronger. Now, the only way to halt something so powerful was when the Three and Three became One.

When he entered the inn, it was already filled with men eating and drinking. He stepped inside, hearing the door close behind him, and scanned over heads for Lord Bathsar. Not immediately seeing him, he started through the crowd to the bar area in the rear of the room. He was almost there when, from across the room, the sounds of raised voices came to him and he recognized one of them as the man he sought. He headed toward the voice.

"My lord, what you ask simply cannot be done."

A hum of loud voices accompanied this proclamation. Men who agreed with the speaker but were not brave enough to speak up alone.

"I do not need to hear the limitations you insist on putting on this endeavor," came the reply. "What I require are your solutions."

"But, my lord." Patrick could imagine the man groveling on his knees. The voice flowed with a whine. "There is no way to get within the walls of the temple."

"Silence." And with that one word, all the chatter was cut off. "We must reach the inner sanctum of the temple to halt my brother's madness. There is no other option."

Patrick stepped to the front just as Eldred stood. When he turned and saw Patrick, he moved through the men toward him.

"My lord," Patrick said by way of greeting, dipping his

head.

Placing his hand on the priest's shoulder, Lord Bathsar turned him back the way he'd come. "Where have you been, old friend? I thought perhaps you gave up on us and left the city."

"Never." The priest hedged for a moment, making a show of watching where he was going, sure not to trip on any of the feet surrounding them. "I've been spending time with the scriptures, my lord. I thought I might find illumination for our dilemma within."

"Ah." Eldred nodded as he followed. "Wouldn't that be a lovely thing."

Quick to change the subject, Patrick stopped and faced Eldred. "Have you heard anything concerning Maya?"

Light flooded the room when the outer door was thrust open. "My lord Bathsar," a man in a cloak shouted above the fray.

"I am here." He stepped toward the man, his arm raised in the air.

The man headed through the crowd toward him. The other men moved back and eased his passage. When he reached Eldred, he leaned close to speak in the lord's ear.

Patrick saw the lord's eyes widen and then a grin split his face. When the man finished speaking, he stepped back, and the lord slapped the man twice on the shoulder. "Thank you, my man. Thank you," he said and, without diminishing his smile, moved to Patrick.

He grasped the priest's arm, turned him toward the back exit, and pulled him through the crowd of men.

"My lord," Patrick panted, keeping up with Eldred Bathsar by sheer will. His body hurt all over, and the grip on his arm felt as if it were causing wounds to reopen.

The lord stopped and spun into the priest. "They've found her." His voice low and intense, he looked to the heavens as if in thanks, repeating the words in a whisper. "They've found her."

67

SYLVAN WOKE. SHE DIDN'T EVEN realize she'd fallen asleep, but here she was, opening her eyes to the same gray existence, the sensation of lost time.

Moving came easier to her this time around. Her head, arms, and legs shifted at her request. When she attempted to sit, her body felt weak as if she'd been sick and abed for a long time.

She pushed through the numbness, the shakiness, and sat. Her hair flowed about her head as if she were underwater, and when she reached to smooth it, her arm flowed upward like the earth pulled at it. She looked up, wondering if she were hanging upside down.

Feeling with her hand, she stretched out in each direction. Nothing stopped her exploration. It was as if she were floating freely in the air.

With no up and no down, a sense of vertigo hit so hard she almost passed out. Taking deep breaths, she closed her eyes and concentrated on the image of Maya's face. She thought of her initially as a newborn babe, up until the morning she ran out of their cabin accompanied by Rory. Calmness settled her, a deep knowing that everything was going to be all right.

When she opened her eyes, the grayness had again lightened. She squinted, straining her eyes to search through the mist to see something, anything. Movement, slight and blurry, caught her attention and she strained harder, but it remained elusive. Perhaps she could move closer. She stretched her body, arms pushing down at her sides, and shifted. It was like swimming through mud, but when she did it again, again she shifted.

Closer she moved, the image gaining in clarity, bit by bit.

Exhausted, she stopped and looked at the scene before her, but she couldn't understand what she saw. She peered out into a room like she were at a window. A beautiful room, but her vantage point was nearer to the floor.

What. Was. Happening.

68

ORSON STOPPED OUTSIDE THE CLOSED door of the room the woman occupied in the temple. This was it. This was the moment. Mikel was holding court in the main room. People from town were there to have their cases heard. Mikel would determine who would be punished and who would be rewarded.

He would show his master how valuable the woman could be. And how valuable he could be.

Orson opened the door. It gave a loud creak as it revealed a room he, at first, thought was empty. When he stepped in and looked around, he found the woman sitting on the floor in the corner. A fire blazed in the hearth, heat filling the room while wood sputtered and popped.

She was in a fresh gown. That was good. Mikel had an unreasonable aversion to the natural scents of a body.

She really was a beauty.

Now clean and brushed, her hair shone with highlights reflected in the flames. Not simply brown, her lush mane defied description, holding all the hues of a sun setting after a storm. Through the tresses, streaks of gray slid. If possible, this flaw made her even more attractive. For just a moment, he thought again to keep her as his own, but then he shook his head. She would serve him better by giving her away.

"Come, my pet." With a hand out to her, he moved forward. A small twinge of fear snaked up his back, making him feel alive. When he caught her gaze, her eyes were a clear blue.

Beautiful.

69

SYLVAN WATCHED THE SCENE IN front of her. Confusion filled her mind.

She didn't understand. Where in the world was she?

When the man approached her, she saw him mouth some words, but she couldn't hear what he said. He spoke so fast, his head tilting, she couldn't begin to read his lips. She scanned his face for some insight into what might be happening.

A small smile hinted at the lines of his face, and his eyes were direct. He seemed to be a friend.

When a delicate hand reached for his from just under where she looked, she gave a start, which had her floating backward in this alien world. She pulled herself forward again to peer down, looking for where the hand had come from. The two hands joined—the man's and the delicate one—and everything shifted. With her perspective changed, she looked out into the room from a greater height, the man now appearing shorter.

He kept the hand in his, motioning with the other toward the door. Then she was moving. Small quakes ran through the world where she found herself. Her body shifted and surged.

The room flowed by and they were in a hallway. Her view didn't shift left or right. Even with no movement in her view, she became dizzy as the hallway flowed by on either side.

She was afraid to look away. Afraid she'd miss something. Something that would give her a clue as to where she was or what was happening.

When they stopped in front of an ornate door, light reflected and illuminated the area. Gold glinted like drops of sunlight. She'd never seen anything so majestic to compare.

The door opened, and she flowed through. Beyond was a room of people. Humble people by the looks of them. Most were clothed in simple homespun fabrics of browns and greens. Along the edges of the room stood soldiers. The first jolt of disquiet moved through her—the soldiers were cloaked in red and black.

Then the small man stepped in front of her, and she again saw the joined hands.

He moved through the mass of people. When they saw it was him, the look of fear came to their faces and they fell back, moving their neighbors with them until he walked freely in a pathway they had created.

Sylvan's attention was caught on the room. She tried to look around, to see more of the area, to identify where she was, but her view was limited by what was in front of her. When they stopped, she searched for a reason why. A sign of what was to come.

Then the image shifted. Her breath expelled in a rush.

There he stood.

Mikel.

She found it difficult to draw in another breath. When he stepped toward her, that look of avarice on his face, her heart finally caught. Then it sped up until she was panting and sweating.

He'd found her. After all this time—a lifetime—he'd found her.

70

WYLIAM SCUFFED HIS SHOES IN the dirt. After a few more paces, he stopped. When he pushed his mop of hair from his eyes, he left a streak of dirt across his sweaty forehead.

He stared into the foliage along the side of the road, searching for any movement. After another moment, he continued walking.

Two days ago, he and the cat had exited Berth. Nathaniel hadn't talked about it, but the boy knew how hard it was for him to leave without Sylvan. Each night, he'd wake to see the cat pacing about their makeshift camp. Lying near their fire, he'd listen while the cat muttered under his breath about what went wrong and things he should have done. He didn't know what to say or what to do, so he remained silent. And today when he woke, the cat was gone.

The day got hotter the longer the boy walked. He didn't know where this road led and didn't know when or if the cat would be back. Maybe, he was on his own.

THE SUN HAD JUST BEGUN its descent into the golden sky when the boy rounded a bend and saw a puff of smoke in the distance. He stopped and thought about fleeing the other way. Strangers weren't to be trusted.

But instead of running, Wyliam walked forward. Soon a cabin came into view, the smoke rising from a stone chimney. A large cultivated field stretched off until it met the forest on the edge of the property, and behind the cabin a small barn stood. In a corral was a scrawny old swayback horse, and when the breeze shifted, the boy smelled pigs.

A newly mended fence ran down the property line, and as Wyliam passed it, he looked back at the open road, searching for the cat. He should be showing up at any time. Then they'd move on together.

As he neared the house, he shoved his hands in the pockets of his trousers, his thumbnail worrying a scab on a forefinger. He was almost to the door when it surged open and a large dog ran at him, barking. Wyliam flew backward, landing on his hind end, a puff of dust ballooning around him and the dog now licking his face with abandon.

The boy pushed at the dog. When he got a little room, he turned on his hands and knees, but the dog still covered him, licking and whining.

"Ben!"

The dog jumped off Wyliam. Alone, dusty, and with dog saliva drying on his cheeks and neck, the boy turned to face the speaker.

"What you want, boy?"

Wyliam looked up from the dust to see a woman staring down at him, the dog sitting beside her. She was middle-aged and round. She wore a stained apron tied tightly over her blouse and skirt, and old, dusty boots peeked from under the hem.

Wyliam sat still, uncertain of what to do.

"Well?" She stepped from the porch and placed her hands on her hips. "You lost your tongue?"

When he still didn't answer, the woman said, "Come on in and have somethin' to eat. Dog won't hurt you," and she turned and walked back into the cabin followed closely by the dog.

Wyliam looked after her, and then, standing, turned to look back the way he'd come.

The cat would come, right?

LATER THAT NIGHT, FED, CLEANED, and lying on a pallet by the fire, Wyliam wondered what had become of Nathaniel. It didn't look like he would be coming back.

Freda, "just call me Fred," was a widow. Just she, the dog, and the old horse worked this farm. She didn't have any family. No children. She'd fed him and made him welcome, and after feeding him, she invited him to stay with her since she thought he was all alone in the world. And perhaps he was. Nathaniel had disappeared.

He'd spend the night. Be warm and safe this night and make his decision in the morning.

Breath coming deep, eyelids drooping, he heard her soft snores in the other room and was comforted.

* * * * *

NATHANIEL SAT IN THE TREE and observed the cabin.

The boy would be safe here. It was a good thing. The woman would give the boy a good life and a future. It was better for them both that Wyliam not travel with him. Where he was going, there would be danger. It was not a place for a child.

Not a leaf was displaced as he jumped from the tree, and only once did he look back. Turning back to the road, he stomped down the ache in his chest and headed back into the city to find his girl.

71

IKEL'S EYES NARROWED AND HIS mouth pursed when he heard Orson's voice coming through the crowd. The small man had failed him.

Turning, he drew in a breath, ready to tell the small man just what a failure he was, already thinking of what his punishment would be. It was a shame. He'd always liked Orson.

Before he could bellow an order, his breath caught in his throat, and for a moment he thought his heart would stop. Standing beside Orson was Sylvan. His beautiful Sylvan.

No one moved. No one spoke.

Orson stepped forward and cleared his throat. "My lord, I've brought you a present."

Unable to tear his eyes from the woman, Mikel gave a nod to acknowledge what he said. "Yes, a present." When he took the first step from the dais, the entire room took a step back. Everyone except the small man and the woman with him.

Mikel moved closer, looking her over from head to foot. Her

gown, an elegant gold, set her hair and skin off to perfection. So many years later, and she was still a beauty. If anything, she was lovelier as a grown woman.

Finally, dragging his gaze from her, he glanced at his servant.

"Orson, my faithful companion. Where did you find her?"

Orson smiled with pride and stepped forward. "She is for you. A gift." It seemed he had no idea the gift she truly was.

"Yes." He nodded. "She is for me. She has always been for me."

The small man's brows drew together, and he looked from Mikel to the woman.

Mikel stepped between Orson and the woman to wrap his hand around her arm.

"My lord—" Orson began, but Mikel turned his back to him and drew the woman up the stairs of the dais. She went with him willingly, even tilted her head to look him in the eye.

Orson watched them, speechless, and then stepped back to wait.

Mikel walked the woman to the chair on the platform. Gold and set with jewels, it was more a throne than a simple chair. When prompted, she sat on the edge gracefully. Standing back from her, Mikel Bathsar clasped his hands together and, projecting a type of glee, rocked back on his heels, a large smile covering his face. Then he turned to the assembly and lifted his voice.

"People. My people." He turned to again look at the woman as if to convince himself she was still there. "I'm so glad you can all be witness to this miracle."

Orson stepped forward, his eyes intent, a small frown forming.

"For years I have searched for my bride, my only love. Now, after all this time, my faithful man, Orson, has brought her to me."

Orson's jaw dropped.

"Please. Welcome my true wife . . . Sylvan."

72

T HE PAIN REVERBERATED THROUGH HIS head to radiate down his neck and spine. He didn't care. It was what he deserved. They'd come for him again. Wanting information, taking his pride and a bit of sanity. Now, once again, he was at their mercy. Only this time he'd given them too much.

With effort, Patrick lifted his head from the floor then, relaxing, allowed it to drop. Again, the pain arced through his system.

So dumb. So weak.

A small sob tried to escape, but in shame he clamped his lips down. But there was nothing he could do to stop a hot tear from rolling down his face to pool at his temple.

Stupid.

Again, he cracked his head to the floor, enjoying the shattering of agony that accompanied his self-punishment.

He deserved far worse. He wished the torturers would come back. Do their worst. Perhaps even put an end to this worthless life. How could he have done it? To betray those who meant the most to him. It was unheard of.

He thought himself made of stronger stock. In his ignorance, he'd thought he'd be able to withstand the ardors of torture. How stupid he'd been.

Now, the deaths of many would be on his head, and there was no way to stop it. If he were lucky, perhaps he could minimize the damage. Save some lives. But first, he had to get out of here.

73

SYLVAN SCREAMED. SHE COULD FEEL the burn of it in her throat, the constriction of the muscles, the collapsing of her lungs as they emptied of air.

No sound. No matter how much she pushed and protested. No matter how much she called out to stop it, the horror continued.

She'd been with Mikel for weeks and he loved to use her to kill. Not her exactly—the other one. The one controlling this body.

She'd finally figured out where she was. Somehow, she was inside herself. She recognized the power—knew it for what it was. Her magic. She remembered what Nathaniel had told her. She'd been without her magic for so long, then it was back but subverted. Strong. It made her a killing machine.

At first, as a simple observer, she was in shock. The barbaric acts, the lack of empathy. How would she remain sane? For a time, she hadn't. Her mind had shut down. For a time, a blessed time, she didn't see or feel anything. But that didn't last long.

Waking, she had shifted within the sack she found herself in. For a wonderful moment, she didn't remember where she was—didn't remember anything. For a wonderful moment, she thought herself back in the cabin in the woods. Snuggled in bed, her daughter cuddled into her, safe and warm.

Then, a light blazed. She looked, and she remembered.

She was in the midst of it—or at least her body was. She didn't know what controlled her, what master she now served. Who was this mimic? This entity that controlled her body?

She stared, transfixed, as the man before her disappeared into a mass of red and gray, indistinguishable from a gut pile at the butcher. No evidence that a man once stood there, once screamed in terror and pain. What had he done to warrant such punishment? And who was she to play executioner?

Luckily, it wasn't all horror. Sometimes there was nothing but a simple wall or hallway. The blank slate of normalcy occurring right in front of her eyes. Staff working, food served, occasionally, even the out of doors. Oh, how she longed to feel the breeze on her face, smell the flowers blooming in the gardens.

Then there were the times of fear. Heart-pounding, brow-beading fear. The common catalyst for the fear was Mikel. He was there for the terror as well but *really* there for the fear. Standing close, touching her, leaning in to whisper in an ear she couldn't hear out of. Just his nearness was enough to cause her to spiral in her cell.

That's how she'd come to think of this place. This constant floating. No way out. No way to be heard or saved. It was a cell, a prison. She couldn't change her situation. All she could be was witness to the madness.

* * * * *

NAV-LYS PACED IN THE SMALL room.

She knew the man Mikel. His face was the one she saw in her dreams. She'd known him the moment she saw him. And she'd felt the terror of the Other. She liked the reaction.

Oh, how she hated the Other. For that alone, she would be with him; to make the Other miserable was one of her goals.

But in addition to this, he gave her such fun playthings. The toys of people. Allowing her to do what she would with them. Clapping his hands and laughing in glee when she worked her wiles. It came with an added benefit. While she felt pleasure, the Other felt pain.

It felt good to use her magic. The surge of it through her, almost an emptying. A release.

Pacing, Nav-lys's brow furrowed. A few nights ago, Cassandra had come to her again in her dreams. It was a wonderful dream of a land where the magic flowed freely, and all the life forms were sucked dry. In the dream she was part of an eternal entity, and with their joining, they would become all-powerful. No one and nothing could stop them, could halt their taking of this world and many others.

Cassandra spoke of her desire to have the man, this Mikel, in the plan. He was still useful to them. For now.

74

O RSON STOOD TO THE SIDE of the dais, partially hidden by a curtain.

Once again, the people had come to the temple to be heard. Each day there were fewer and fewer. They were understanding their complaints would be met with violence. Not that he minded—all he'd ever known, all he'd ever wanted, was violence.

In the past week he'd come to believe the woman was *the* woman. The one they'd all been looking for. He'd searched for her for two decades, and with her recovery, he'd witnessed his master become more crazed. He was obsessed with the woman—his wife. He loved the things she could do. Loved the power she gave him. No one could stand in his way.

And she responded to him. Never had he seen her react with anything but compliance when he was present. He didn't know if she recognized him from before or if it was that Mikel allowed her to kill. Hell, he insisted on it.

Since that day he presented her to his master, there hadn't

been any further talk about Orson's failure. Once again, he was a favorite. A trusted servant. He'd even participated in the killing spree of a band of miscreants. The three of them — the woman, Mikel, and Orson — had turned the room in the dungeon into a blood bath. The pleasure had been intense.

Now he watched her from the sidelines. She was a treasure. A treasure he had begun to covet. Mikel's Sylvan. His Nav-lys.

75

"Y OU CHECK ON THAT SOW today, boy."
Wyliam nodded and finished the meal Fred laid
before him.

It had been a week since he'd come to her farm. A week
since the cat had disappeared. Every day, while working either
in the fields or with the animals, he would stop and look toward
the road, certain he would see the cat trotting down the dirt
path, come to collect him. But it remained empty.

Freda had accepted him readily. Even at only six years of
age, he was a hard worker. He knew animals and how to tend
to the garden. He'd never been one to complain, so he eased her
days. She wouldn't admit it, but she was lonely—just her and
the dog. He didn't talk much more than the dog, Ben, but she
seemed to enjoy his company.

Only seven days had passed, but they'd found a routine, a
rhythm.

Each day, after breaking his fast, he headed out to take care
of the animals. Ben accompanied him, and they'd become fast

friends. It wasn't like the cat, but even though he couldn't talk, the dog was smart and friendly.

The horse, old and gentle, did its best when worked in the fields, but Wyliam knew it wouldn't be too long before they'd be needing another. And his nose was right—there were pigs on the place. A sow with a new litter. Freda bred her with a neighbor's boar, and when grown, she would owe him one of the litter. For now, however, Wyliam fed and tended her, keeping a wary eye out. Pigs, he remembered, could be aggressive when they had young. He didn't want to become that sow's next meal.

Working in the fields was the hardest part. It was physically taxing for a boy his age, but at least they did the work together. In the beginning of the day, his mind wandered. He thought not only of the cat but of Sylvan. Where she might be. The last clear memory of her was in the never-ending hall in the church. His memories were scanty and missing after that.

Was she still alive? In his heart, he thought she was. He would like to see her again someday. Maybe the cat and the woman would come to visit.

He finished his mash, and when he slid off the chair, the dog lifted his head from his spot by the door.

"Come, Ben."

He'd been speaking more and more during his time with Freda. She didn't know his past; he had nothing to hide while with her. His life could continue from this point. He could become anything and anyone he wanted.

Walking to the door, he grabbed a jacket Freda had given

him. It was too large so he had to roll up the arms, but one day he'd grow into it. When he opened the door, Ben trotted through and the boy followed the dog to the barn. The horse lifted its head and looked their way as birds called in the distance and the sun broke over the horizon.

For a moment, Wyliam stopped and enjoyed this moment. The smells and the breeze against his skin. He squinted into the rising sun but enjoyed its warmth.

When he dropped his gaze, it was to see the big dog moving along the fence to the barn. Tucking his hands into his pockets, the boy followed the dog. He had work to do.

76

I T HAD BEEN A ROUTING. They'd lost over half of their men. Eldred looked around the tavern. Bloody and exhausted, his men caught his eye and then looked away. How had they been betrayed? What had gone wrong?

He picked himself up, a groan warbling from his lips.

They'd barely gotten themselves out with their lives.

The guards had been waiting for them—that was obvious. As they neared the temple, the streets had filled from all sides with armor-clad men. Red and black cloaks were awash for as far as he could see.

And then, he'd almost panicked, almost lost his mind when he saw Maya in the fray. Fighting like a demon.

His lips turned up in a small smile, pride filling his mind, which before had held only regrets. She was a sight to see, swords flashing in the sunlight. He was amazed he and Sylvan had produced such a force.

Now, back in the tavern, he wandered among his men, stopping to say a word of hope or encouragement, or help with bandaging a wound.

They would have to regroup. Plan for another incursion. The men would not be so willing to do battle with the temple soldiers now that they'd been shown how ill-matched they were. This was going to take planning. But they couldn't quit. Mikel must be stopped. The land must be saved.

And now the information had come that he had a queen. An evil queen.

77

MIKEL WALKED IN THE DOOR, and Nav-lys left the consciousness of the body. She had no desire to be present for this. She wanted him happy—or at least Cassandra wanted him happy. Nav-lys needed to keep the body safe for her use, but urges of the flesh were beneath her. She didn't find it necessary to be present.

What she did find interesting, a bit like ripping the legs from an insect to watch it squirm, was to allow Sylvan to experience his attentions. The Other would experience it but have no power to stop it. Her anguish was so rewarding.

* * * * *

SYLVAN BLINKED AND STIRRED. SHE'D slept again.
Manipulating her body within her existence had become easier, like a muscle well used. She looked toward the faded light of her window into the world. This had become a habit, too. An aligning of where she was.

A room. She sighed. At least she wasn't in the room with the throne. It seemed, often, that was where the killing took place. She hated to awaken within that room. To know what was to come.

She could only see a tile floor. Her body stood on a floor, the tips of her toes poking from beneath the edges of a white gown. The fabric looked soft and light.

It came to her then that she was wearing a nightgown. She must be in her chambers, and it must be evening. Just before bed.

A hand holding hers came into view. They were both in front of where she stood, her arm extended back to her body. She squinted at the joining. Who was with her? Larger and of a darker hue, the hand appeared to belong to a man.

A shiver ran up her back and across her shoulders.

The hands moved and she was walking. The large masculine hands moved to her shoulders, and her body was being turned. Her view changed and she sat. A man stood in front of her. There could be no doubt about it now. From this perspective she could only see him from chest to knees, but the body facing her was a man. A man in a dressing gown.

He reached out to her chin and her head rose. Up his chest to shoulders, neck, and then the face of her visitor. Breath drawn in a harsh gasp, she was unable to release it. Everything in her quivered, and finally the breath came out.

Mikel.

She didn't need to ask what he wanted. It was what he had always wanted from her. Now when she was defenseless, he would take it.

He leaned down to look her in the eye, said something she couldn't hear, and ran a hand through her hair. From her temple to the ends of her hair, he caressed, looking her over, speaking to her.

With a hand back on her shoulder, he leaned in, lying her back.

Oh, no. No, this must be stopped.

Struggling, intent on breaking through the walls that contained her, she thrashed. It did no good. She was not in control. In this, she was truly a victim.

In her prison of gray, Sylvan could only watch the face that filled her vision. There was no sound, but this time she felt. She wished to return to her ignorance, the inability to know the air of the room and the feeling of another on her skin. Her breath quickened and the burn of nausea rose in her throat. His eyes on her, ownership and ecstasy saturating them, she shut her own, but still the motion of her body taking his thrusts continued.

When she thought she couldn't take it anymore, that she would go insane, everything stopped. Still she waited, afraid it might begin again. After a time, she peered out at the world, leery of what she might see. Darkness. Blessed darkness welcomed her. She lay in her world, tears rolling down her face, mourning for a life and an innocence that would never be again.

78

NATHANIEL SCOURED THE CITY. UNLESS he found a body, he could only assume Sylvan was alive. He couldn't even entertain the thought that she might be gone. And, although he was unusual as pedagogues went—an actual being, born in the real world—when the heir died, so did the pedagogue. If Sylvan were dead, wouldn't he cease to exist? At least in this time and place.

That thought gave him the confidence to continue his search. To keep his faith that he would once again find her. But he felt lost, not sure what to do. All that could be done, he decided, was to go back to the beginning, to the day he'd lost her. He would go to the church, tear it apart for any sign of her, watch, and listen. He could be stealthy—invisible. If he didn't find anything, then he would move on. It would be time-consuming, but in the end, all he had was time.

The front entrance, the one Sylvan and Wyliam went through, didn't seem like the smart move. Nathaniel had a feeling the alley where he found the boy was going to foster a better result. He'd been around the entire building but was never lucky enough, or perhaps never in the right place at the right time to locate another entrance. He'd wait in the alley for something to happen or someone to come. And then he'd find her.

IT WAS DAYS LATER AND the cat wondered if he'd chosen the wrong location. He'd been here, within a few feet of where he'd found Wyliam, afraid to leave for fear of missing some little occurrence.

He was considering moving somewhere else when a sweet scent wafted by his location and drew his attention. A moment later, he heard a low creak, and there was a shift in the mountain of garbage partway down the alley and along the other side.

With his head raised and his ears perked forward, he studied the location.

When a panel opened, he was prepared for it but still surprised to see two men enter the alley. Between them, they hauled a body. It looked to be male but was so damaged the cat wasn't completely sure. They moved down the alley and, setting down their load, moved some of the garbage.

Nathaniel's head spun back and he stared at the still-open portal. With a sideways glance at the men, he padded across the alley and entered the church.

The recesses of the building were dim, lanterns mounted sporadically in the interior hall. It was plenty of light for a determined feline, however, and Nathaniel made his way quickly from the door.

He'd traveled quite a way before hearing voices. Even though his magic was active, the ability to see him limited, he moved stealthily. He wasn't the only magic user in this world. It wouldn't be good to be found out at this stage.

Farther along the corridor, it emptied into two rooms. Peering into one, he ensured it was empty. The other, just a bit farther on, he heard something.

As he neared, he could make out individual voices. Most of them were the deep tones of men, but interspersed were the softer ones of women. Slipping around the corner, he slid into the room and made his way down the wall. Perhaps he could find something out about the running of this institution that would assist him in finding Sylvan.

The overall feeling of the people in the room was jovial, and the speech crass. At first, Nathaniel was confused, not seeing this as something he'd encountered before in a church. He realized that this was no ordinary church—perhaps not a church at all.

What had he sent his girl and the child into?

Most of the people in the room were eating, consuming large hanks of meat he had trouble identifying. Soon enough, they finished and began to filter out.

Back to their work?

He made his way to the exit and watched them leave. Deciding to follow, the large group traversed down a hallway. They continued to joke and push each other, their voices loud in the small space.

When they opened a heavy door and made their way

through, he slipped between legs and got to the other side before the door clanged shut.

Against the wall, he forgot for a moment he was following the group. Moans issued from a multitude of rooms along both sides of the walls. *No*, he thought, *not rooms*. Cells. Each door had a small window in it, and the windows were crisscrossed with bars.

The smell in this portion of the building was harsh. Filled with waste and death. No breeze moved through the corridor to help dissipate the stench. It hung like fog from the rafters.

His nose wrinkled, Nathaniel scanned the area and then followed the group. Their conversation changed now. They barely spoke and when they did, the tones were deeper, threatening. Down the corridor, they began to branch off. A few of them rapped loudly on the entries with canes they pulled from their belts. Within, the sounds fell silent.

A disquiet filled Nathaniel. He could tell what this place was, and it wasn't a church. He needed to locate his girl, and he needed to do it quickly.

He moved down the hallways until the one he was in split and veered off into the distance. Down this one, screams echoed. His ears laid flat and he hissed, unable to control his reaction. This entire facility had his nerves jumping.

When he heard footsteps coming, he pressed against the wall and waited. Soon, two people moved by him. The one in the lead was dressed as the groups had been—black clothing and long-sleeved shirts. This one, however, wore some sort of a mask over his nose and mouth. He couldn't tell what it was or what purpose it served.

Behind the one in black, another person walked. This person was attached to the first by a leash anchored to a collar that encircled her neck. She went with the leader willingly, mumbling something about the fine meal that awaited her.

Nathaniel was doubly confused, but he didn't need to understand this place. He just needed to find his girl and get her out of here.

Silently and quickly, he continued down the hall. The sounds of screaming became louder the farther he got. His tail, always so luxurious and smooth, now stood straight up and was twice its normal size.

When the screams abruptly cut off, he stopped, one paw in the air. A door a bit farther down the hall opened and a man in black stepped out. Taking a glance back into the cell, he closed the door and headed toward where Nathaniel stood.

Nathaniel watched him pass. The man had barely walked on when, in his wake, a whiff of Sylvan came to the cat. His head wrenched around, and he watched the man. Her scent confirmed the feline's worst fears. Hurrying now, he followed.

79

ELDRED SAT IN THE NEAR silence and stared at his daughter. What a crafty woman he and Sylvan had made. She had come up with the perfect plan for getting them close to Mikel for a killing strike.

Looking out into the room, he realized how far they had come from the life he'd envisioned as a young man. Peace, prosperity, a loving wife, and children—one day he had hoped to have many children. Would he have sent Sylvan away that day if he'd known she was pregnant? Yes, he thought, but he would have gone with her.

Now, he didn't know where she was. Maya had been unable to locate her. Unable to find even a trace. They didn't know whether she was even alive.

Shaking himself from the fast-approaching depression that this topic always brought, Eldred thought of Maya's plan again. It was a good plan. Better than any they had come up with. Now to tear it apart. See where it may fail—for this time, they must not fail.

He moved to stare down at his daughter who so quickly had filled his heart. He would keep her here, protected, if he thought he could get away with it.

When she looked up at him, her green gaze direct, so like his own, he knew she'd never stand for being left behind. Protected. Coddled.

"And do you know who you'd want to accompany you on this raid?"

When she smiled and stood, he knew he'd made the right choice. He just hoped his heart would survive it.

80

THE CASTLE HAD THE FEELING of a space long-unused as Caleb moved through the main room. Where might his sister be? It was rare when she didn't show for an extended time. Rare when she didn't come to poke at him about their contest and how she would be the victor. Even rarer were the occurrences of him coming into her space.

In the center of the dimly lit room, an enormous table occupied most of the area. Upon the table sat a large candelabra. With a wave of his hand, the candles lit, their flames wavering in a slight breeze that always seemed to move through this room. He stepped from the table and made a slow circle around the room, searching for a clue to the whereabouts of Cassandra. It was unlike her to leave with so much on the line.

When he passed her scrying bowl, the inky fluid surged and splashed. He stopped to look over his shoulder at the basin. "Seeing" in this way had never been something he was drawn to. Ever since she was a small child, Cassandra had enjoyed peeking into other worlds. She once confided in him, when they were still confiding their secrets to each other, that she felt powerful when she knew secrets. Now, wondering if it might give him some insight into her whereabouts, he reversed his direction and stepped to the bowl.

Ancient and inscribed, the vessel was beautiful. The water surged at his nearness, and he had an impression of life and consciousness when he regarded it. If it could talk, what secrets could it tell?

A bit hesitant, he reached out and placed his hands on the rim. The water calmed, becoming clear and smooth as a pane of glass. With pursed lips, he stepped forward and looked into the image appearing in the basin.

A room was half-filled with people. There was a commotion at the rear of the room. Against his better judgment, he was captivated. His fists tightened on the basin, and he leaned forward, curious what this would show him.

Some of the players he knew. Some were his allies. He also recognized his enemies, Cassandra's lackey and minions. What would bring them all to this one place?

81

IDDEN BESIDE THE DAIS, ORSON watched the spectacle unfold.

When the girl and her father walked through the door, he wasn't even surprised. It seemed inevitable. His destiny would play out this day. Years before, his mistress, Cassandra, had promised him great things. Told him that *he* would be great. Over the years of service to Mikel Bathsar, he'd forgotten that promise. Put it aside to fulfill Mikel's destiny.

Now desire reared its head. Desire to take what he wanted. He would be great, and Nav-lys would be his. With her, it would be *he* who ruled this land, and no one else.

He barely heard the exchange of words. He was uninterested in the dealings of these people. Only the outcome.

His eyes remained glued to Mikel. If he became fixated on the girl and Mikel's brother, he may be vulnerable. Slowly, Orson moved forward until he was within a step of the dais. He was quick. He had always been quick.

With a furtive movement, Orson pulled his dagger from the

sheath at his belt. He held the weapon down along his leg, hidden from the many soldiers. Almost casually, he sent his gaze around the room, but everyone was focused on the scene before them. No one thought of the threat that might be coming from behind.

Watching Mikel, thinking his time was at hand, Orson barely had a moment to move within striking distance when the scene changed.

Stupefied, he watched the girl grab a weapon from a soldier and run it through Mikel.

Half of Mikel's body lay on the steps. Blood dripped in slow globules onto the tile floor and spread around his remains. It was as if a vacuum had occurred; all the sound sucked out of the room.

Nav-lys, his beloved, stood alone on the stage. The girl yelled something. He saw her mouth move, but no sound came to him. When Nav-lys responded, it was as if a cork popped, and the sound came rushing in louder than he could imagine. Screams and the stomping of fleeing feet.

Mikel's brother rushed forward, throwing the girl from the line of fire. He was engulfed and then shattered. As bits of him rained down on the steps, the girl—that red-haired witch who started all the trouble—screamed and labored forward, pulling against the warrior who held her.

Orson stared, spellbound, when the girl's eyes shone blue.

When the building rocked, he ripped his gaze from her to survey the room. People ran toward the exits, yelling. Chaos was everywhere. When the skylight dome exploded, he jumped back and cowered, peering up as glass rained down. His brows pulled together, he stood in a kind of shock as vines flowed over the edge of the open dome and into the room.

He stumbled back, grabbing the wall when the floor again heaved. This time, the tile cracked. Roots surged through the opening.

He had to get Nav-lys out of here. She must be kept safe. She was his priority.

He turned back toward the dais and started for her just as a vine wrapped around her waist and pulled her back. She screeched, letting loose a mass of gray ooze that flowed over the vine, turning it dry and brown. She twisted and chopped downward with her arm, hitting the dead vine and breaking it from her. Undaunted, she turned to engage more of the foliage.

82

WHEN MIKEL DROPPED TO THE stage and the room erupted, the soldier behind Patrick rushed around him and forward. Seeing his chance, Patrick stumbled to his feet and ran.

Leaving it all behind, fleeing down a hall, he turned at the first juncture and continued on. He turned at intersections of hallways without thought, his only desire to get away. His body was a mass of pain, especially his arm. With the motion of his flight, a throbbing had begun in the hand that was no longer there.

His mind tried to pull him back into the memory of earlier—the taking of his hand, the torturer, his cleaver.

Patrick shook his head as he pushed himself to move faster. He needed to stay in the here and now and get himself out. Guilt dragged at his feet. He'd left his friends behind. How could he have first betrayed them so completely and now run and not even attempt to help?

The priest tripped, almost going down. Stopping, he bent

over, gasping. Sobs racked his body and pain shot through him, both physical and emotional. Taking a deep breath, he tilted his head and looked down the hallway. Straightening, he continued his limping path away from the center of the temple.

He told himself he would be unable to give aid in the final conflict if he were killed now. He would find a safe place to recover from his wounds and experiences within the temple. And he would watch—for the coming of the Three.

* * * * *

CRACKS BOOMED AS THE FLOOR continued to disintegrate under the onslaught of the plants. The room was filling with their vines and roots. Surging and swirling, the door was pushed from within and ripped from its hinges to fly across the outer hall. Nav-lys stood on the dais staring out into the room, looking for the child. It felt like days that she had been battling the plants. Where had they come from? For the first time in this existence, exhaustion overwhelmed her, and still the plants came. The use of her magic was taking a toll.

A cracking sound sent her gaze upward just as the ceiling split. Great chunks of stone rained down. Launching herself backward, Nav-lys hit the edge of the dais and rolled to safety.

"My pet."

She heard the voice, and through a mental fog, she swung her head to find the small man beside her. He gestured to her, then his gaze jumped between her and the vines overhead.

"Come, come with me." When he held out his hand, she

took it and he helped her to her feet. Leading her around obstacles and from the room, they moved down a long hall. Behind them the crashing continued, and under it all, the insidious whisper of the plants.

* * * * *

ORSON LED THE WOMAN INTO the safety of the cavern. They had barely escaped the temple. This day, he had become the master.

Now he had her. Now the power would be his. They would stay hidden—for a time. They would grow stronger, and when they were ready, they would once again do the bidding of his mistress. Cassandra would see he was the one to bring her this world. He was all she needed.

But first, they would regroup.

Then, they would conquer.

* * * * *

This ends *The Pedagogue Chronicles, Book II:*
Sylvan's Guise.
Continue the story with *The Pedagogue Chronicles, Book III:*
Tessa's Flight.

ACKNOWLEDGMENTS

Driven Digital Services

Kingsman Editing Services

Did you enjoy this book? Visit your favorite retailer
and leave a review to help other readers discover the magic
of *The Pedagogue Chronicles*.

* * * * *

VickiBWilliamson.com

Facebook.com/FindingPoppies

Made in the USA
Middletown, DE
14 November 2021

51831562R00210